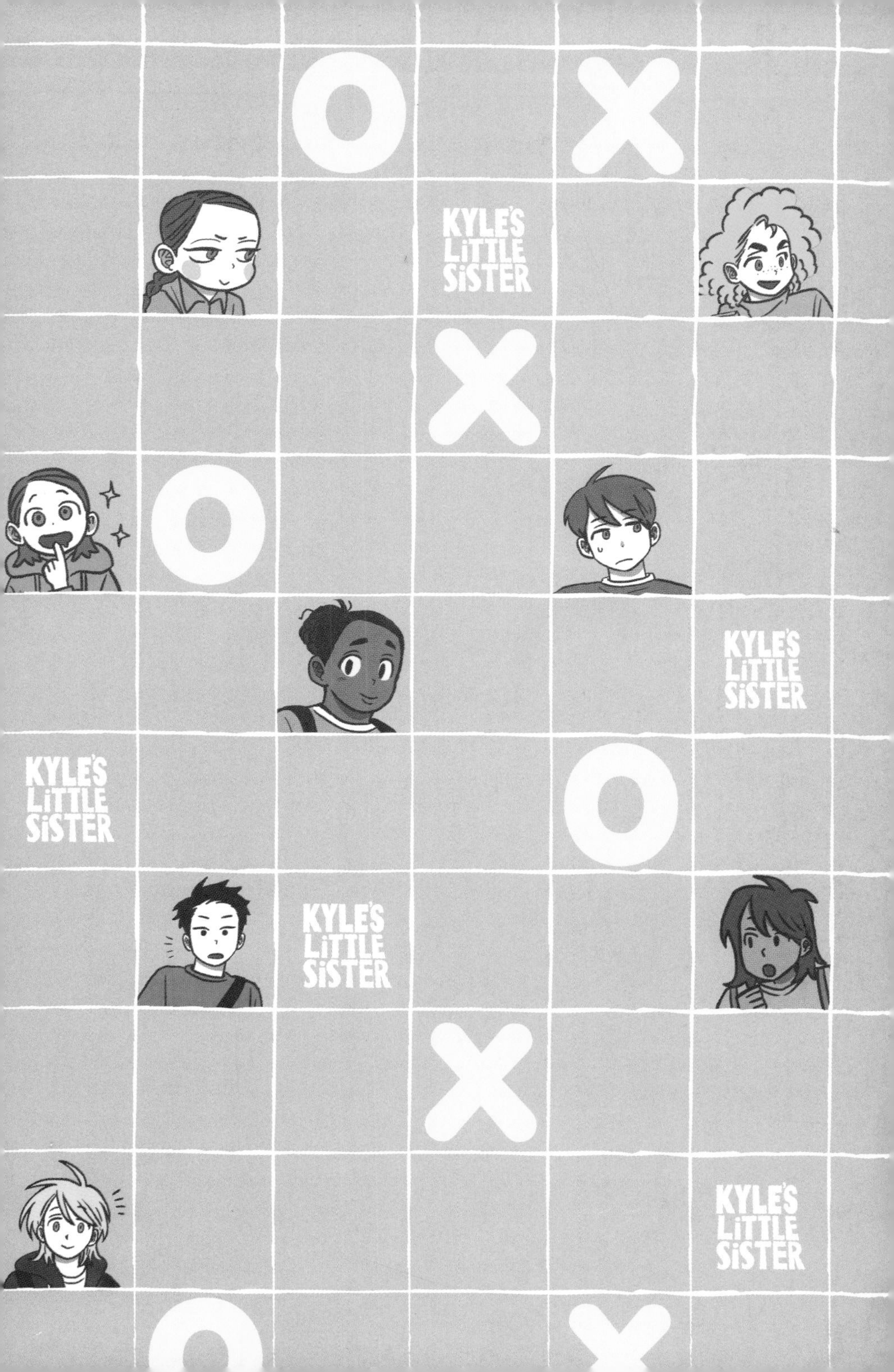
KYLE'S LITTLE SISTER

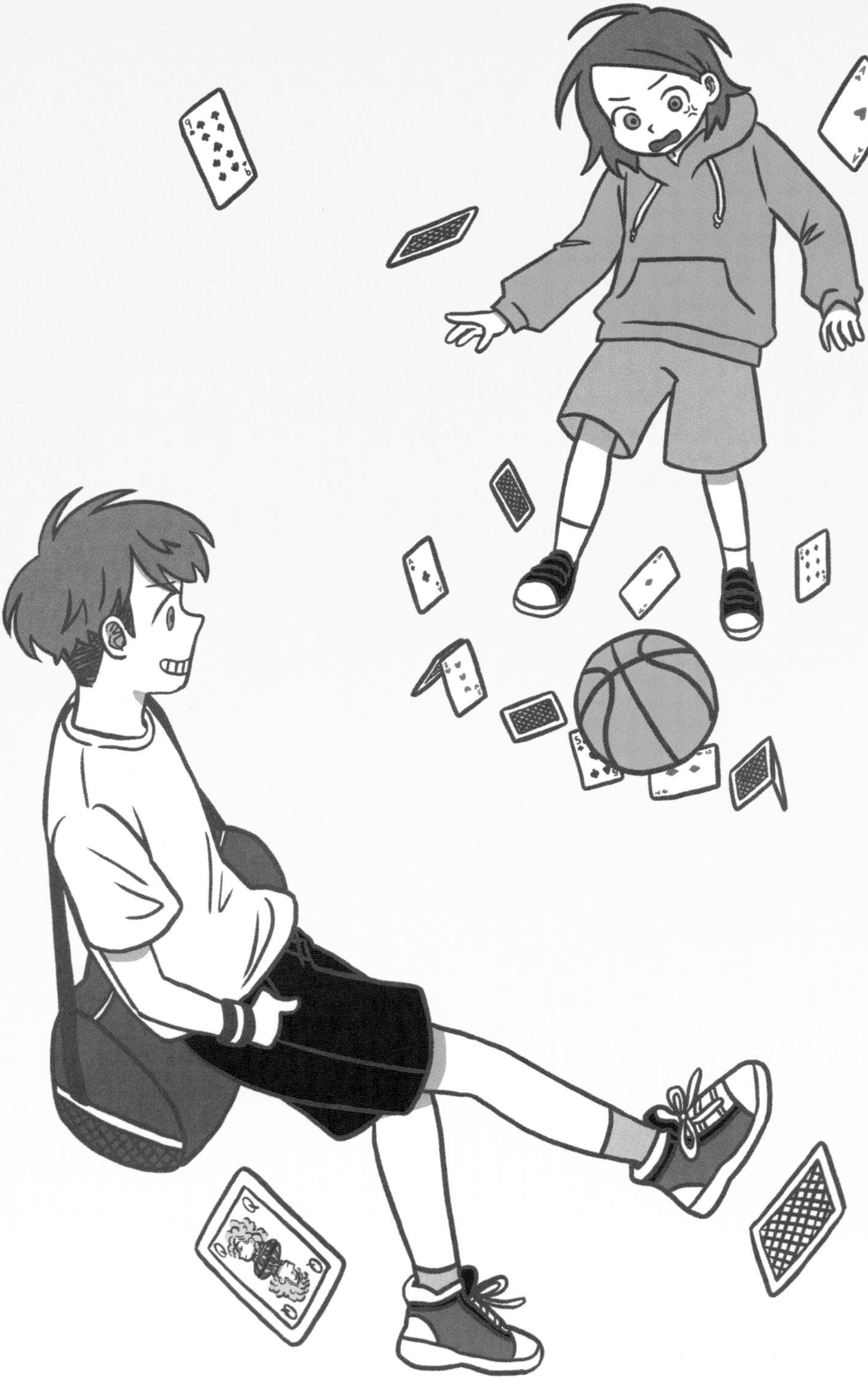

KYLE'S LITTLE SISTER

Story & Art by

BonHyung Jeong

New York

KYLE'S LiTTLE SiSTER

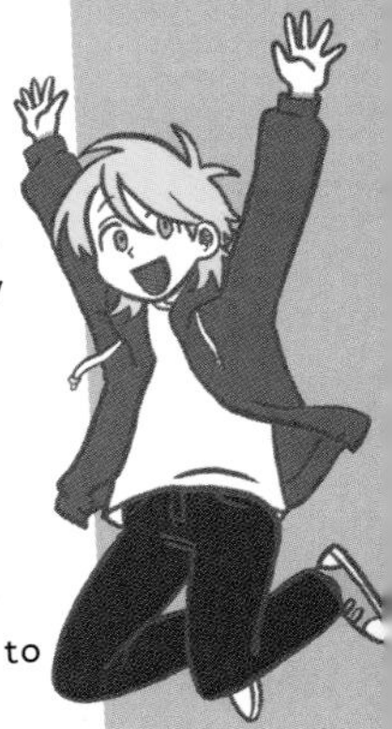

BONHYUNG JEONG
LETTERING: JY EDITORIAL

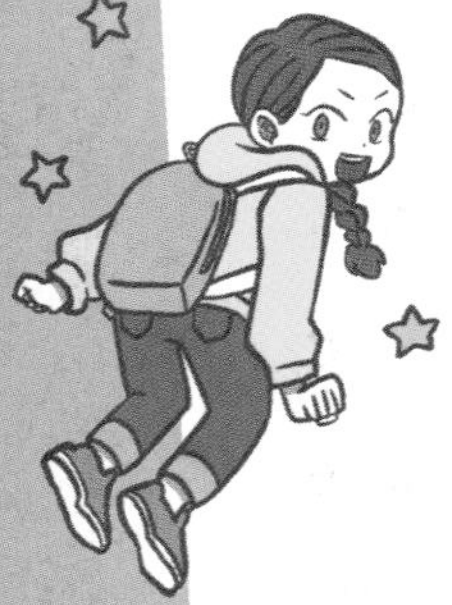

JY
150 West 30th Street, 19th Floor
New York, NY 10001

Visit us at jyforkids.com
facebook.com/jyforkids • twitter.com/jyforkids
jyforkids.tumblr.com • instagram.com/jyforkids

First JY Edition: June 2021

JY is an imprint of Yen Press, LLC.
The JY name and logo are trademarks of Yen Press, LLC.

The publisher is not responsible for websites (or their content) that are not owned by the publisher.

Library of Congress Control Number: 2021934049

ISBNs: 978-1-9753-3589-2 (hardcover)
978-1-9753-1654-9 (paperback)
978-1-9753-3590-8 (ebook)

10 9 8 7 6 5 4 3 2 1

LSC-C

Printed in the United States of America

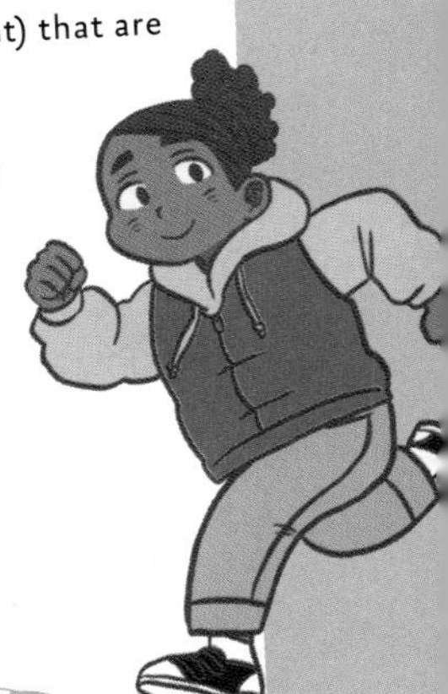

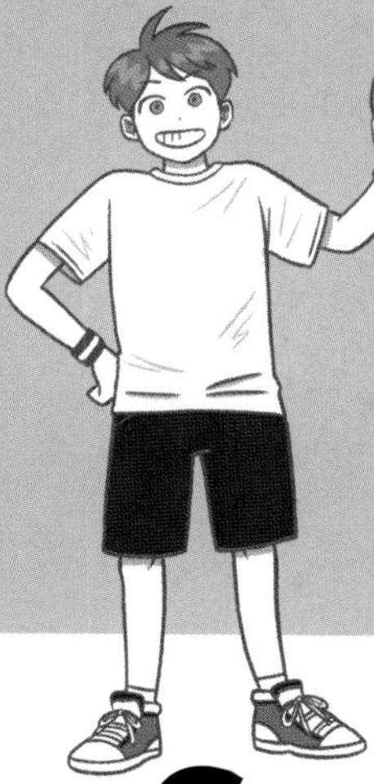

Table of Contents

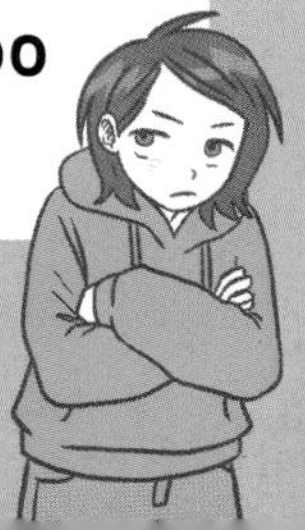

CHAPTER 1

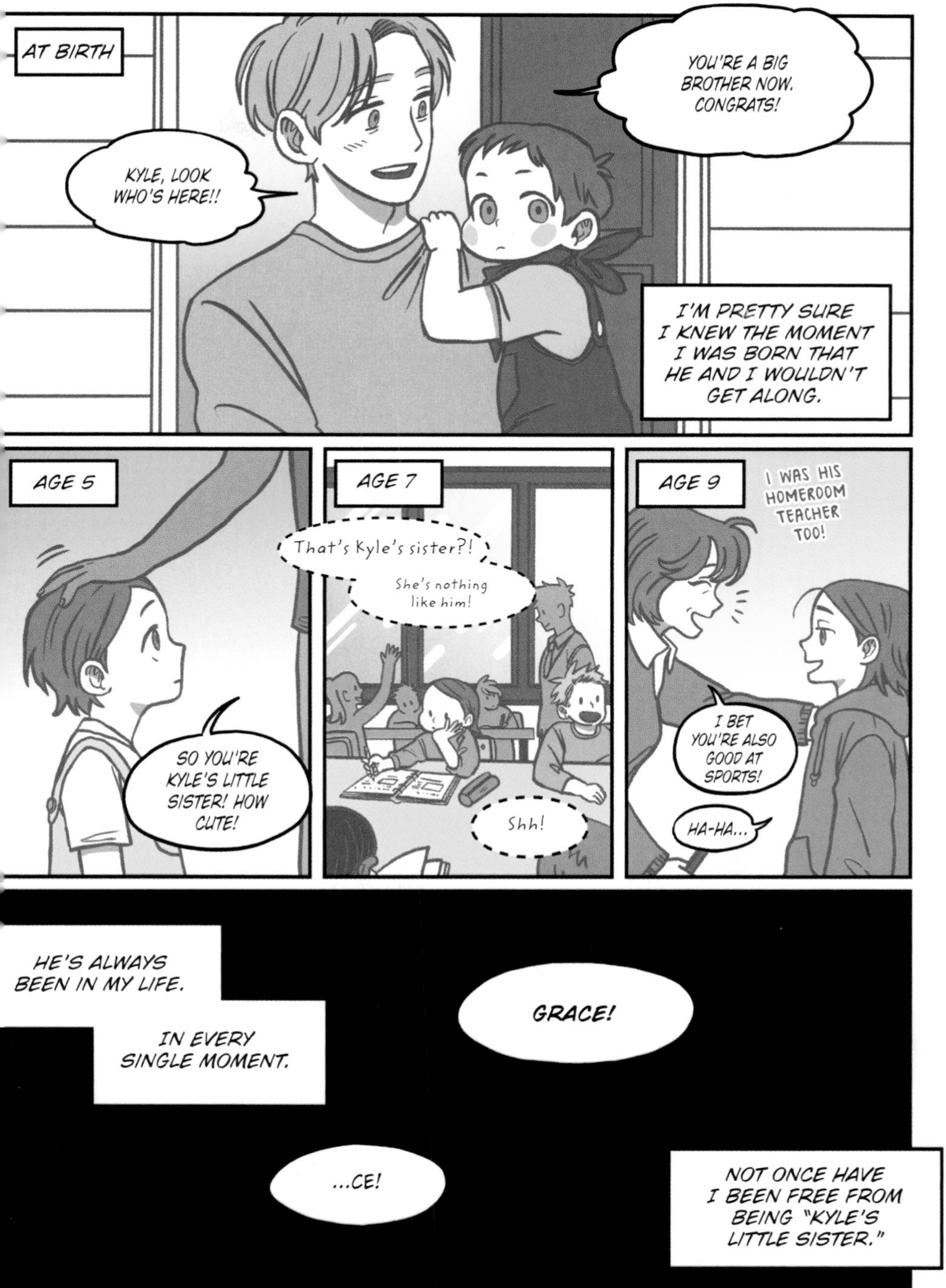
AT BIRTH
KYLE, LOOK WHO'S HERE!!
YOU'RE A BIG BROTHER NOW. CONGRATS!
I'M PRETTY SURE I KNEW THE MOMENT I WAS BORN THAT HE AND I WOULDN'T GET ALONG.
AGE 5
SO YOU'RE KYLE'S LITTLE SISTER! HOW CUTE!
AGE 7
That's Kyle's sister?!
She's nothing like him!
Shh!
AGE 9
I WAS HIS HOMEROOM TEACHER TOO!
I BET YOU'RE ALSO GOOD AT SPORTS!
HA-HA...
HE'S ALWAYS BEEN IN MY LIFE.
IN EVERY SINGLE MOMENT.
GRACE!
...CE!
NOT ONCE HAVE I BEEN FREE FROM BEING "KYLE'S LITTLE SISTER."

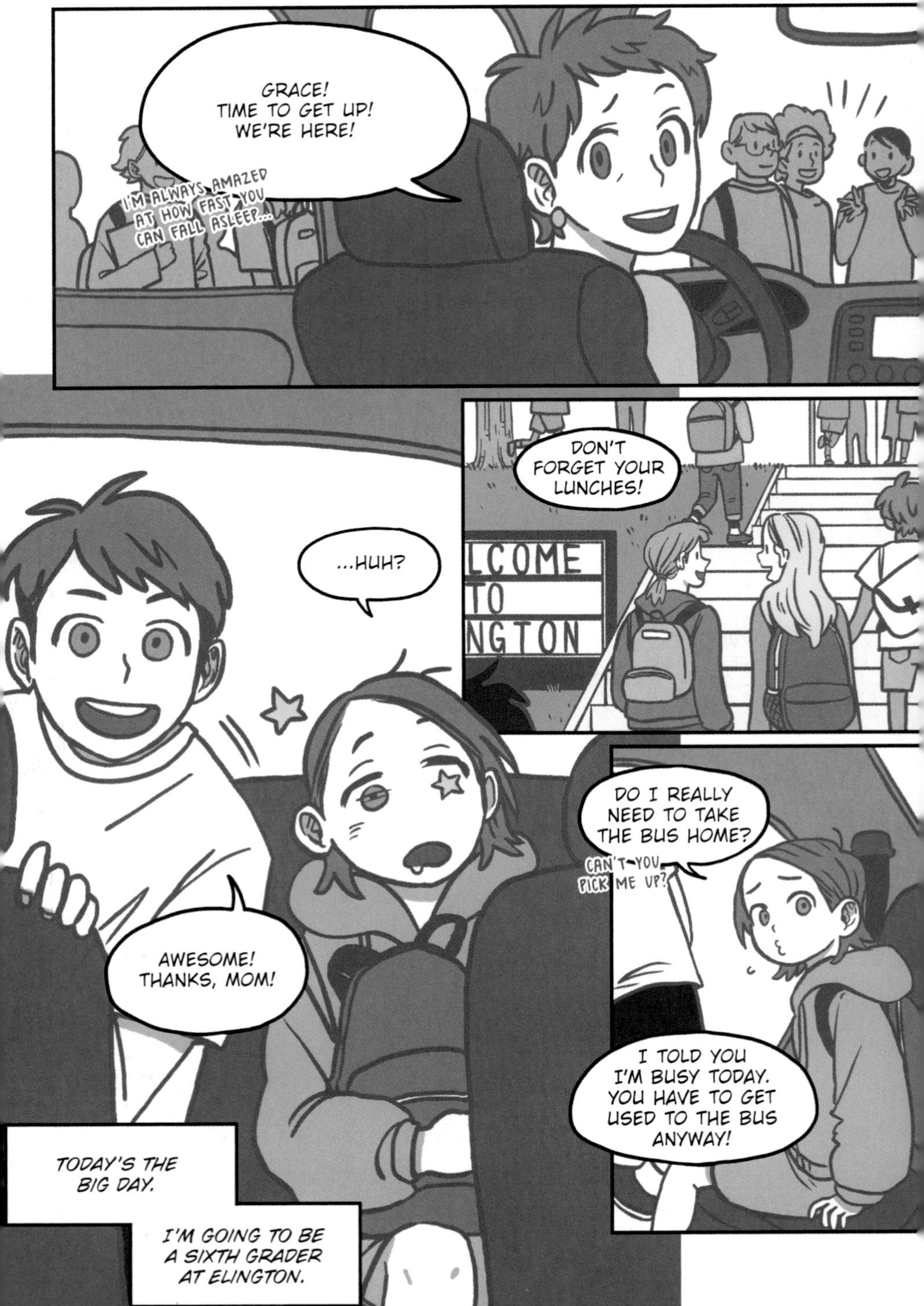
GRACE!
TIME TO GET UP!
WE'RE HERE!
I'M ALWAYS AMAZED AT HOW FAST YOU CAN FALL ASLEEP...
...HUH?
AWESOME! THANKS, MOM!
TODAY'S THE BIG DAY.
I'M GOING TO BE A SIXTH GRADER AT ELINGTON.
DON'T FORGET YOUR LUNCHES!
LCOME TO NGTON
DO I REALLY NEED TO TAKE THE BUS HOME?
CAN'T YOU PICK ME UP?
I TOLD YOU I'M BUSY TODAY. YOU HAVE TO GET USED TO THE BUS ANYWAY!

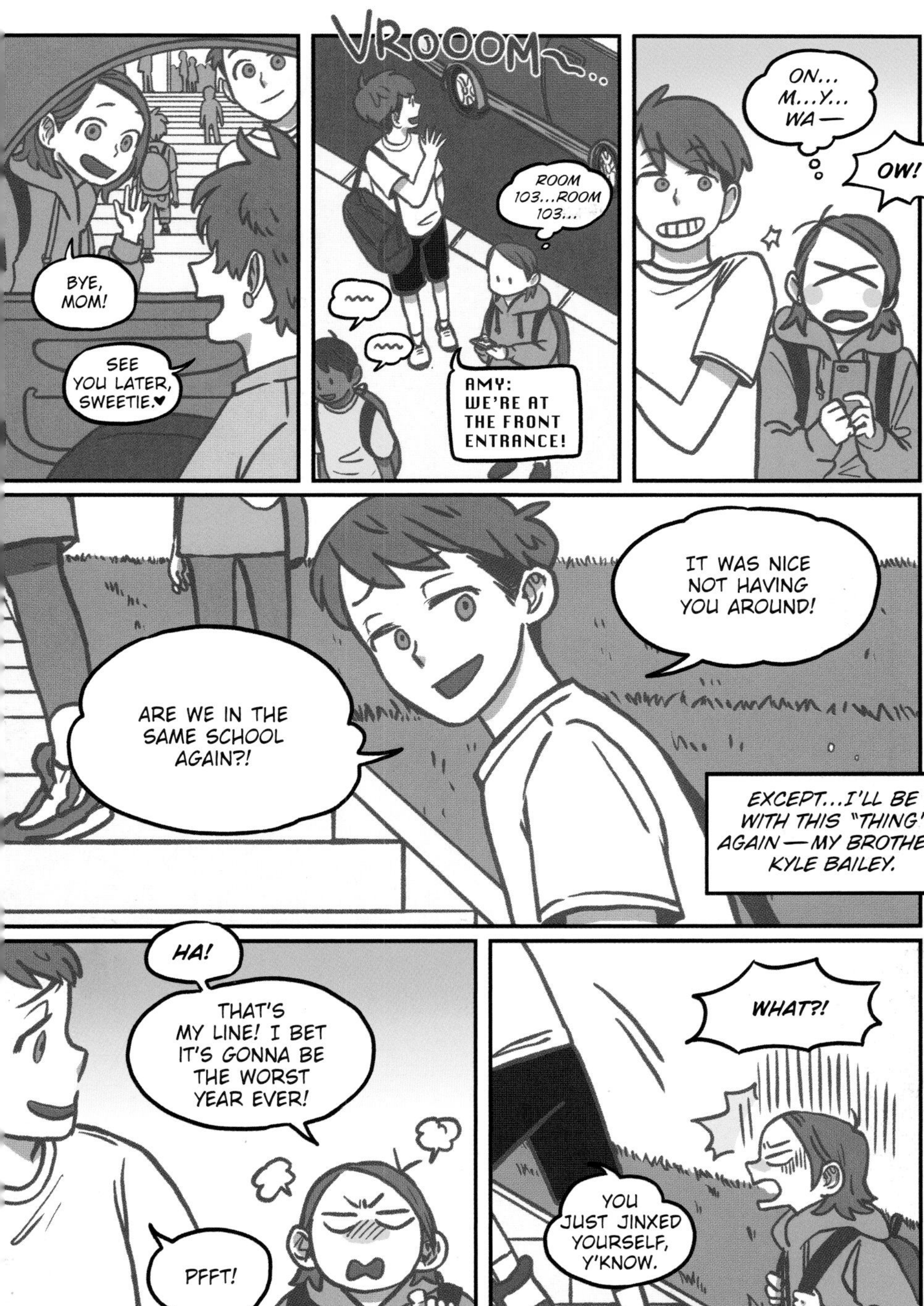
BYE, MOM!
SEE YOU LATER, SWEETIE.♥
VROOOM~...
ROOM 103...ROOM 103...
AMY: WE'RE AT THE FRONT ENTRANCE!
ON... M...Y... WA—
OW!
IT WAS NICE NOT HAVING YOU AROUND!
ARE WE IN THE SAME SCHOOL AGAIN?!
EXCEPT...I'LL BE WITH THIS "THING" AGAIN—MY BROTHER, KYLE BAILEY.
HA!
THAT'S MY LINE! I BET IT'S GONNA BE THE WORST YEAR EVER!
PFFT!
WHAT?!
YOU JUST JINXED YOURSELF, Y'KNOW.

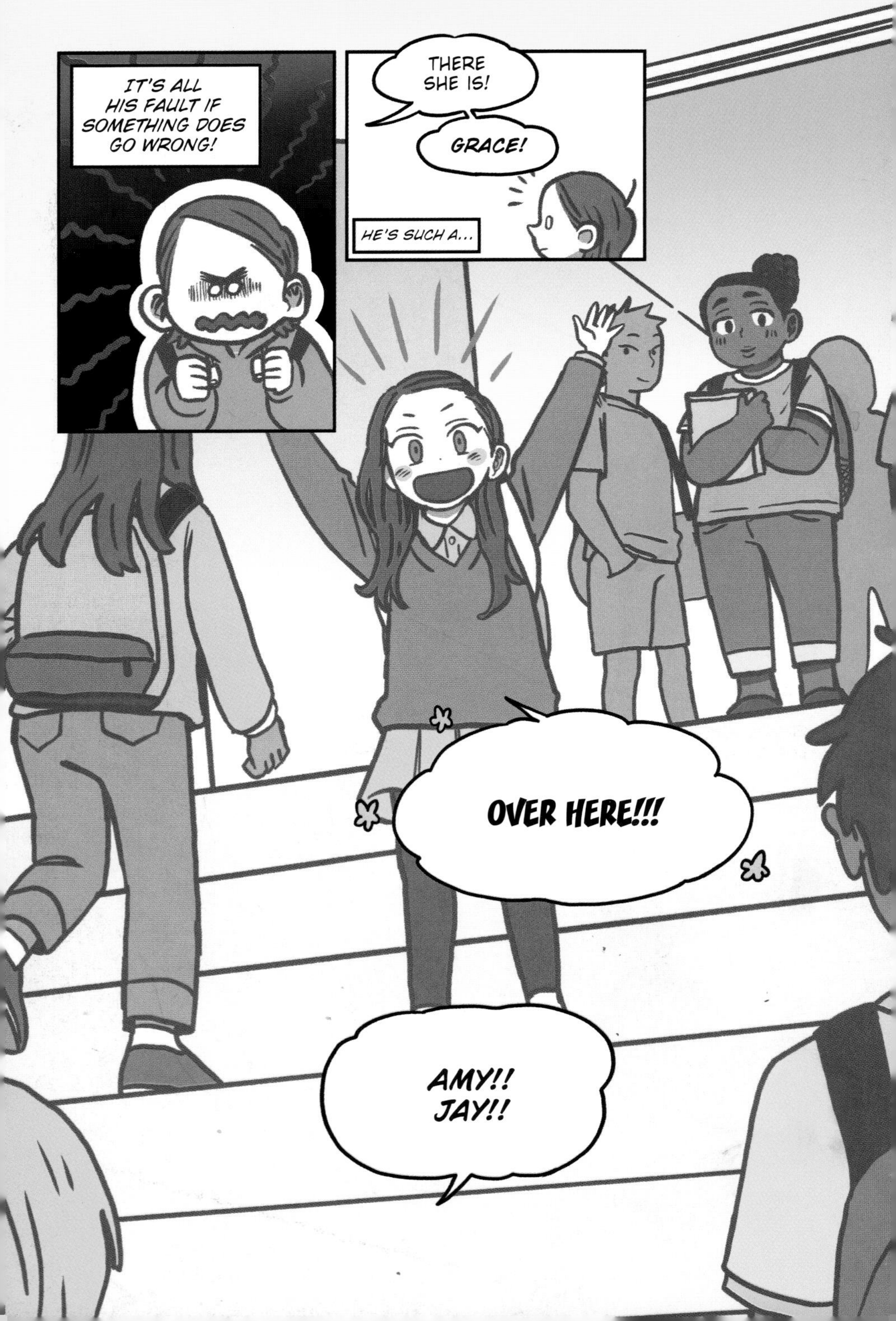
IT'S ALL HIS FAULT IF SOMETHING DOES GO WRONG!
THERE SHE IS!
GRACE!
HE'S SUCH A...
OVER HERE!!!
AMY!! JAY!!

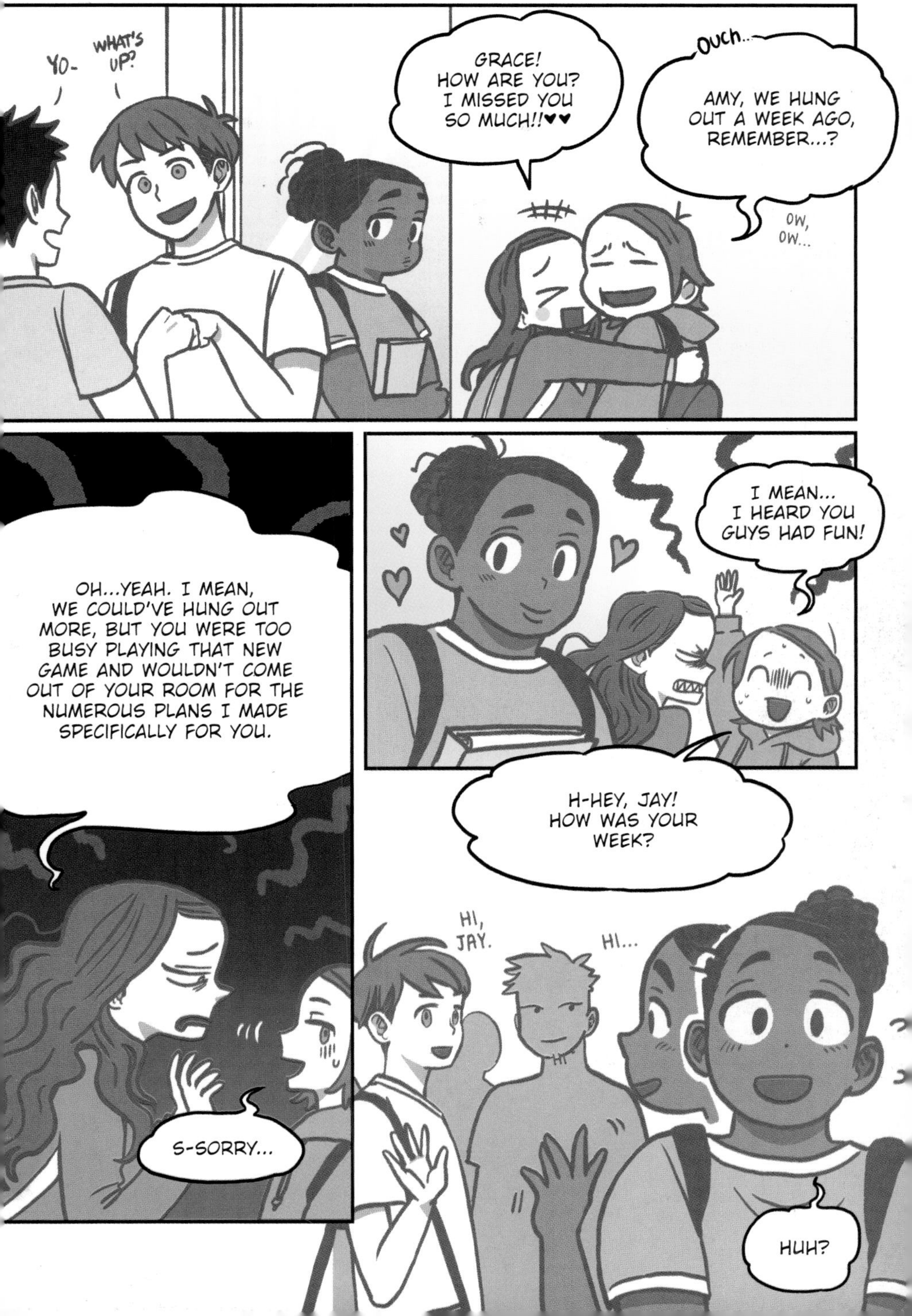
YO-
WHAT'S UP?
GRACE! HOW ARE YOU? I MISSED YOU SO MUCH!!♥♥
Ouch...
AMY, WE HUNG OUT A WEEK AGO, REMEMBER...?
OW, OW...
OH...YEAH. I MEAN, WE COULD'VE HUNG OUT MORE, BUT YOU WERE TOO BUSY PLAYING THAT NEW GAME AND WOULDN'T COME OUT OF YOUR ROOM FOR THE NUMEROUS PLANS I MADE SPECIFICALLY FOR YOU.
I MEAN... I HEARD YOU GUYS HAD FUN!
H-HEY, JAY! HOW WAS YOUR WEEK?
S-SORRY...
HI, JAY.
HI...
HUH?

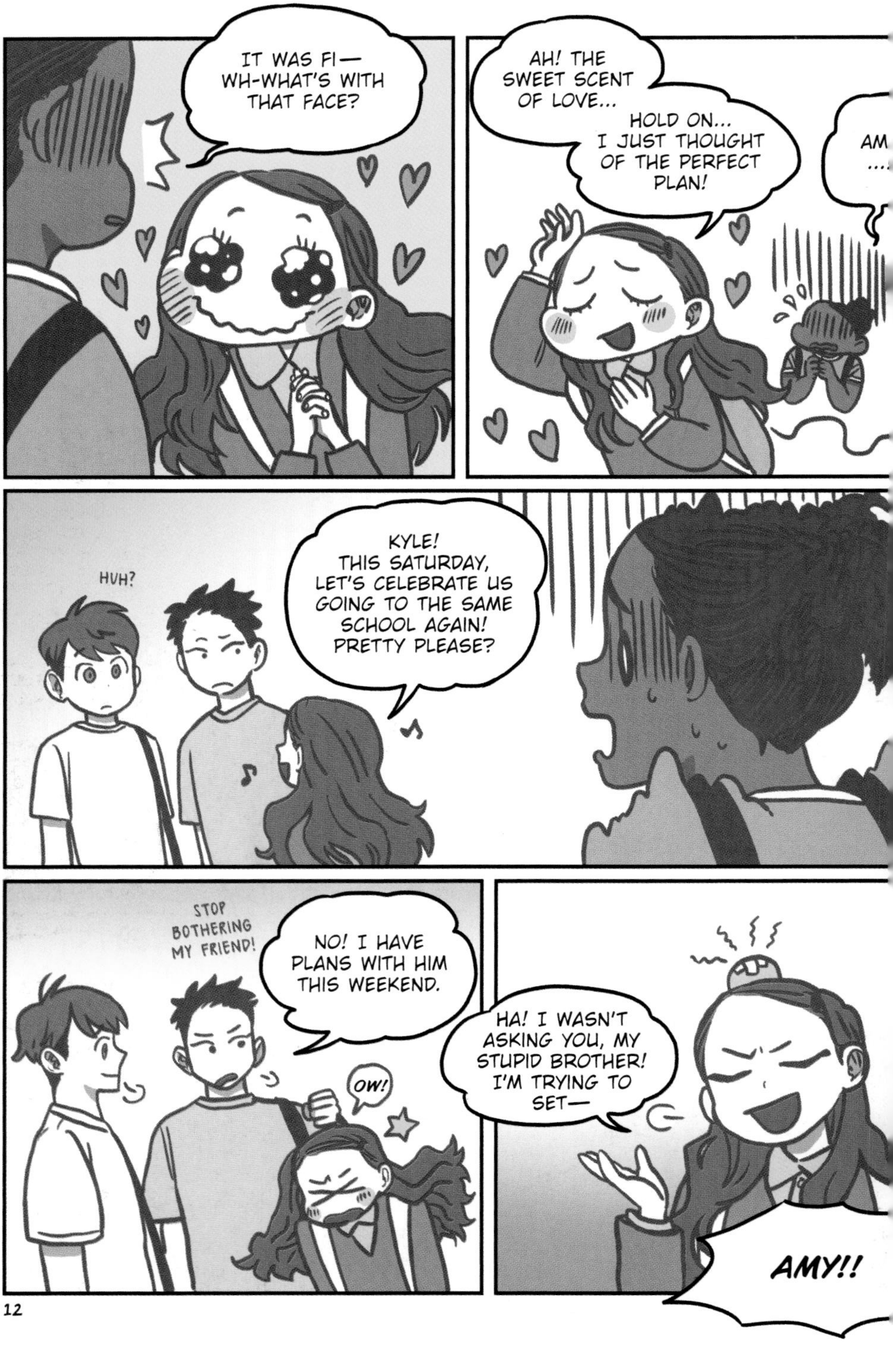
IT WAS FI— WH-WHAT'S WITH THAT FACE?
AH! THE SWEET SCENT OF LOVE...
HOLD ON... I JUST THOUGHT OF THE PERFECT PLAN!
HUH?
KYLE! THIS SATURDAY, LET'S CELEBRATE US GOING TO THE SAME SCHOOL AGAIN! PRETTY PLEASE?
STOP BOTHERING MY FRIEND!
NO! I HAVE PLANS WITH HIM THIS WEEKEND.
OW!
HA! I WASN'T ASKING YOU, MY STUPID BROTHER! I'M TRYING TO SET—
AMY!!

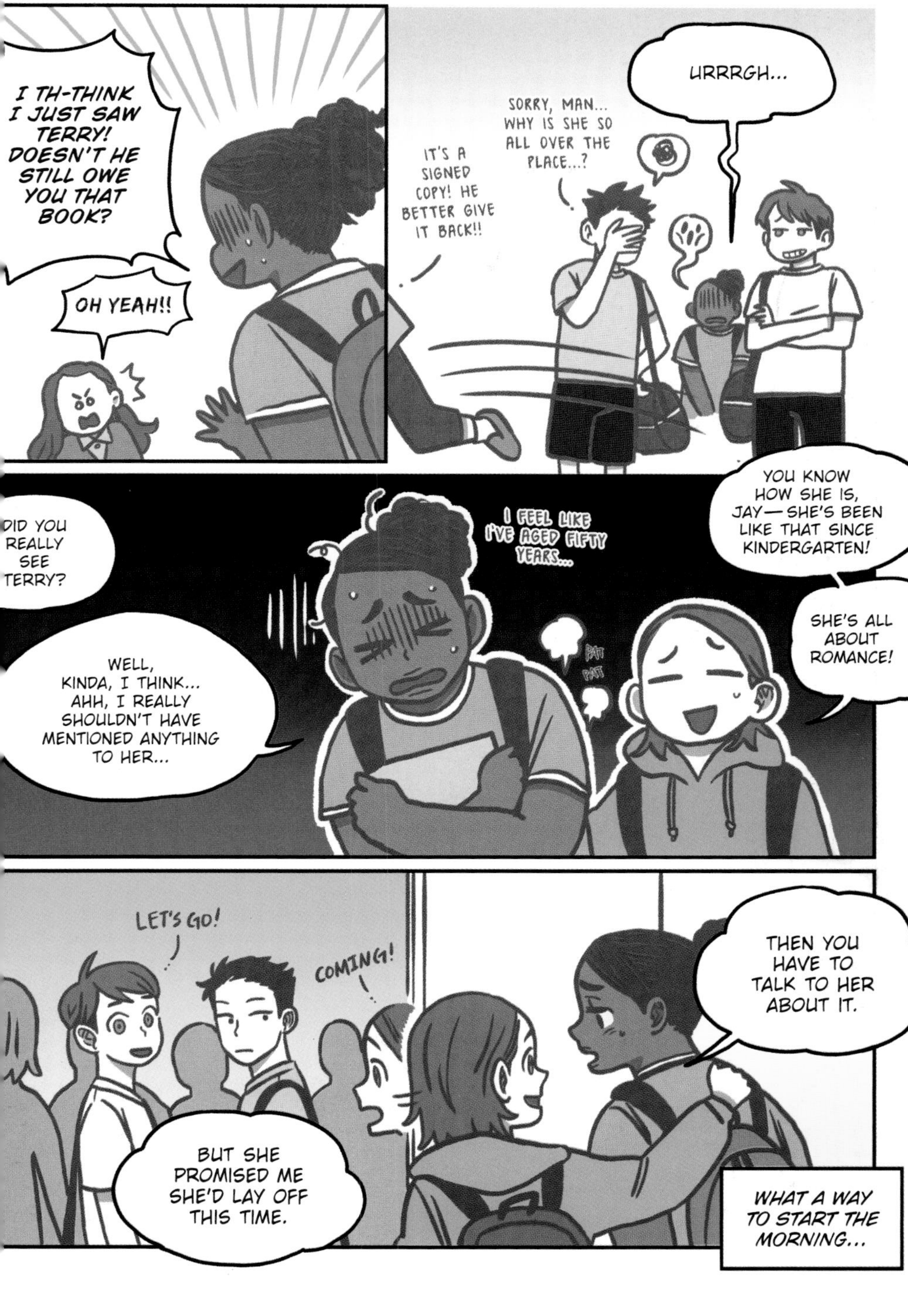
I TH-THINK I JUST SAW TERRY! DOESN'T HE STILL OWE YOU THAT BOOK?
OH YEAH!!
IT'S A SIGNED COPY! HE BETTER GIVE IT BACK!!
SORRY, MAN... WHY IS SHE SO ALL OVER THE PLACE...?
URRRGH...
DID YOU REALLY SEE TERRY?
WELL, KINDA, I THINK... AHH, I REALLY SHOULDN'T HAVE MENTIONED ANYTHING TO HER...
I FEEL LIKE I'VE AGED FIFTY YEARS...
PAT
PAT
YOU KNOW HOW SHE IS, JAY— SHE'S BEEN LIKE THAT SINCE KINDERGARTEN!
SHE'S ALL ABOUT ROMANCE!
LET'S GO!
COMING!
BUT SHE PROMISED ME SHE'D LAY OFF THIS TIME.
THEN YOU HAVE TO TALK TO HER ABOUT IT.
WHAT A WAY TO START THE MORNING...

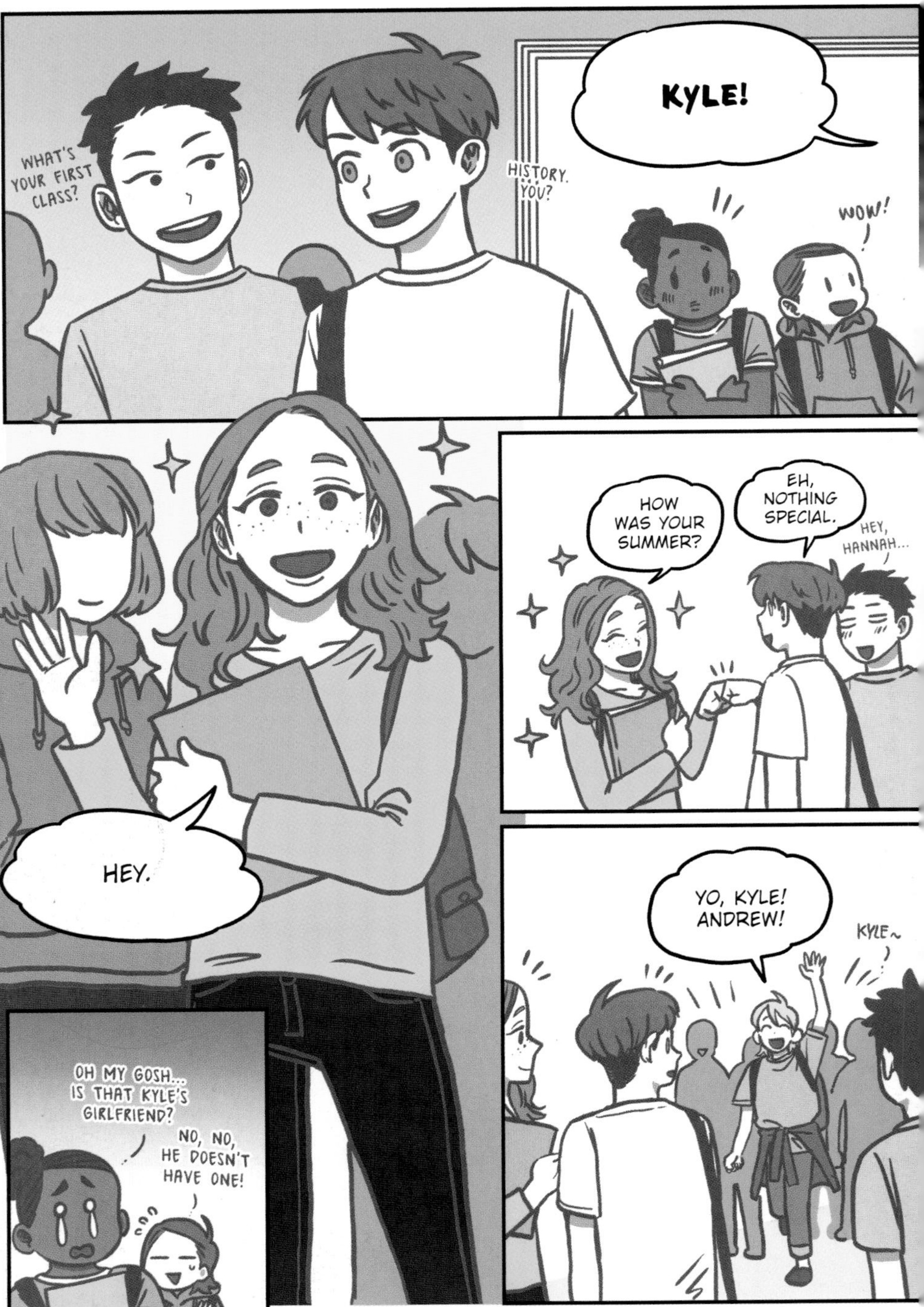
WHAT'S YOUR FIRST CLASS?
HISTORY. YOU?
KYLE!
WOW!
HEY.
HOW WAS YOUR SUMMER?
EH, NOTHING SPECIAL.
HEY, HANNAH...
OH MY GOSH... IS THAT KYLE'S GIRLFRIEND?
NO, NO, HE DOESN'T HAVE ONE!
YO, KYLE! ANDREW!
KYLE~

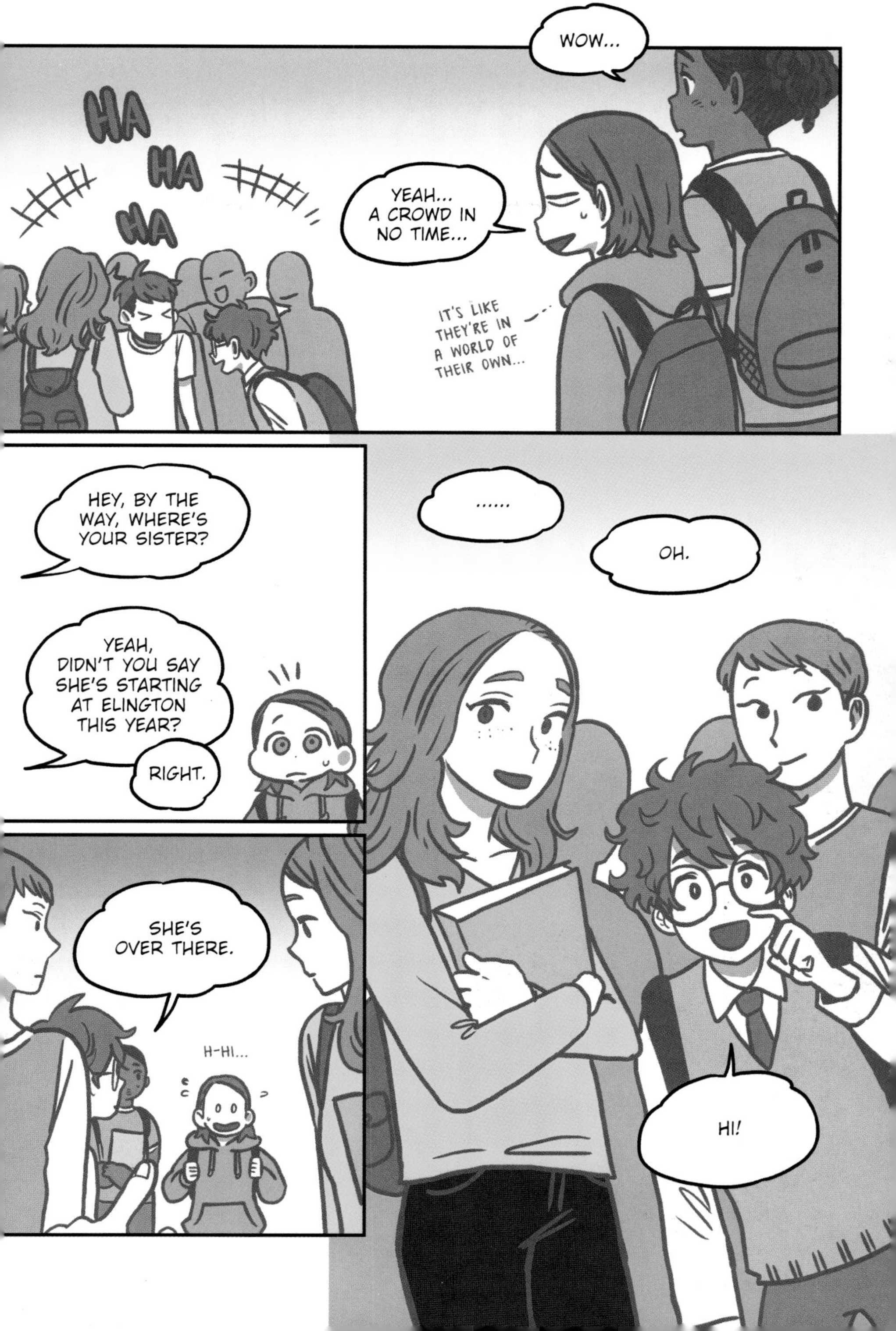
HA HA HA
WOW...
YEAH... A CROWD IN NO TIME...
IT'S LIKE THEY'RE IN A WORLD OF THEIR OWN...
HEY, BY THE WAY, WHERE'S YOUR SISTER?
YEAH, DIDN'T YOU SAY SHE'S STARTING AT ELINGTON THIS YEAR?
RIGHT.
SHE'S OVER THERE.
H-HI...
......
OH.
HI!

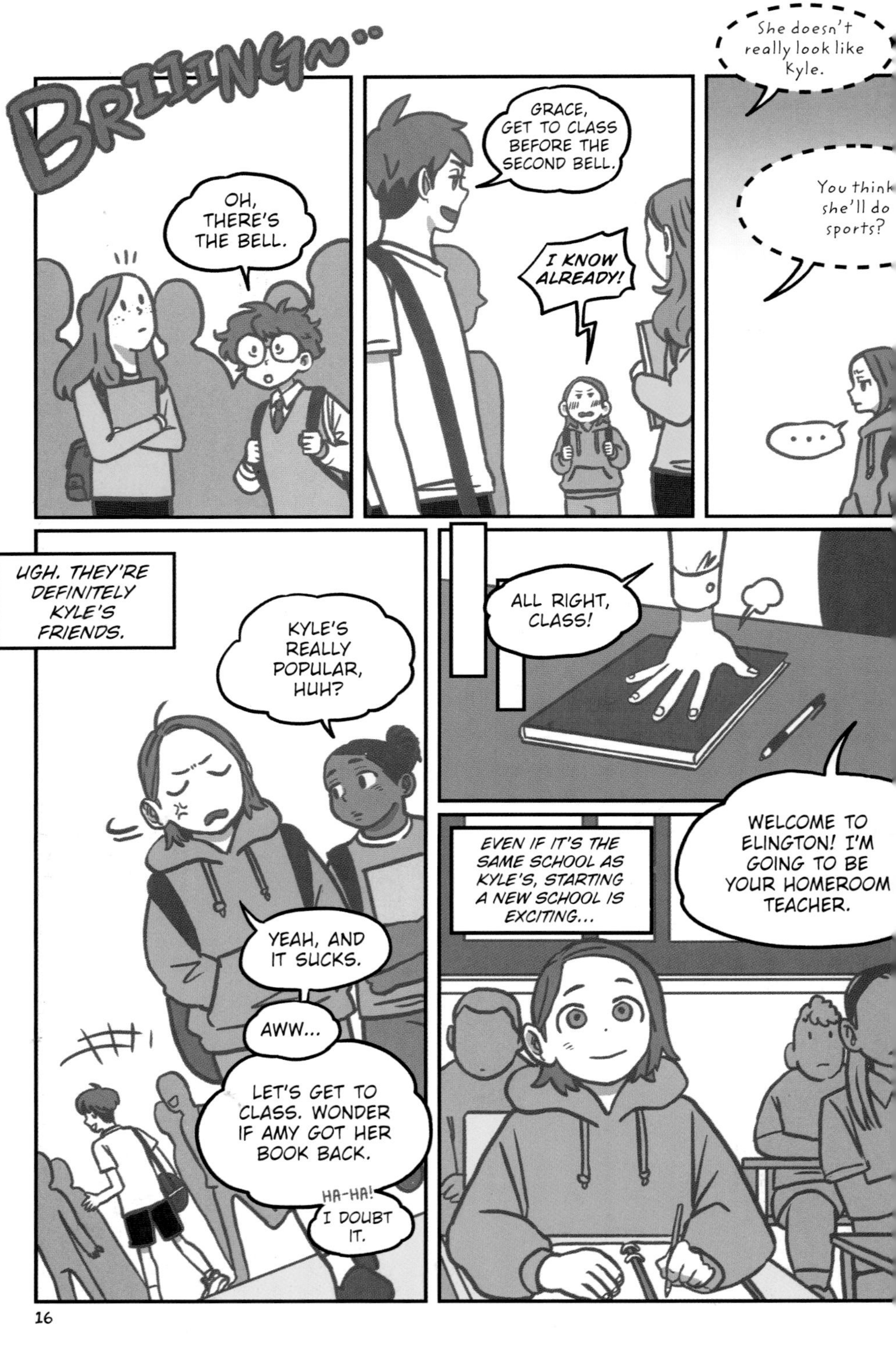
BRIIIING~
OH, THERE'S THE BELL.
GRACE, GET TO CLASS BEFORE THE SECOND BELL.
I KNOW ALREADY!
She doesn't really look like Kyle.
You think she'll do sports?
...
UGH. THEY'RE DEFINITELY KYLE'S FRIENDS.
KYLE'S REALLY POPULAR, HUH?
YEAH, AND IT SUCKS.
AWW...
LET'S GET TO CLASS. WONDER IF AMY GOT HER BOOK BACK.
HA-HA! I DOUBT IT.
ALL RIGHT, CLASS!
EVEN IF IT'S THE SAME SCHOOL AS KYLE'S, STARTING A NEW SCHOOL IS EXCITING...
WELCOME TO ELINGTON! I'M GOING TO BE YOUR HOMEROOM TEACHER.

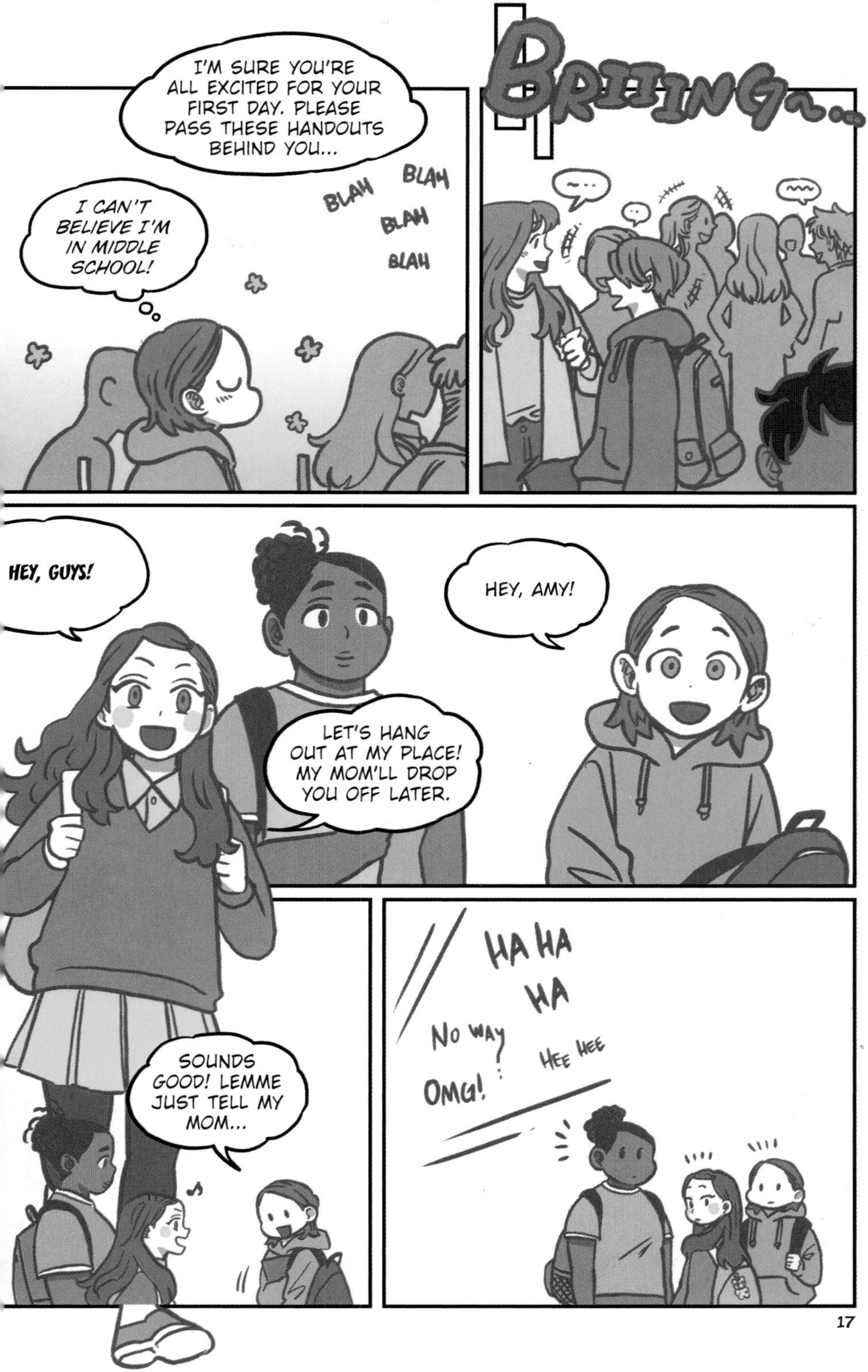
I'M SURE YOU'RE ALL EXCITED FOR YOUR FIRST DAY. PLEASE PASS THESE HANDOUTS BEHIND YOU...
I CAN'T BELIEVE I'M IN MIDDLE SCHOOL!
BLAH BLAH BLAH BLAH
BRIIING~...
HEY, GUYS!
HEY, AMY!
LET'S HANG OUT AT MY PLACE! MY MOM'LL DROP YOU OFF LATER.
SOUNDS GOOD! LEMME JUST TELL MY MOM...
HA HA HA
NO WAY
HEE HEE
OMG!

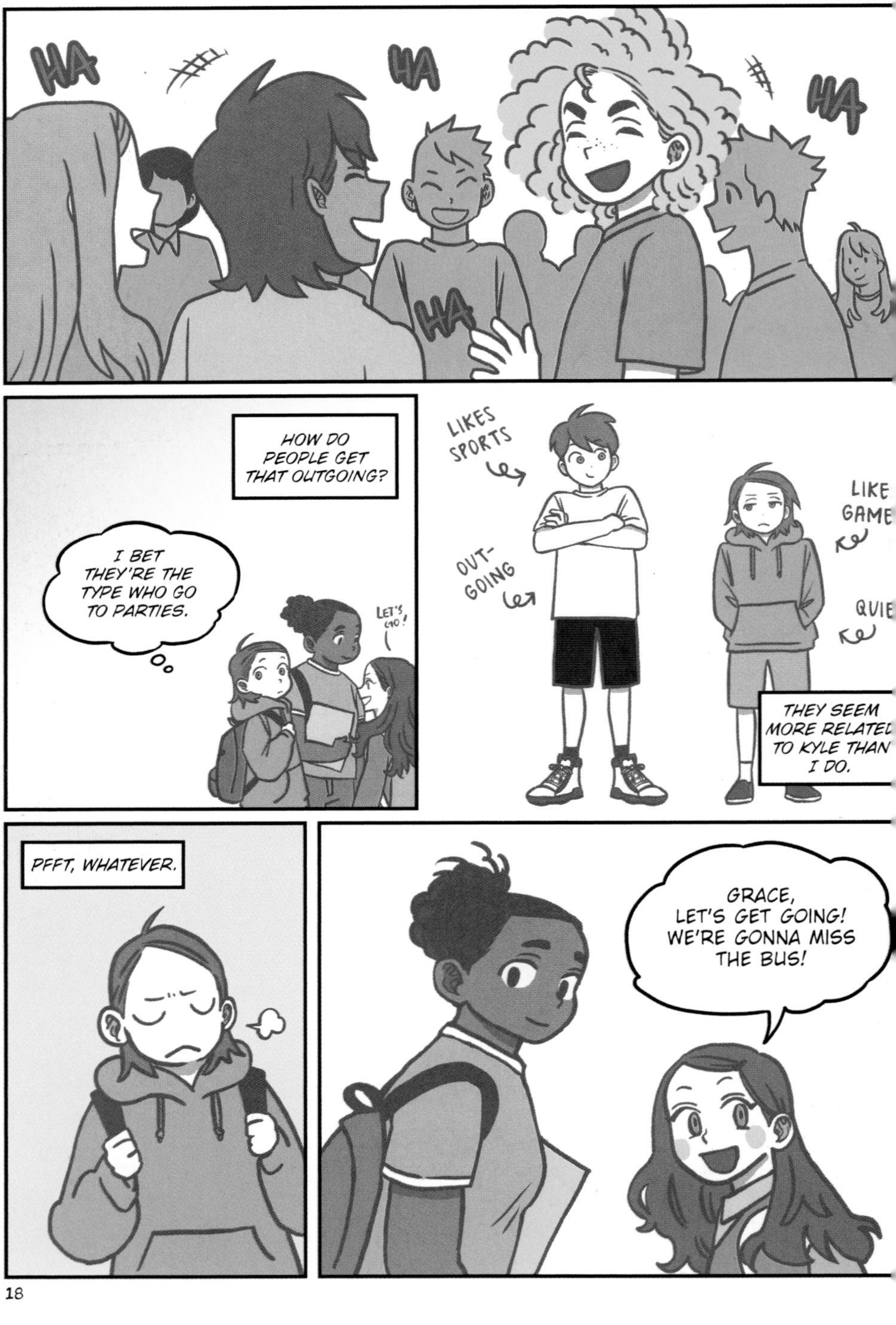

HA
HA
HA
HA
HOW DO PEOPLE GET THAT OUTGOING?
I BET THEY'RE THE TYPE WHO GO TO PARTIES.
LET'S GO!
LIKES SPORTS
OUT-GOING
LIKE GAME
QUIE
THEY SEEM MORE RELATED TO KYLE THAN I DO.
PFFT, WHATEVER.
GRACE, LET'S GET GOING! WE'RE GONNA MISS THE BUS!

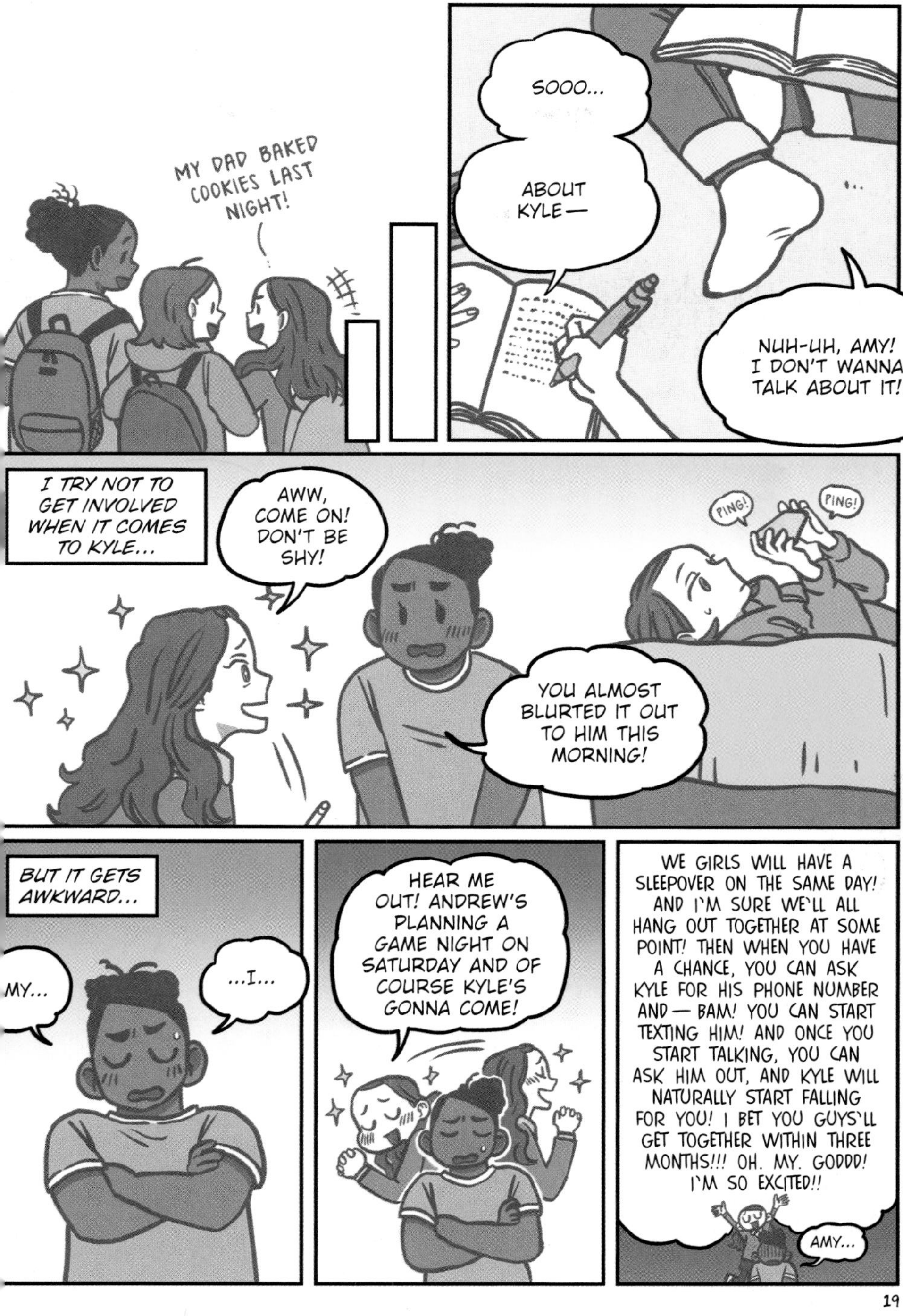
MY DAD BAKED COOKIES LAST NIGHT!
SOOO...
ABOUT KYLE—
...
NUH-UH, AMY! I DON'T WANNA TALK ABOUT IT!
I TRY NOT TO GET INVOLVED WHEN IT COMES TO KYLE...
AWW, COME ON! DON'T BE SHY!
PING!
PING!
YOU ALMOST BLURTED IT OUT TO HIM THIS MORNING!
BUT IT GETS AWKWARD...
MY...
...I...
HEAR ME OUT! ANDREW'S PLANNING A GAME NIGHT ON SATURDAY AND OF COURSE KYLE'S GONNA COME!
WE GIRLS WILL HAVE A SLEEPOVER ON THE SAME DAY! AND I'M SURE WE'LL ALL HANG OUT TOGETHER AT SOME POINT! THEN WHEN YOU HAVE A CHANCE, YOU CAN ASK KYLE FOR HIS PHONE NUMBER AND—BAM! YOU CAN START TEXTING HIM! AND ONCE YOU START TALKING, YOU CAN ASK HIM OUT, AND KYLE WILL NATURALLY START FALLING FOR YOU! I BET YOU GUYS'LL GET TOGETHER WITHIN THREE MONTHS!!! OH. MY. GODDD! I'M SO EXCITED!!
AMY...

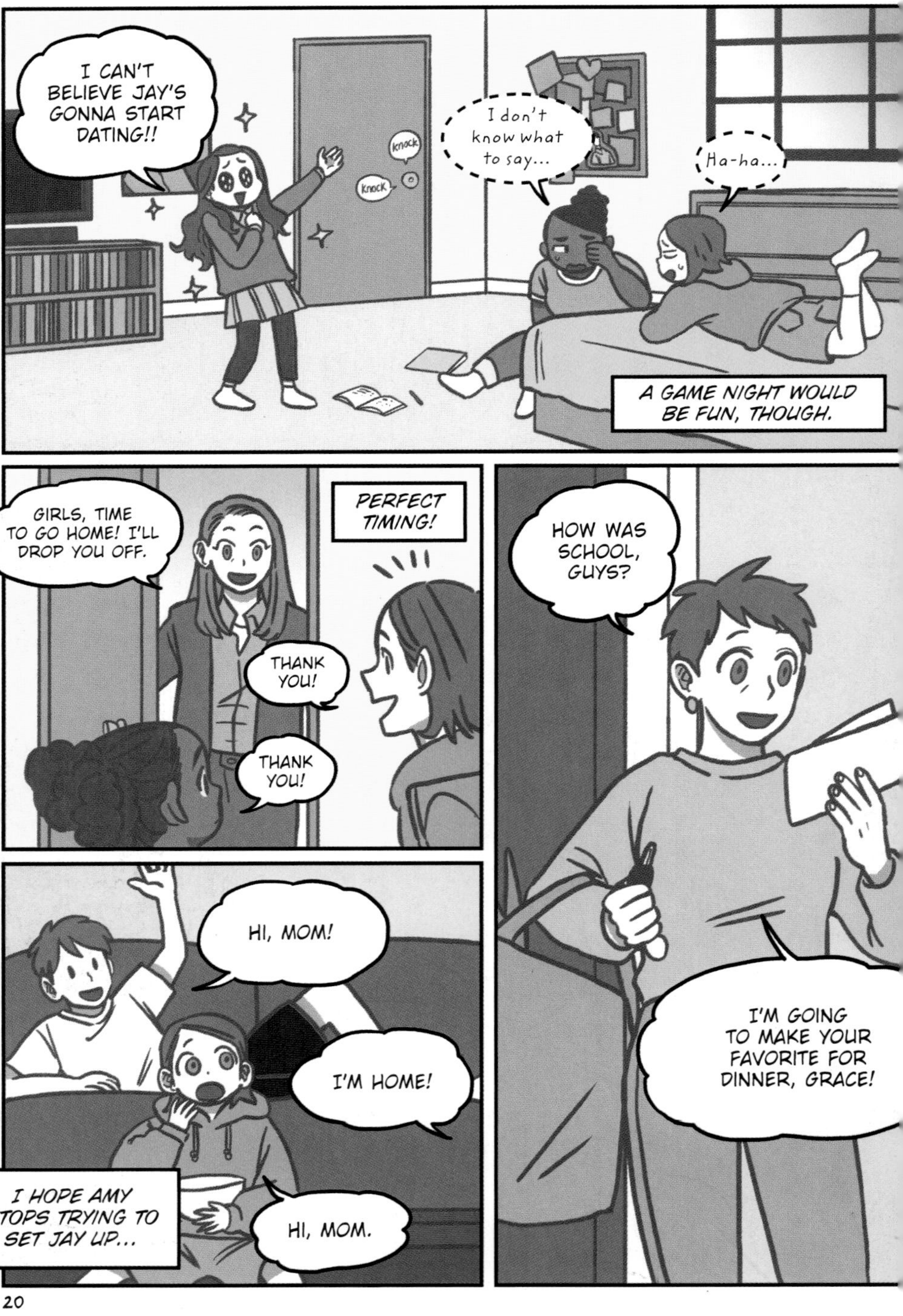
I CAN'T BELIEVE JAY'S GONNA START DATING!!
knock
knock
I don't know what to say...
Ha-ha...
A GAME NIGHT WOULD BE FUN, THOUGH.
GIRLS, TIME TO GO HOME! I'LL DROP YOU OFF.
PERFECT TIMING!
THANK YOU!
THANK YOU!
HI, MOM!
I'M HOME!
I HOPE AMY STOPS TRYING TO SET JAY UP...
HI, MOM.
HOW WAS SCHOOL, GUYS?
I'M GOING TO MAKE YOUR FAVORITE FOR DINNER, GRACE!

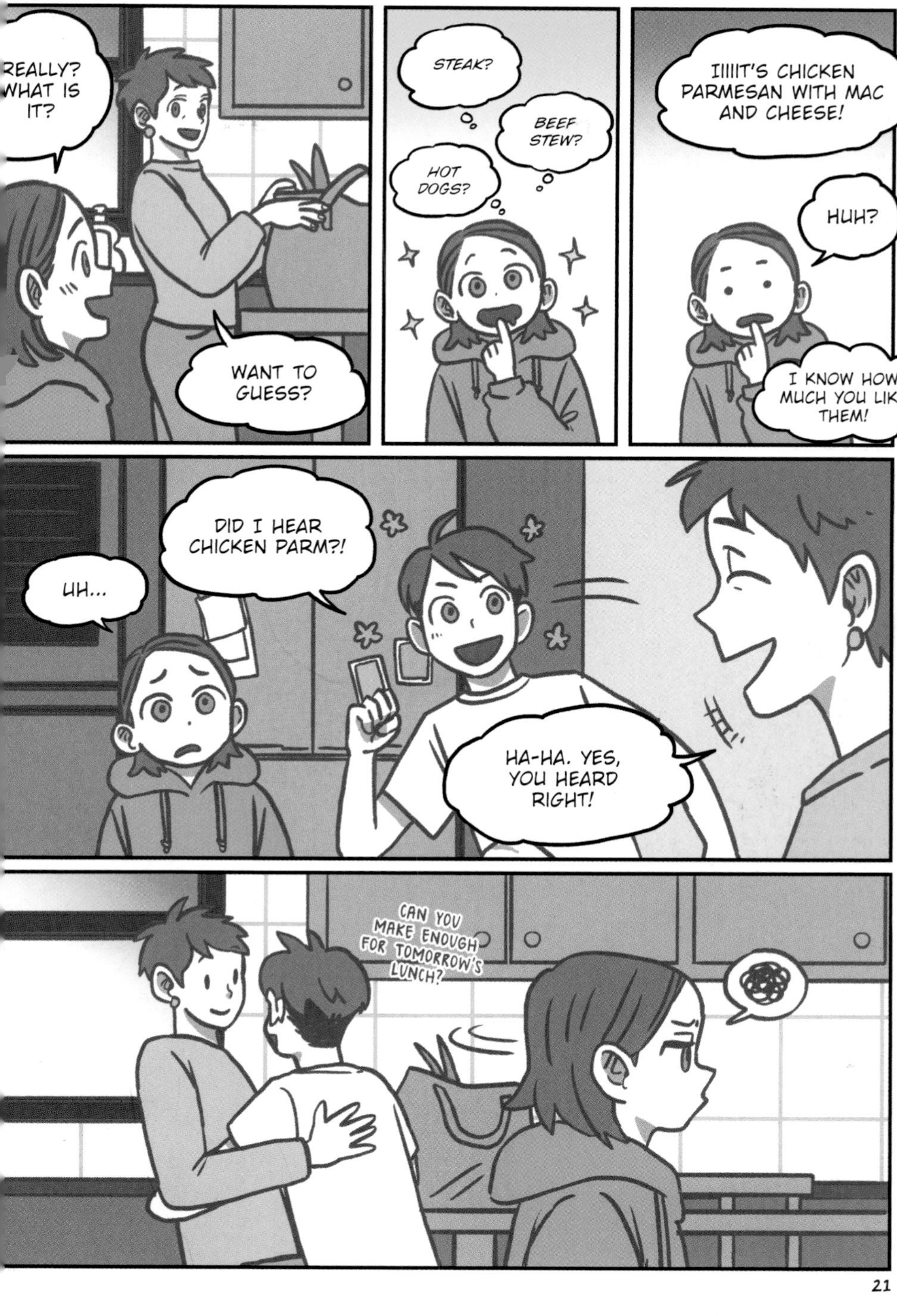
REALLY? WHAT IS IT?
WANT TO GUESS?
STEAK?
BEEF STEW?
HOT DOGS?
IIIIIT'S CHICKEN PARMESAN WITH MAC AND CHEESE!
HUH?
I KNOW HOW MUCH YOU LIKE THEM!
DID I HEAR CHICKEN PARM?!
UH...
HA-HA. YES, YOU HEARD RIGHT!
CAN YOU MAKE ENOUGH FOR TOMORROW'S LUNCH?

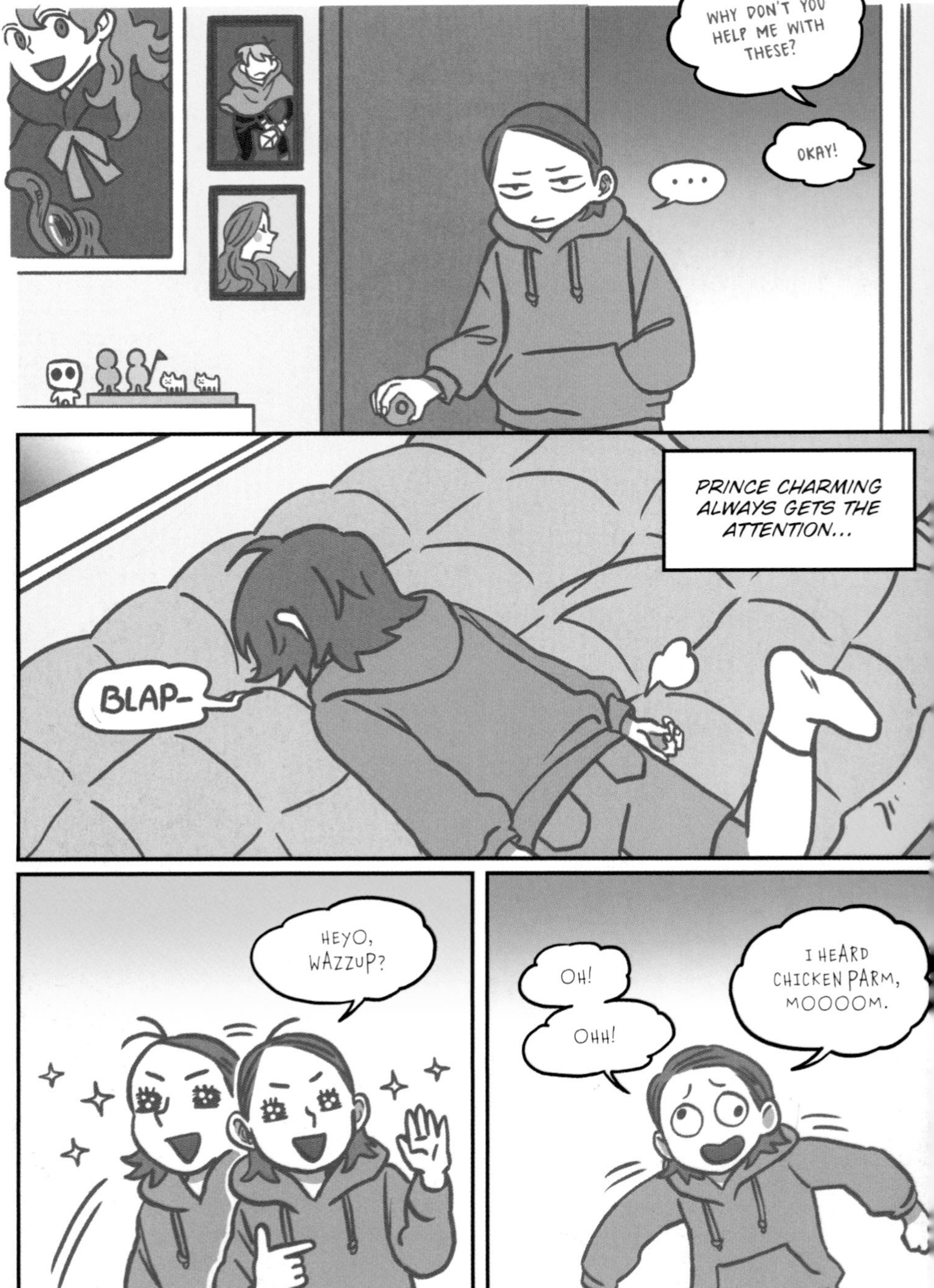
WHY DON'T YOU HELP ME WITH THESE?
OKAY!
...
PRINCE CHARMING ALWAYS GETS THE ATTENTION...
BLAP-
HEYO, WAZZUP?
OH!
OHH!
I HEARD CHICKEN PARM, MOOOOM.

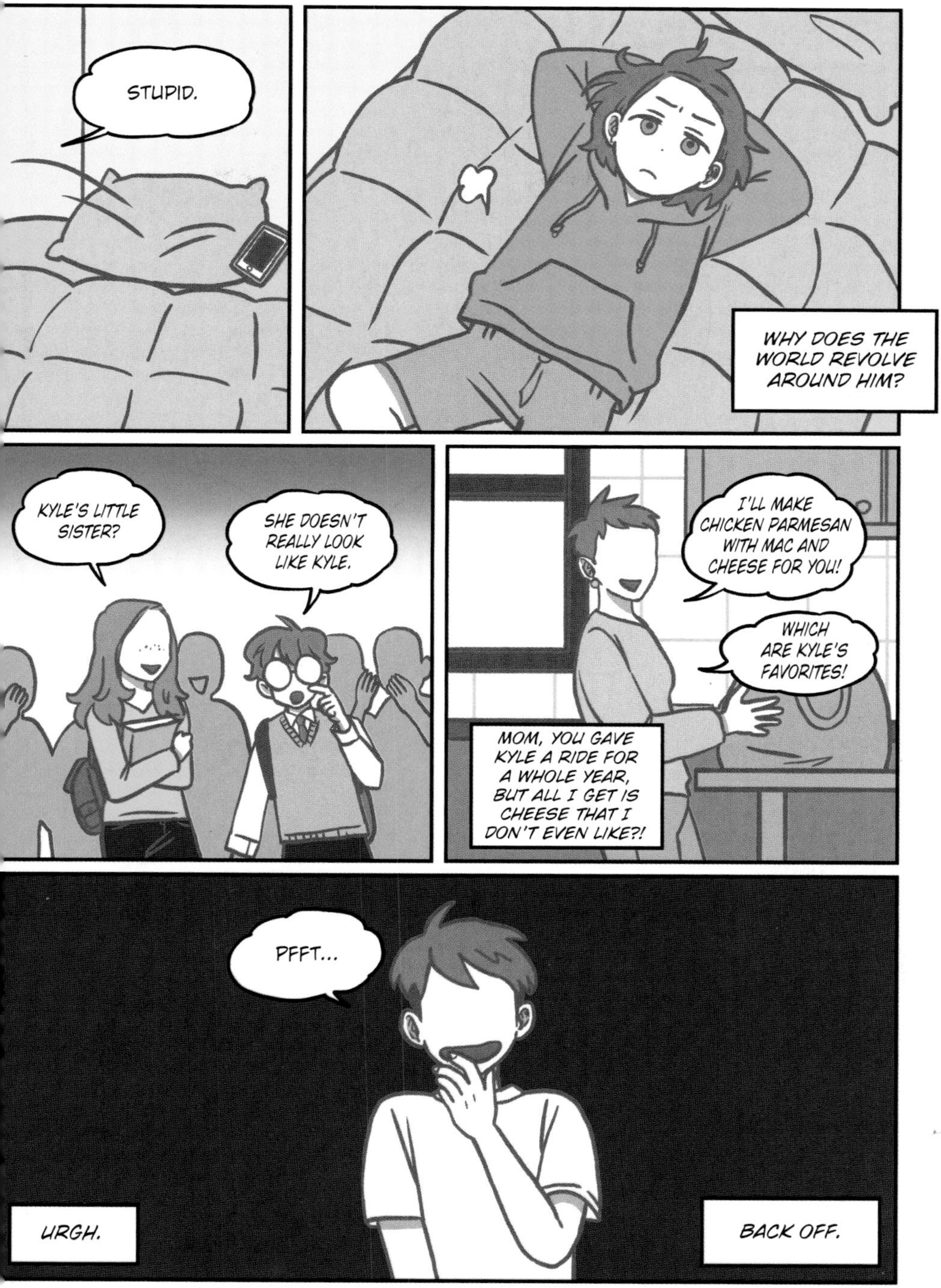
STUPID.
WHY DOES THE WORLD REVOLVE AROUND HIM?
KYLE'S LITTLE SISTER?
SHE DOESN'T REALLY LOOK LIKE KYLE.
I'LL MAKE CHICKEN PARMESAN WITH MAC AND CHEESE FOR YOU!
WHICH ARE KYLE'S FAVORITES!
MOM, YOU GAVE KYLE A RIDE FOR A WHOLE YEAR, BUT ALL I GET IS CHEESE THAT I DON'T EVEN LIKE?!
PFFT...
URGH.
BACK OFF.

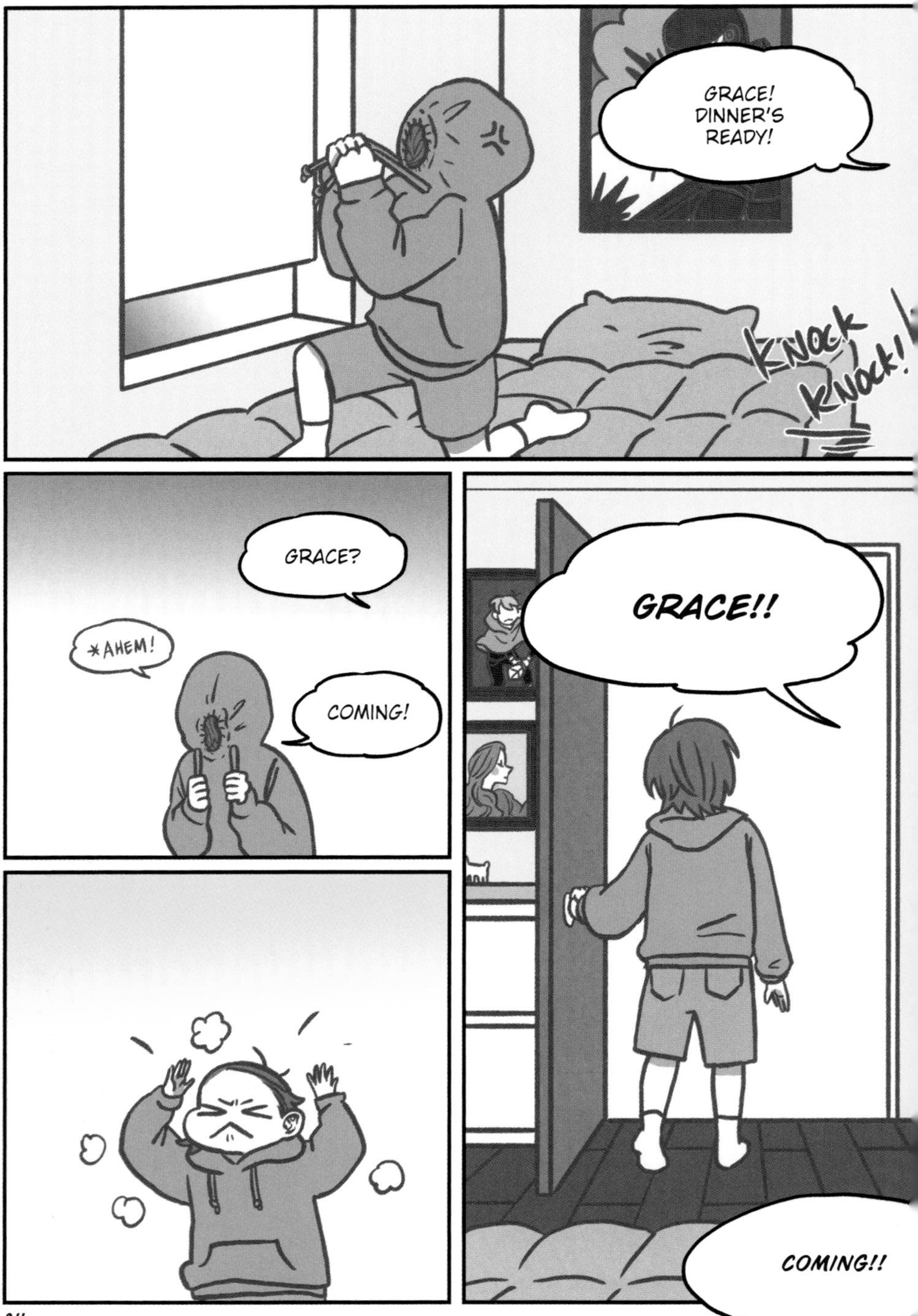
GRACE! DINNER'S READY!
KNOCK KNOCK!
GRACE?
*AHEM!
COMING!
GRACE!!
COMING!!

CHAPTER 2

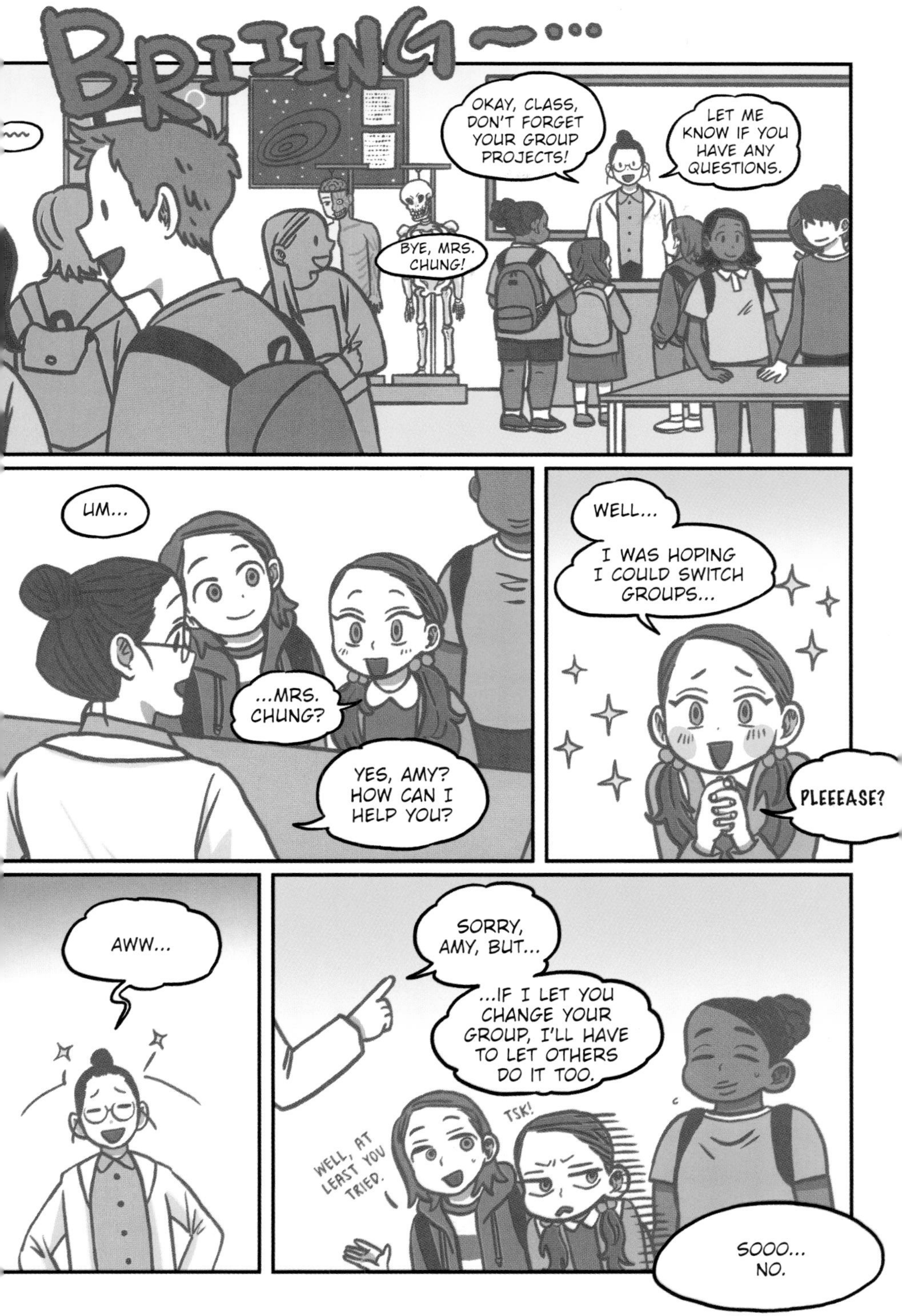
BRIIING~...
~~~
OKAY, CLASS, DON'T FORGET YOUR GROUP PROJECTS!
LET ME KNOW IF YOU HAVE ANY QUESTIONS.
BYE, MRS. CHUNG!
UM...
...MRS. CHUNG?
YES, AMY? HOW CAN I HELP YOU?
WELL...
I WAS HOPING I COULD SWITCH GROUPS...
PLEEEASE?
AWW...
SORRY, AMY, BUT...
...IF I LET YOU CHANGE YOUR GROUP, I'LL HAVE TO LET OTHERS DO IT TOO.
TSK!
WELL, AT LEAST YOU TRIED.
SOOO... NO.
~~~

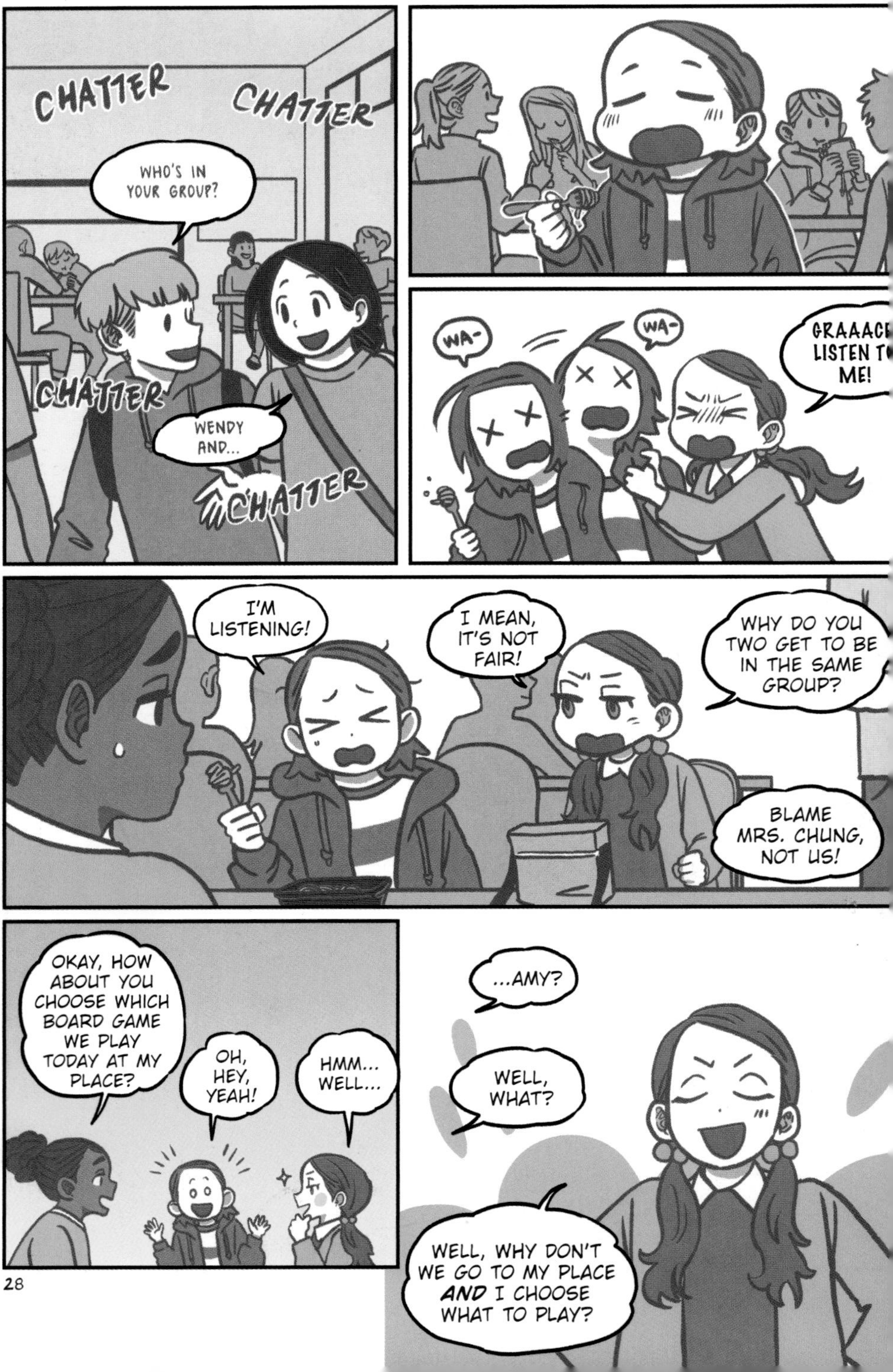
CHATTER
CHATTER
WHO'S IN YOUR GROUP?
CHATTER
WENDY AND...
CHATTER
WA-
WA-
GRAAACE LISTEN TO ME!
I'M LISTENING!
I MEAN, IT'S NOT FAIR!
WHY DO YOU TWO GET TO BE IN THE SAME GROUP?
BLAME MRS. CHUNG, NOT US!
OKAY, HOW ABOUT YOU CHOOSE WHICH BOARD GAME WE PLAY TODAY AT MY PLACE?
OH, HEY, YEAH!
HMM... WELL...
...AMY?
WELL, WHAT?
WELL, WHY DON'T WE GO TO MY PLACE AND I CHOOSE WHAT TO PLAY?

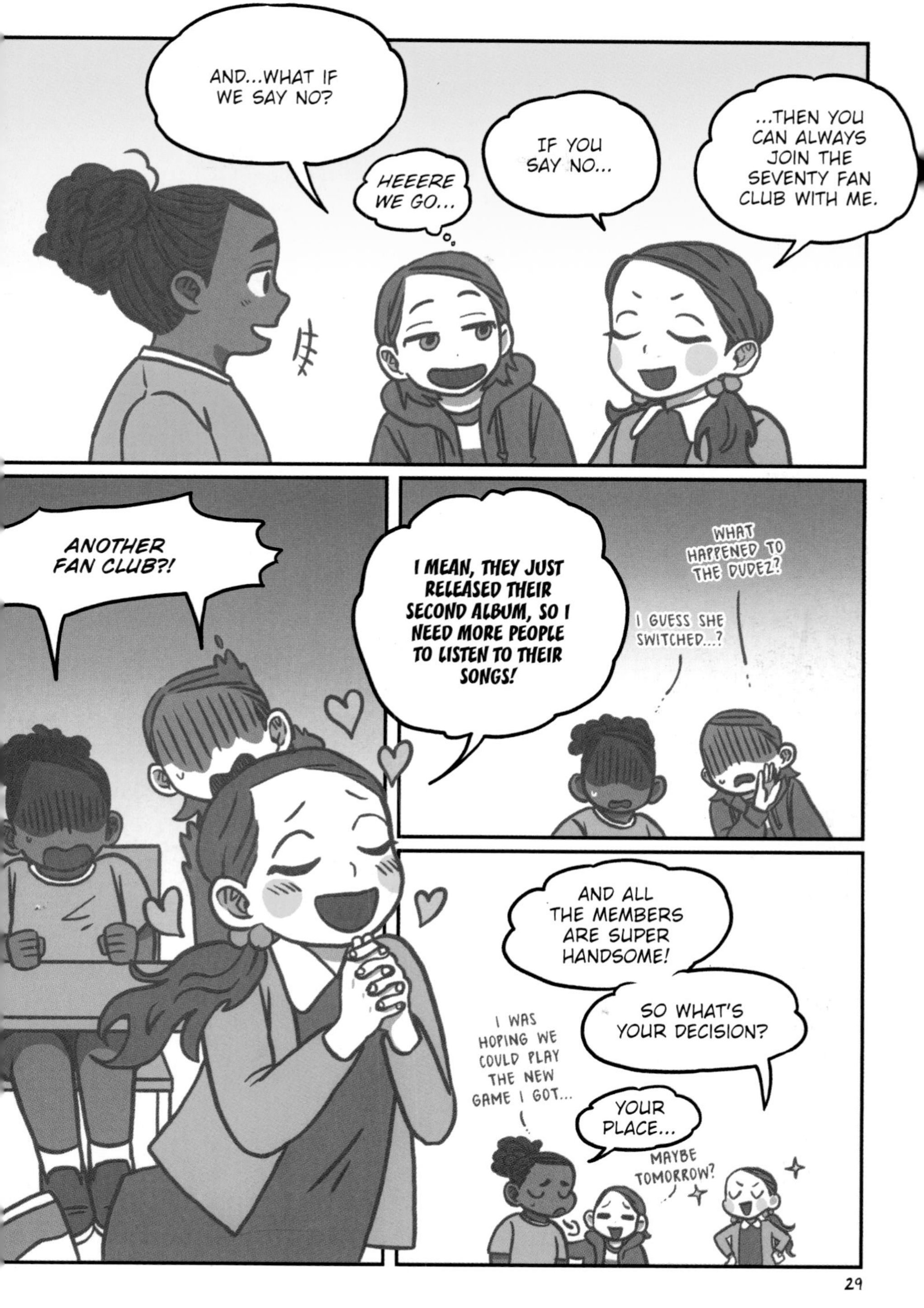
AND...WHAT IF WE SAY NO?
HEEERE WE GO...
IF YOU SAY NO...
...THEN YOU CAN ALWAYS JOIN THE SEVENTY FAN CLUB WITH ME.
ANOTHER FAN CLUB?!
I MEAN, THEY JUST RELEASED THEIR SECOND ALBUM, SO I NEED MORE PEOPLE TO LISTEN TO THEIR SONGS!
WHAT HAPPENED TO THE DUDEZ?
I GUESS SHE SWITCHED...?
AND ALL THE MEMBERS ARE SUPER HANDSOME!
SO WHAT'S YOUR DECISION?
I WAS HOPING WE COULD PLAY THE NEW GAME I GOT...
YOUR PLACE...
MAYBE TOMORROW?

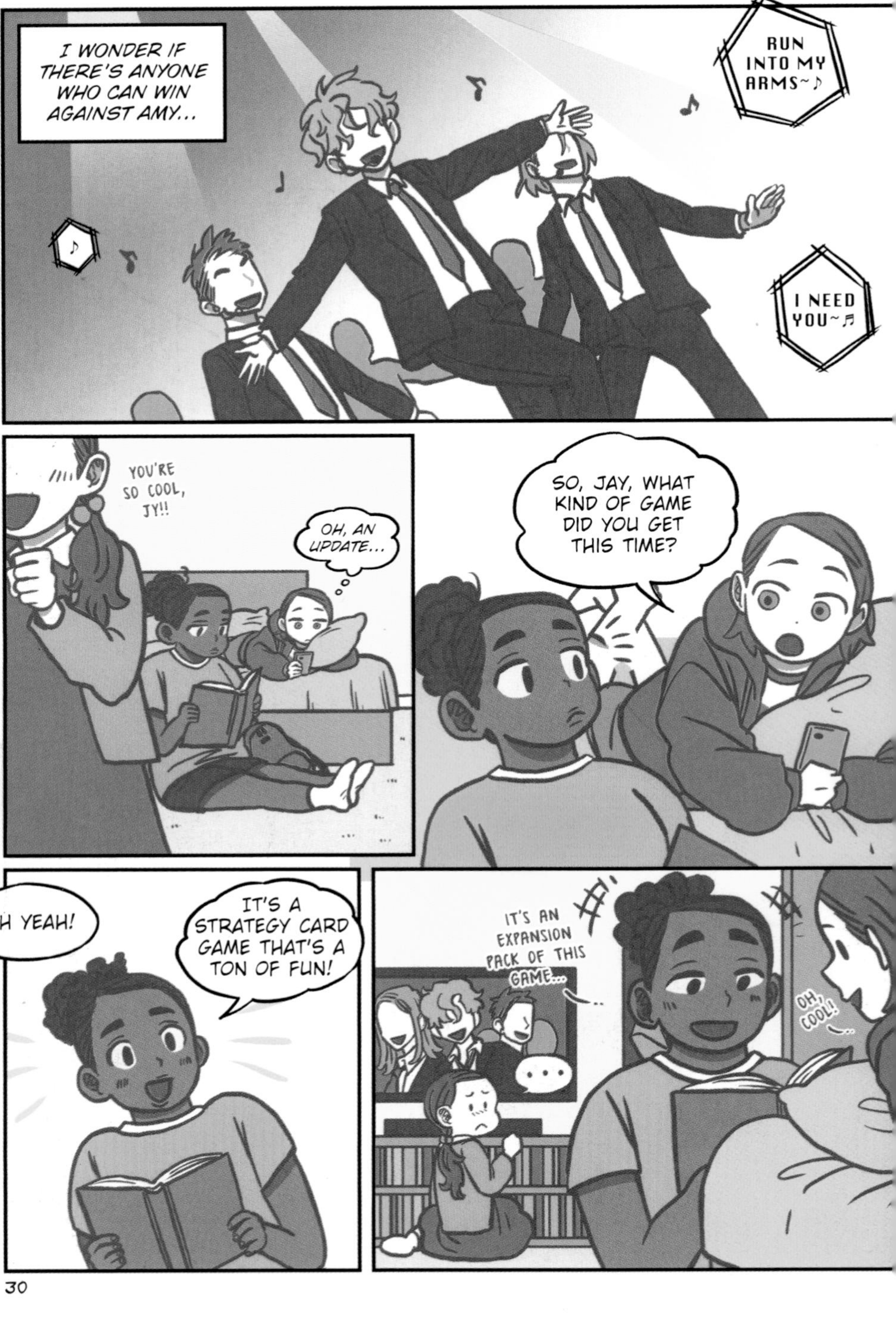
I WONDER IF THERE'S ANYONE WHO CAN WIN AGAINST AMY...
RUN INTO MY ARMS~♪
♪
I NEED YOU~♬
YOU'RE SO COOL, JY!!
OH, AN UPDATE...
SO, JAY, WHAT KIND OF GAME DID YOU GET THIS TIME?
OH YEAH!
IT'S A STRATEGY CARD GAME THAT'S A TON OF FUN!
IT'S AN EXPANSION PACK OF THIS GAME...
...
OH, COOL!

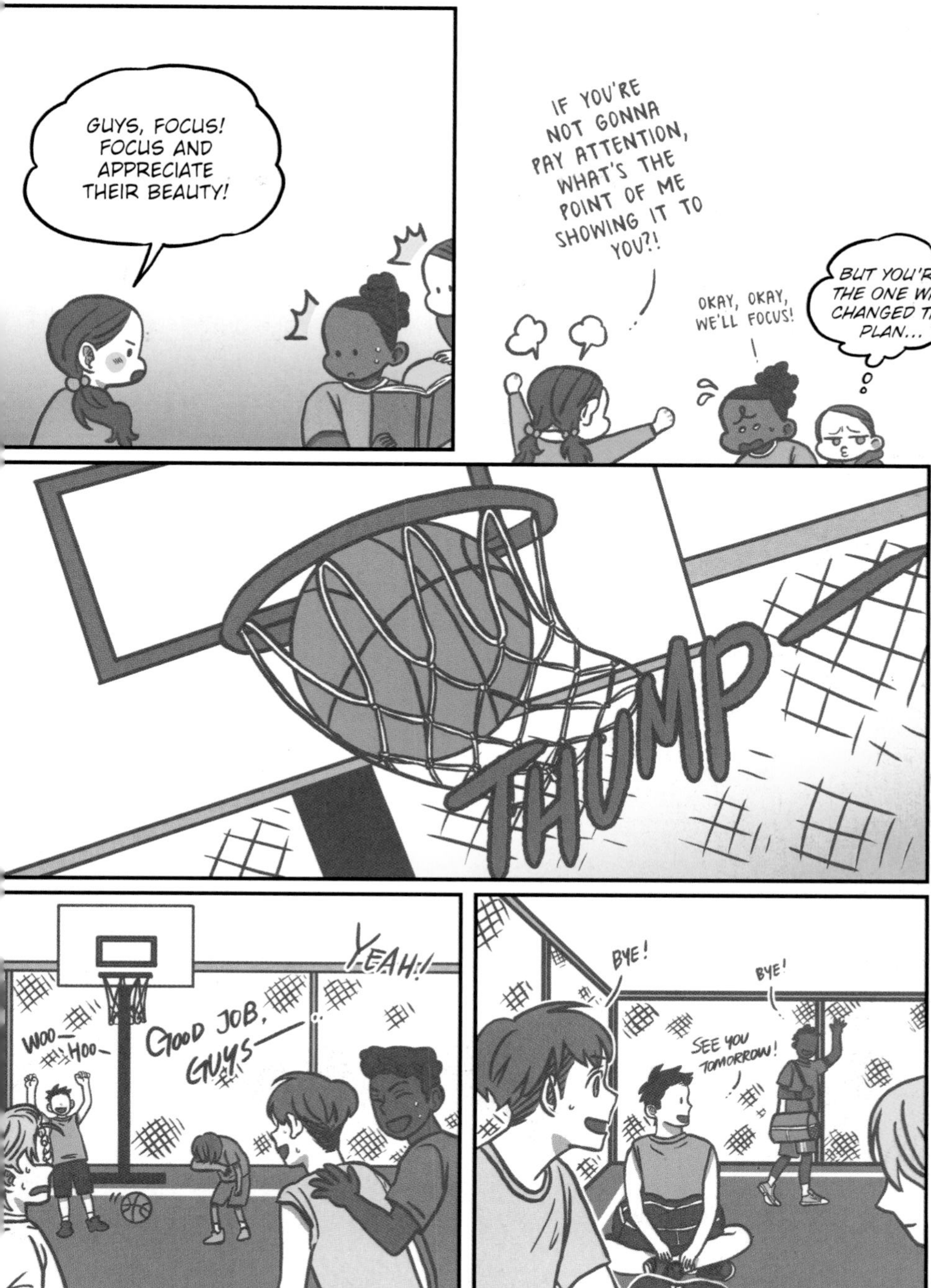
GUYS, FOCUS! FOCUS AND APPRECIATE THEIR BEAUTY!
IF YOU'RE NOT GONNA PAY ATTENTION, WHAT'S THE POINT OF ME SHOWING IT TO YOU?!
OKAY, OKAY, WE'LL FOCUS!
BUT YOU'RE THE ONE WHO CHANGED THE PLAN...
THUMP
YEAH!
WOO-HOO-
GOOD JOB, GUYS
BYE!
BYE!
SEE YOU TOMORROW!

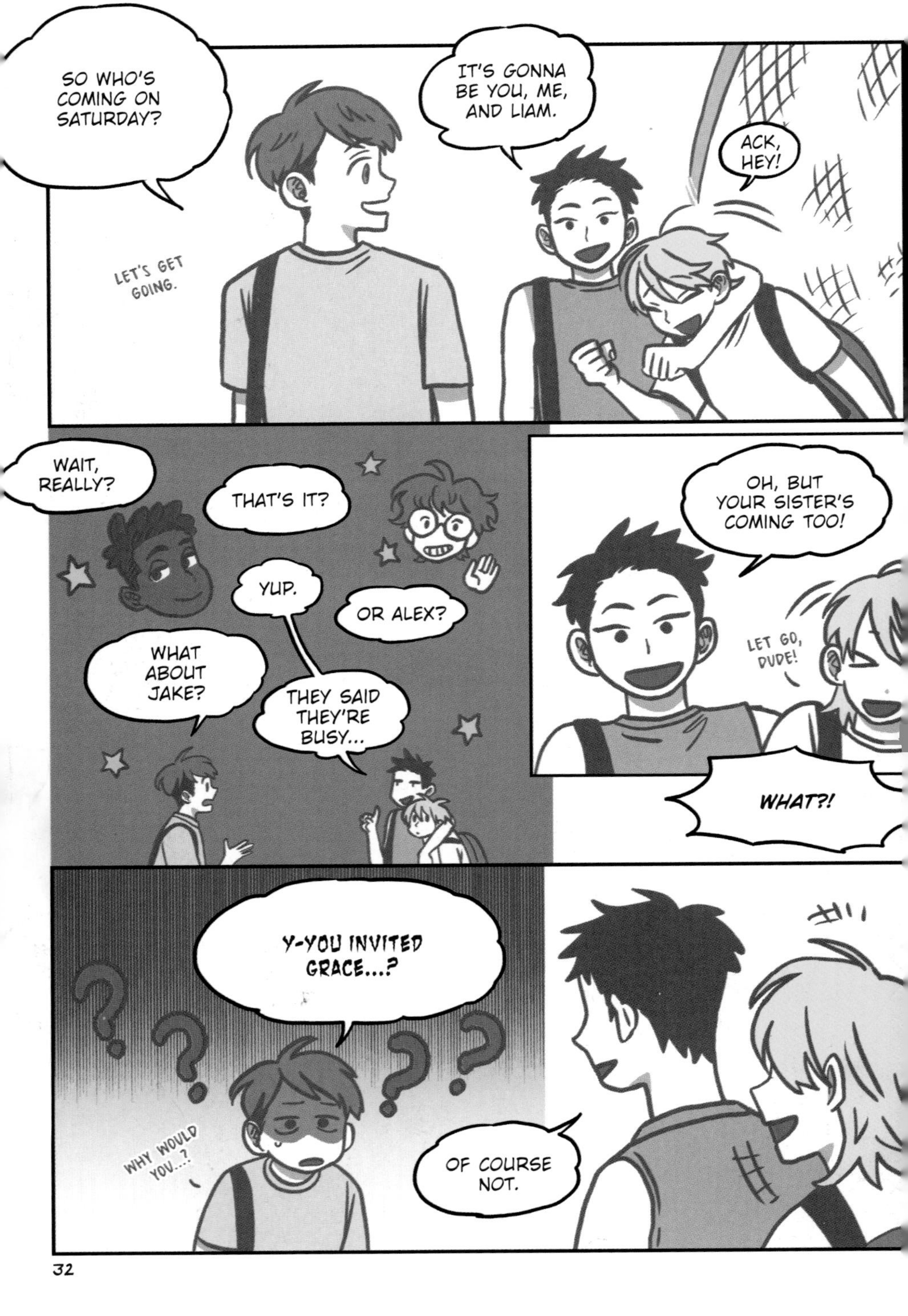
SO WHO'S COMING ON SATURDAY?
IT'S GONNA BE YOU, ME, AND LIAM.
ACK, HEY!
LET'S GET GOING.
WAIT, REALLY?
THAT'S IT?
YUP.
OR ALEX?
WHAT ABOUT JAKE?
THEY SAID THEY'RE BUSY...
OH, BUT YOUR SISTER'S COMING TOO!
LET GO, DUDE!
WHAT?!
Y-YOU INVITED GRACE...?
WHY WOULD YOU...?
OF COURSE NOT.

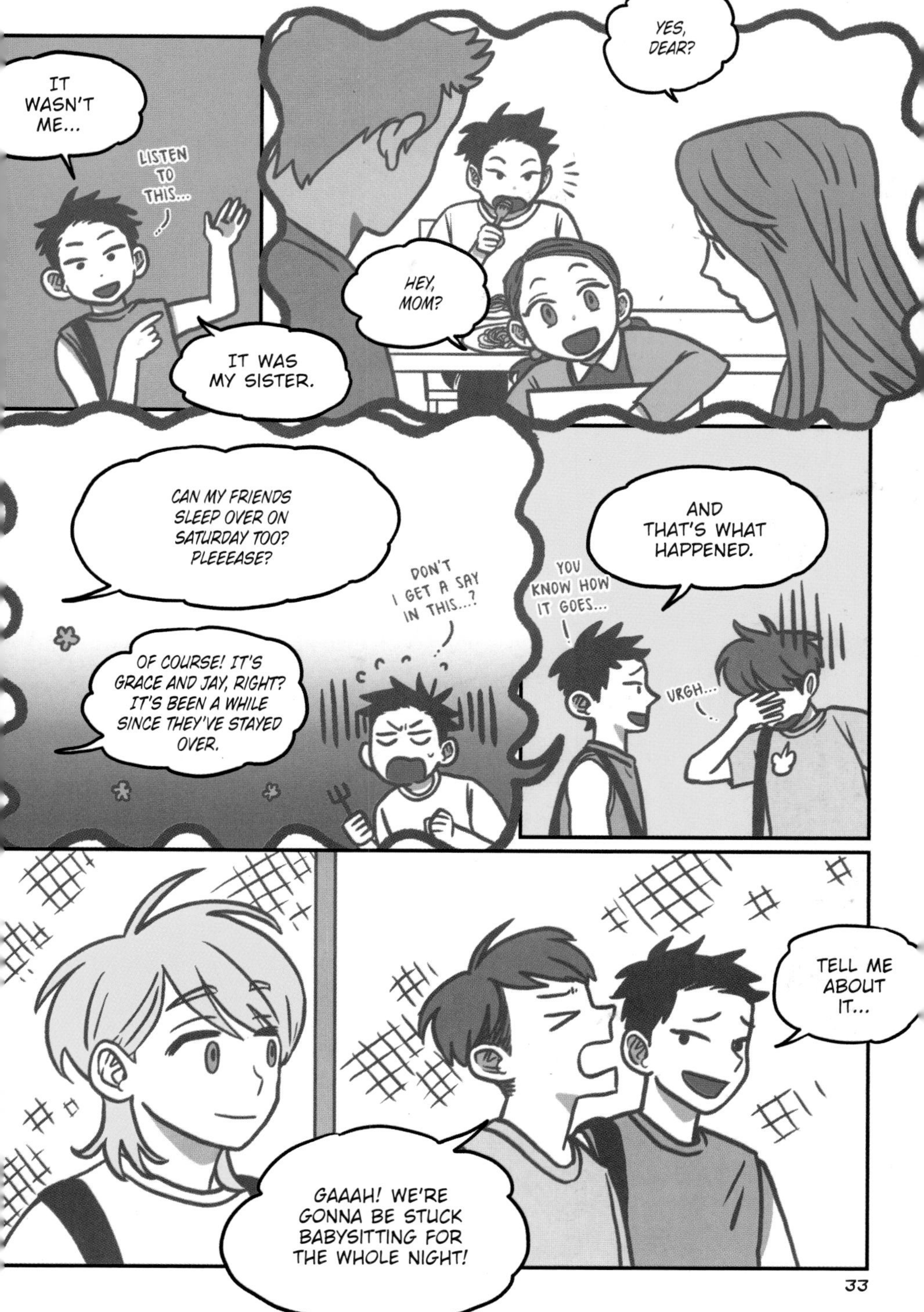
IT WASN'T ME...
LISTEN TO THIS...
IT WAS MY SISTER.
YES, DEAR?
HEY, MOM?
CAN MY FRIENDS SLEEP OVER ON SATURDAY TOO? PLEEEASE?
OF COURSE! IT'S GRACE AND JAY, RIGHT? IT'S BEEN A WHILE SINCE THEY'VE STAYED OVER.
DON'T I GET A SAY IN THIS...?
AND THAT'S WHAT HAPPENED.
YOU KNOW HOW IT GOES...
URGH...
TELL ME ABOUT IT...
GAAAH! WE'RE GONNA BE STUCK BABYSITTING FOR THE WHOLE NIGHT!

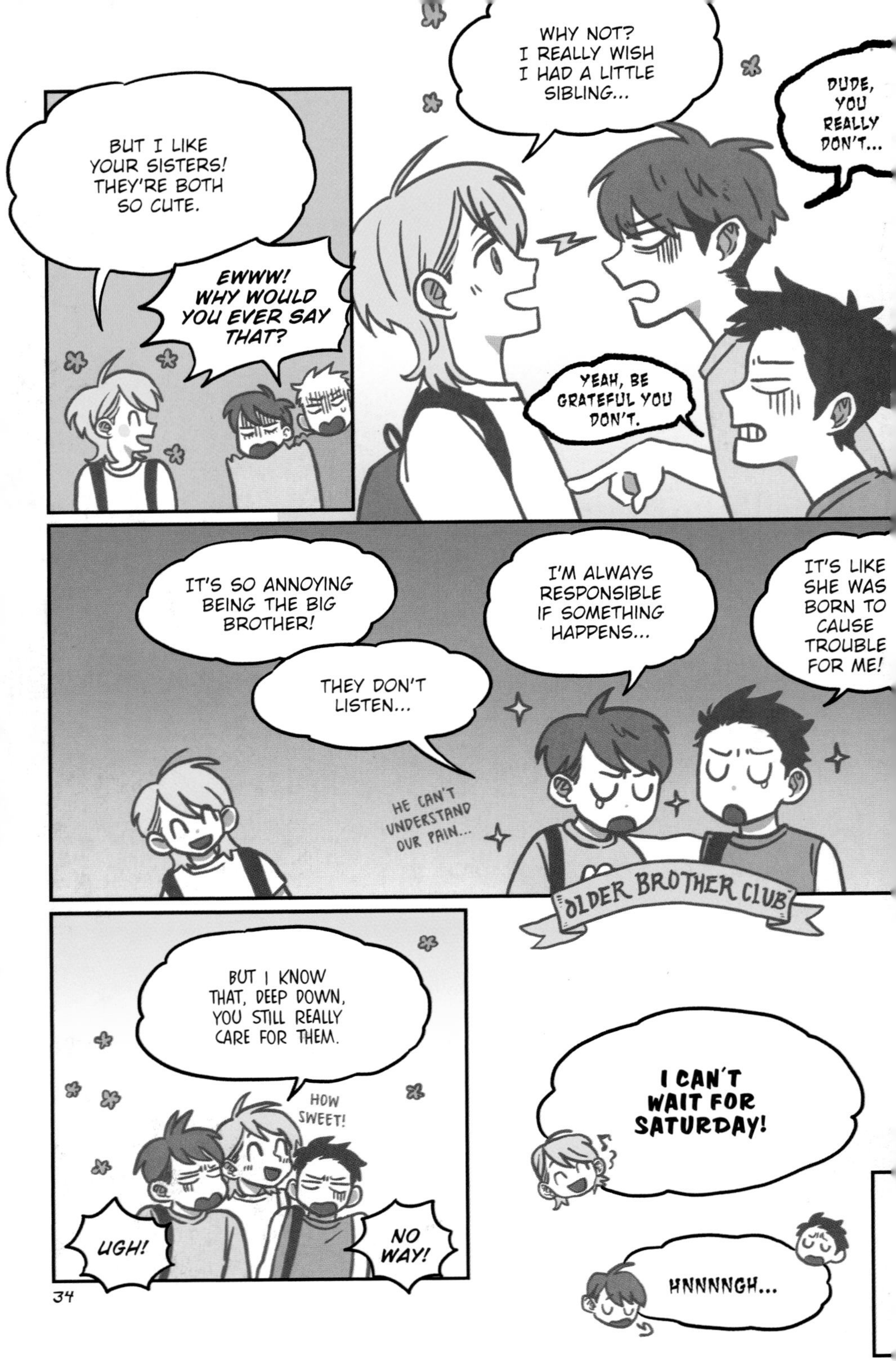
BUT I LIKE YOUR SISTERS! THEY'RE BOTH SO CUTE.
EWWW! WHY WOULD YOU EVER SAY THAT?
WHY NOT? I REALLY WISH I HAD A LITTLE SIBLING...
DUDE, YOU REALLY DON'T...
YEAH, BE GRATEFUL YOU DON'T.
IT'S SO ANNOYING BEING THE BIG BROTHER!
THEY DON'T LISTEN...
I'M ALWAYS RESPONSIBLE IF SOMETHING HAPPENS...
IT'S LIKE SHE WAS BORN TO CAUSE TROUBLE FOR ME!
HE CAN'T UNDERSTAND OUR PAIN...
OLDER BROTHER CLUB
BUT I KNOW THAT, DEEP DOWN, YOU STILL REALLY CARE FOR THEM.
HOW SWEET!
UGH!
NO WAY!
I CAN'T WAIT FOR SATURDAY!
HNNNNGH...

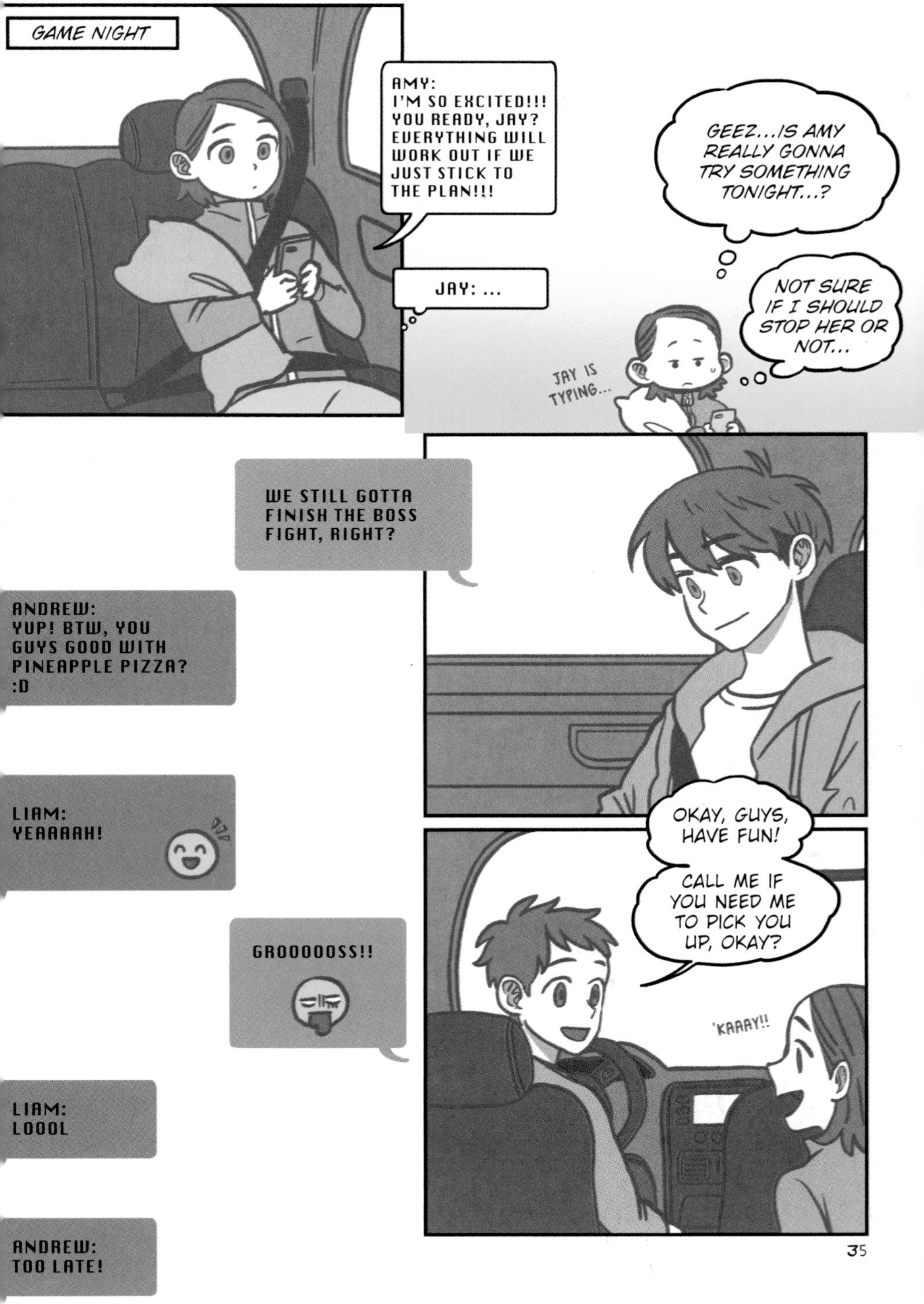
GAME NIGHT
AMY: I'M SO EXCITED!!! YOU READY, JAY? EVERYTHING WILL WORK OUT IF WE JUST STICK TO THE PLAN!!!
JAY: ...
GEEZ...IS AMY REALLY GONNA TRY SOMETHING TONIGHT...?
NOT SURE IF I SHOULD STOP HER OR NOT...
JAY IS TYPING...
WE STILL GOTTA FINISH THE BOSS FIGHT, RIGHT?
ANDREW: YUP! BTW, YOU GUYS GOOD WITH PINEAPPLE PIZZA? :D
LIAM: YEAAAAH!
GROOOOOOSS!!
LIAM: LOOOL
ANDREW: TOO LATE!
OKAY, GUYS, HAVE FUN!
CALL ME IF YOU NEED ME TO PICK YOU UP, OKAY?
'KAAAY!!

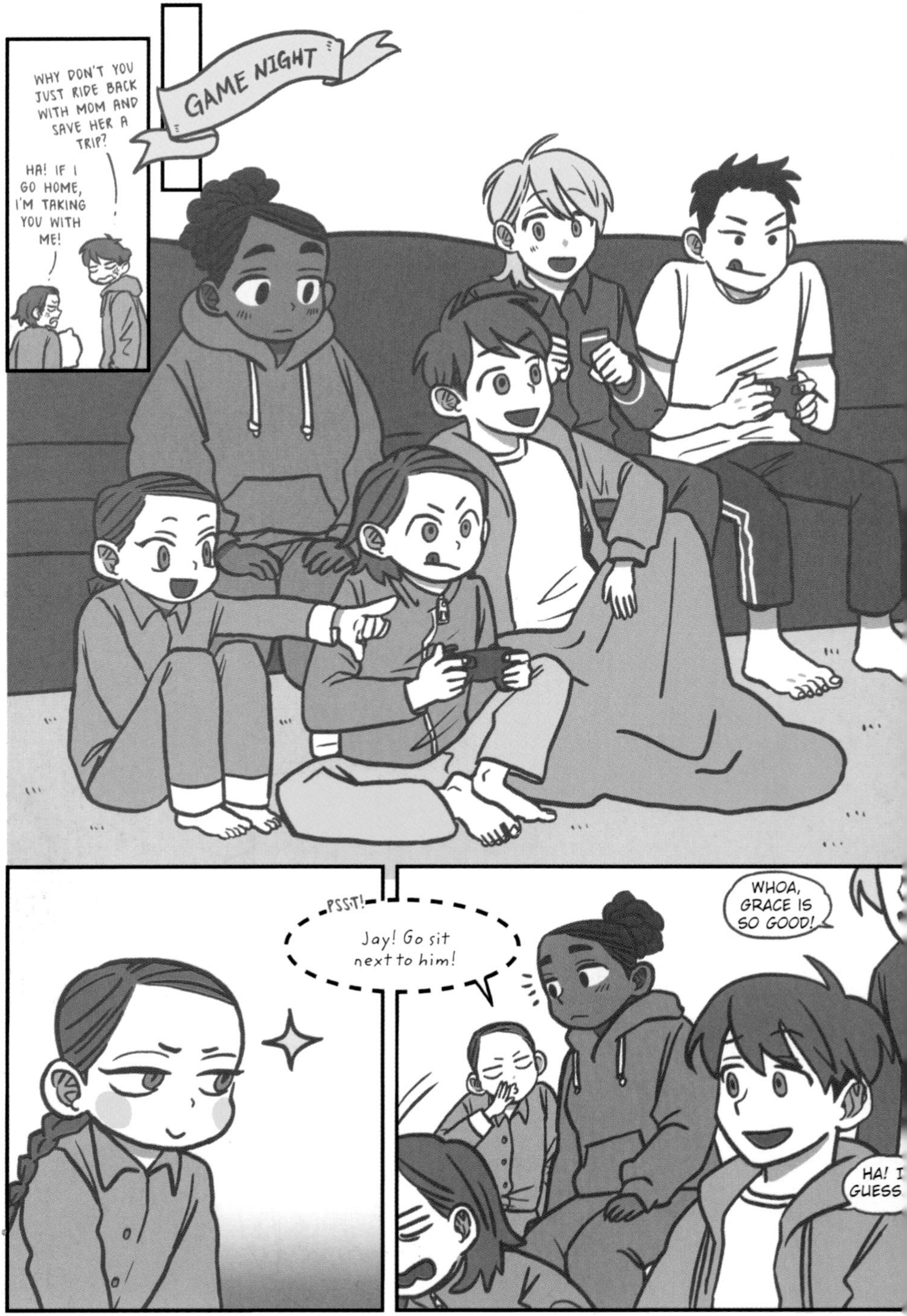
WHY DON'T YOU JUST RIDE BACK WITH MOM AND SAVE HER A TRIP?
HA! IF I GO HOME, I'M TAKING YOU WITH ME!
GAME NIGHT
PSST!
Jay! Go sit next to him!
WHOA, GRACE IS SO GOOD!
HA! I GUESS

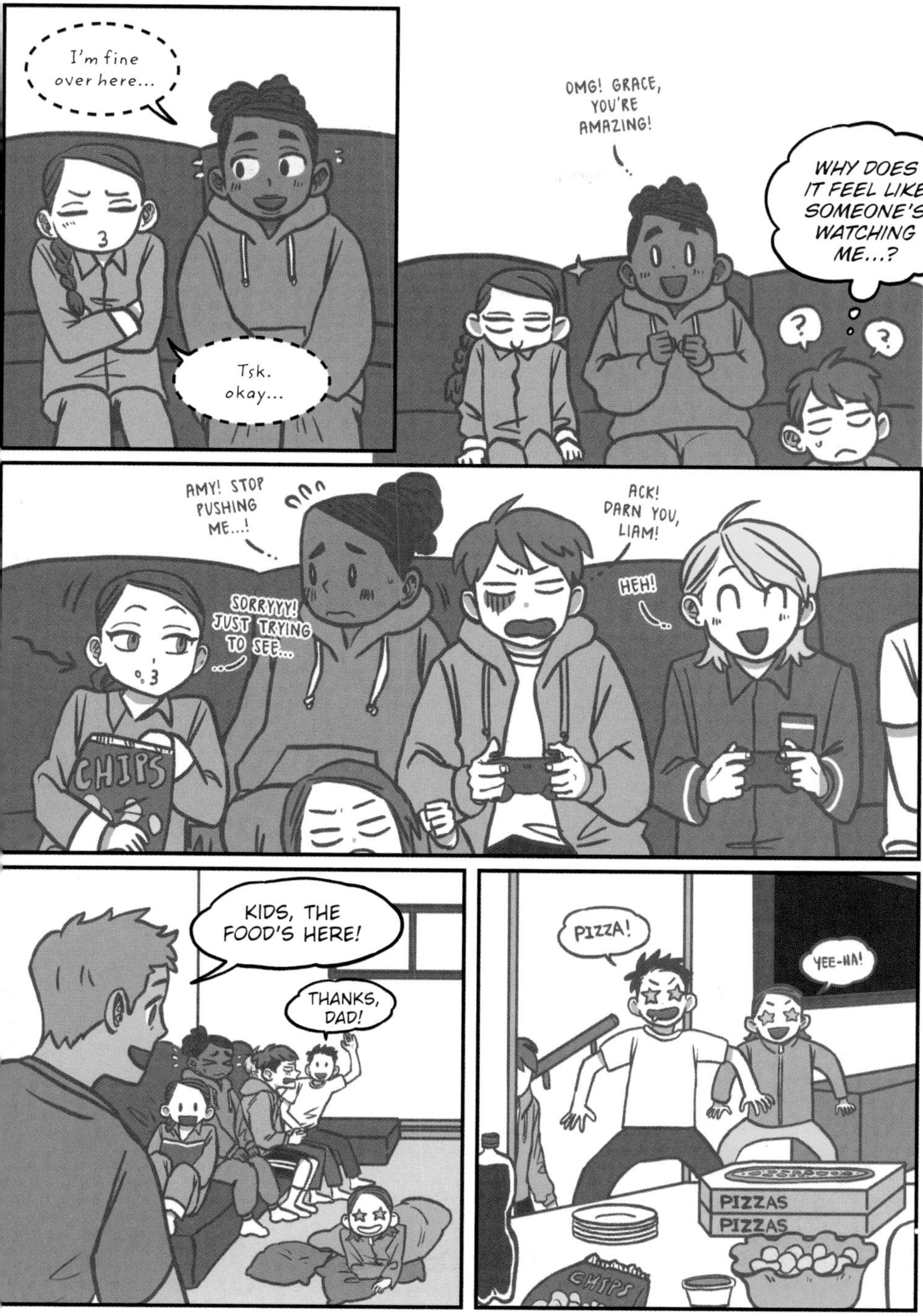
I'm fine over here...
Tsk. okay...
OMG! GRACE, YOU'RE AMAZING!
WHY DOES IT FEEL LIKE SOMEONE'S WATCHING ME...?
AMY! STOP PUSHING ME...!
SORRYYY! JUST TRYING TO SEE...
ACK! DARN YOU, LIAM!
HEH!
CHIPS
KIDS, THE FOOD'S HERE!
THANKS, DAD!
PIZZA!
YEE-HA!
PIZZAS
PIZZAS
CHIPS

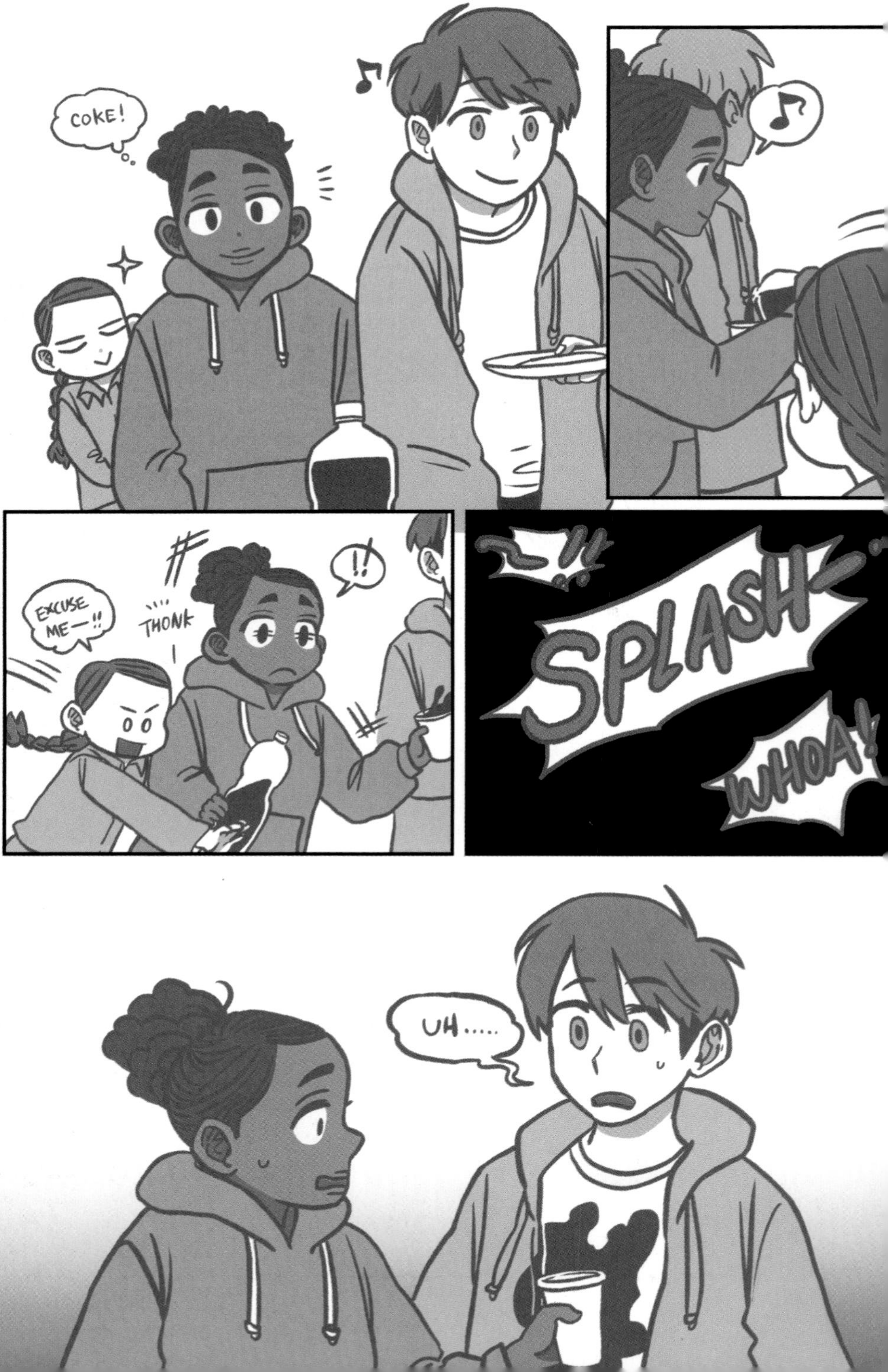
COKE!
EXCUSE ME—!!
THONK
!!
SPLASH
WHOA!
UH.....

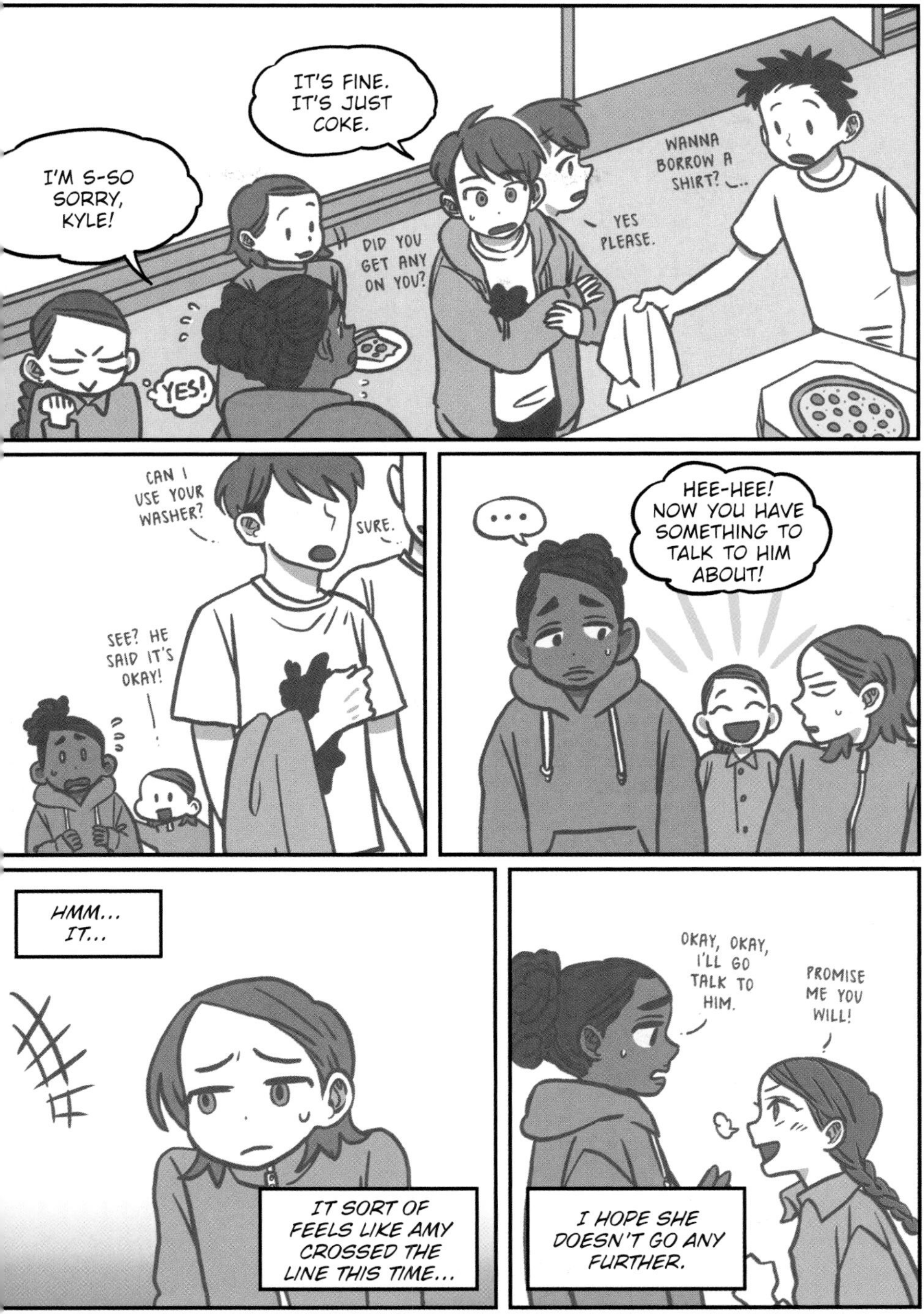
I'M S-SO SORRY, KYLE!
YES!
IT'S FINE. IT'S JUST COKE.
DID YOU GET ANY ON YOU?
WANNA BORROW A SHIRT?
YES PLEASE.
CAN I USE YOUR WASHER?
SURE.
SEE? HE SAID IT'S OKAY!
...
HEE-HEE! NOW YOU HAVE SOMETHING TO TALK TO HIM ABOUT!
HMM... IT...
IT SORT OF FEELS LIKE AMY CROSSED THE LINE THIS TIME...
OKAY, OKAY, I'LL GO TALK TO HIM.
PROMISE ME YOU WILL!
I HOPE SHE DOESN'T GO ANY FURTHER.

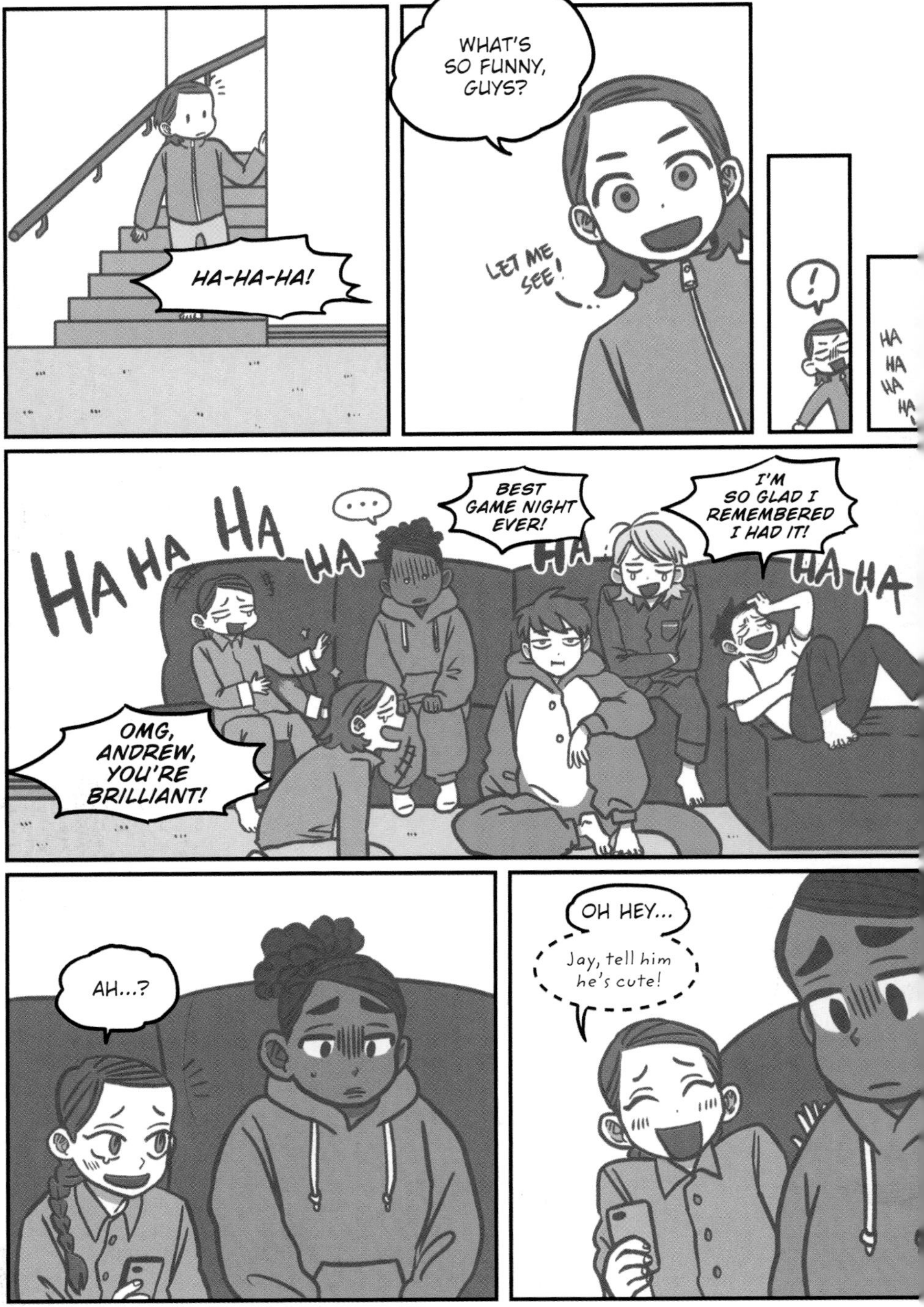
HA-HA-HA!
WHAT'S SO FUNNY, GUYS?
LET ME SEE!
!
HA HA HA HA
HA HA HA HA HA HA HA HA
...
BEST GAME NIGHT EVER!
I'M SO GLAD I REMEMBERED I HAD IT!
OMG, ANDREW, YOU'RE BRILLIANT!
AH...?
OH HEY...
Jay, tell him he's cute!

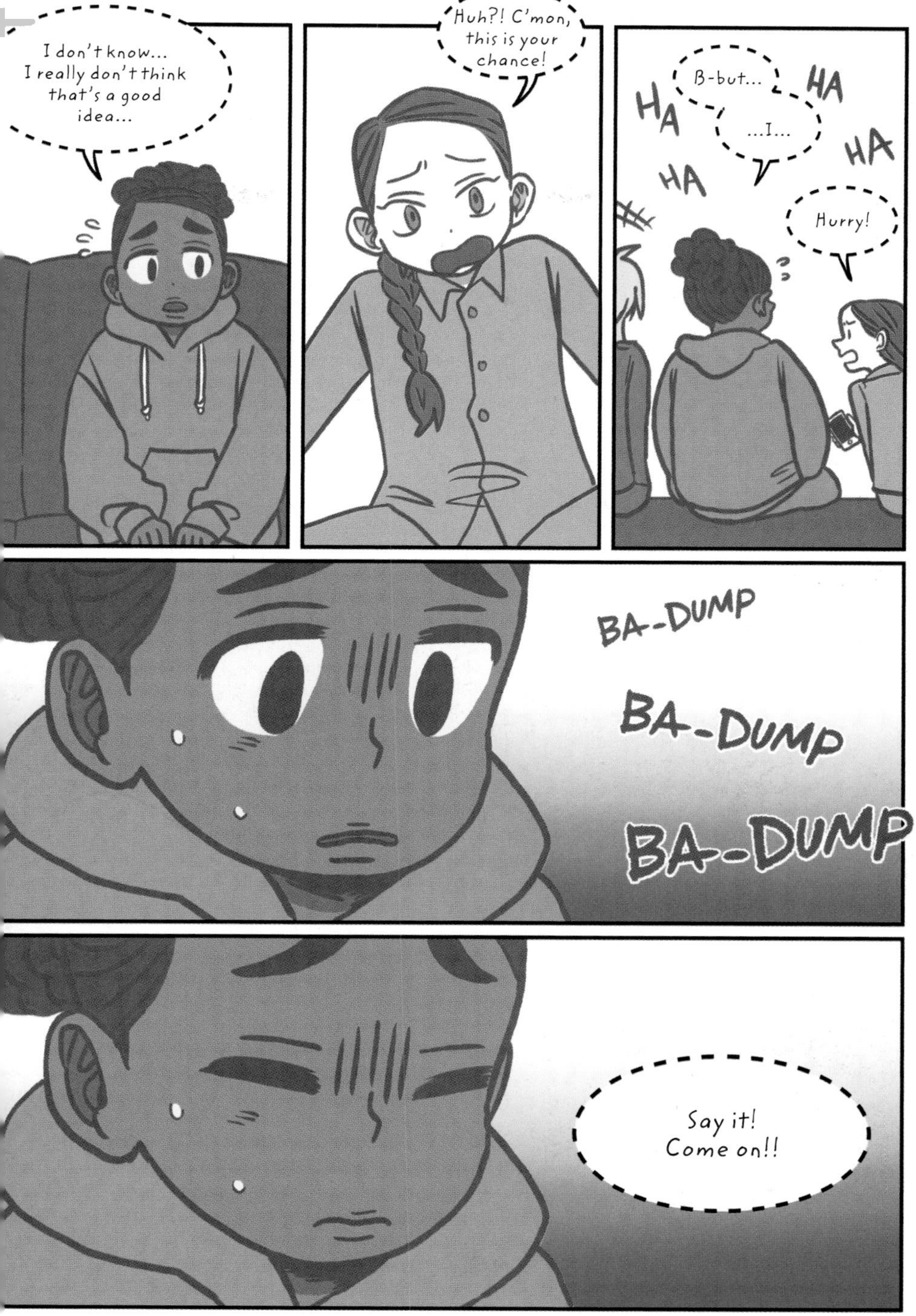
I don't know... I really don't think that's a good idea...
Huh?! C'mon, this is your chance!
HA
B-but...
HA
...I...
HA
HA
Hurry!
BA-DUMP
BA-DUMP
BA-DUMP
Say it! Come on!!

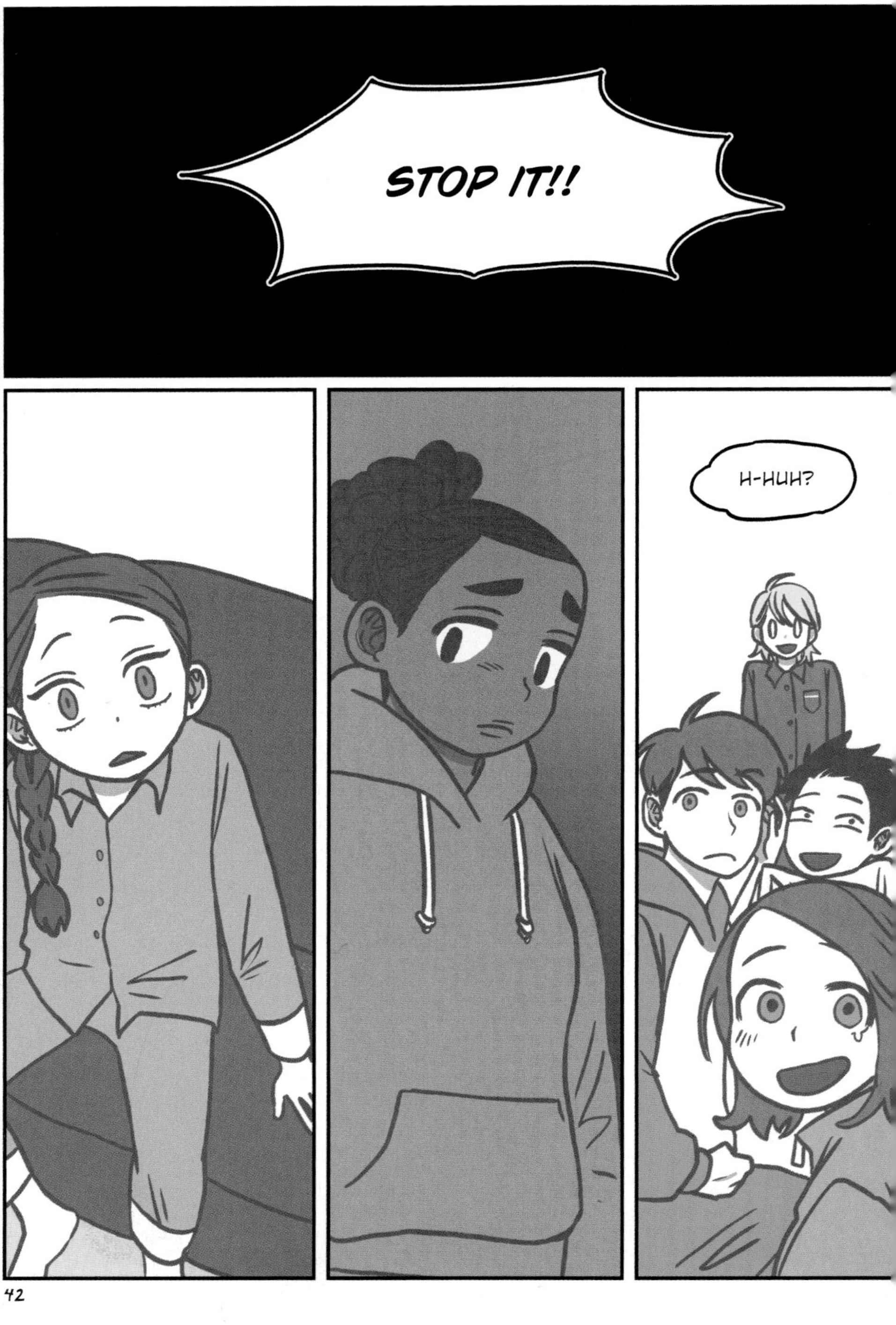
STOP IT!!
H-HUH?

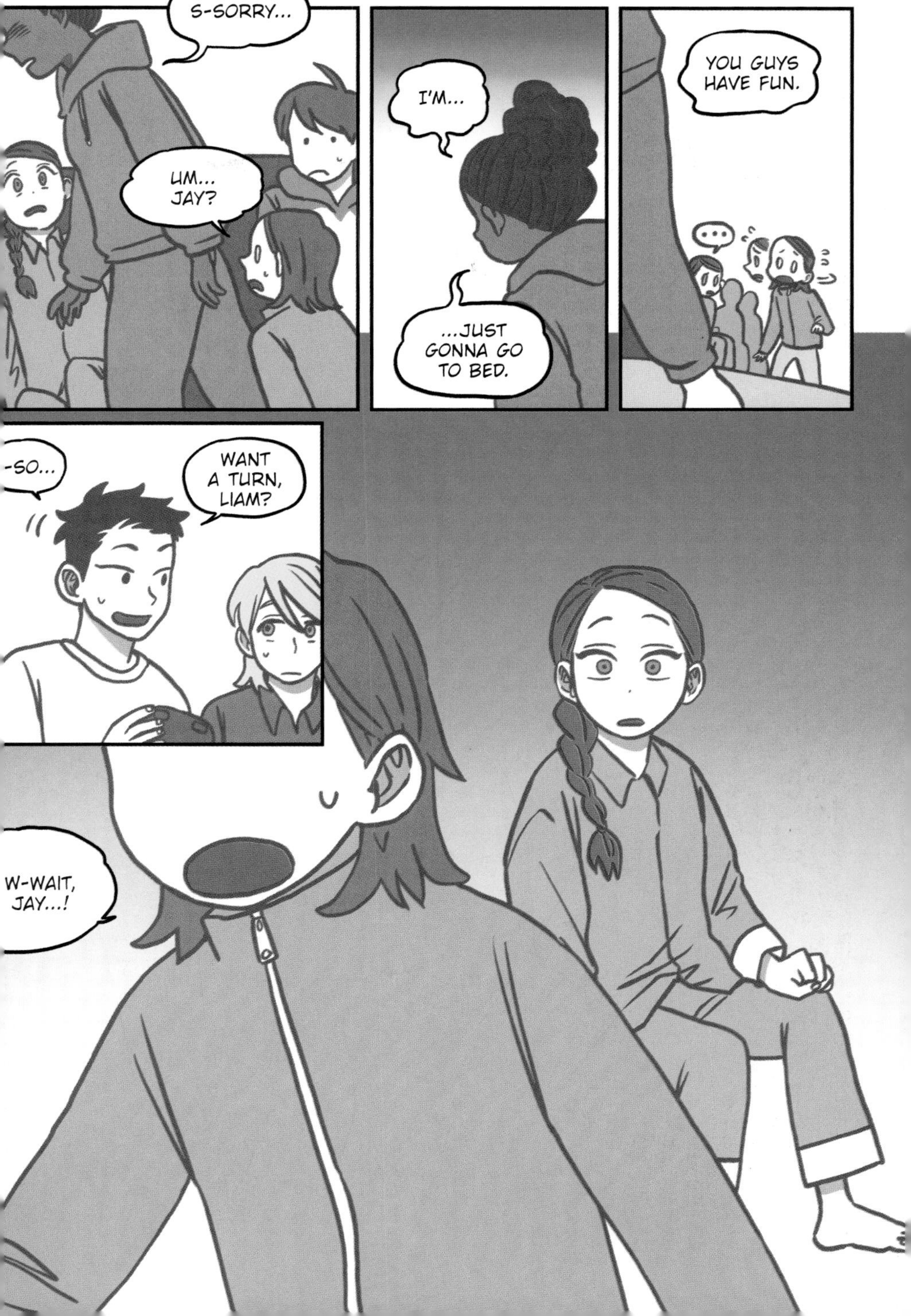
S-SORRY...
UM... JAY?
I'M...
...JUST GONNA GO TO BED.
YOU GUYS HAVE FUN.
...
-SO...
WANT A TURN, LIAM?
W-WAIT, JAY...!

CHAPTER 3

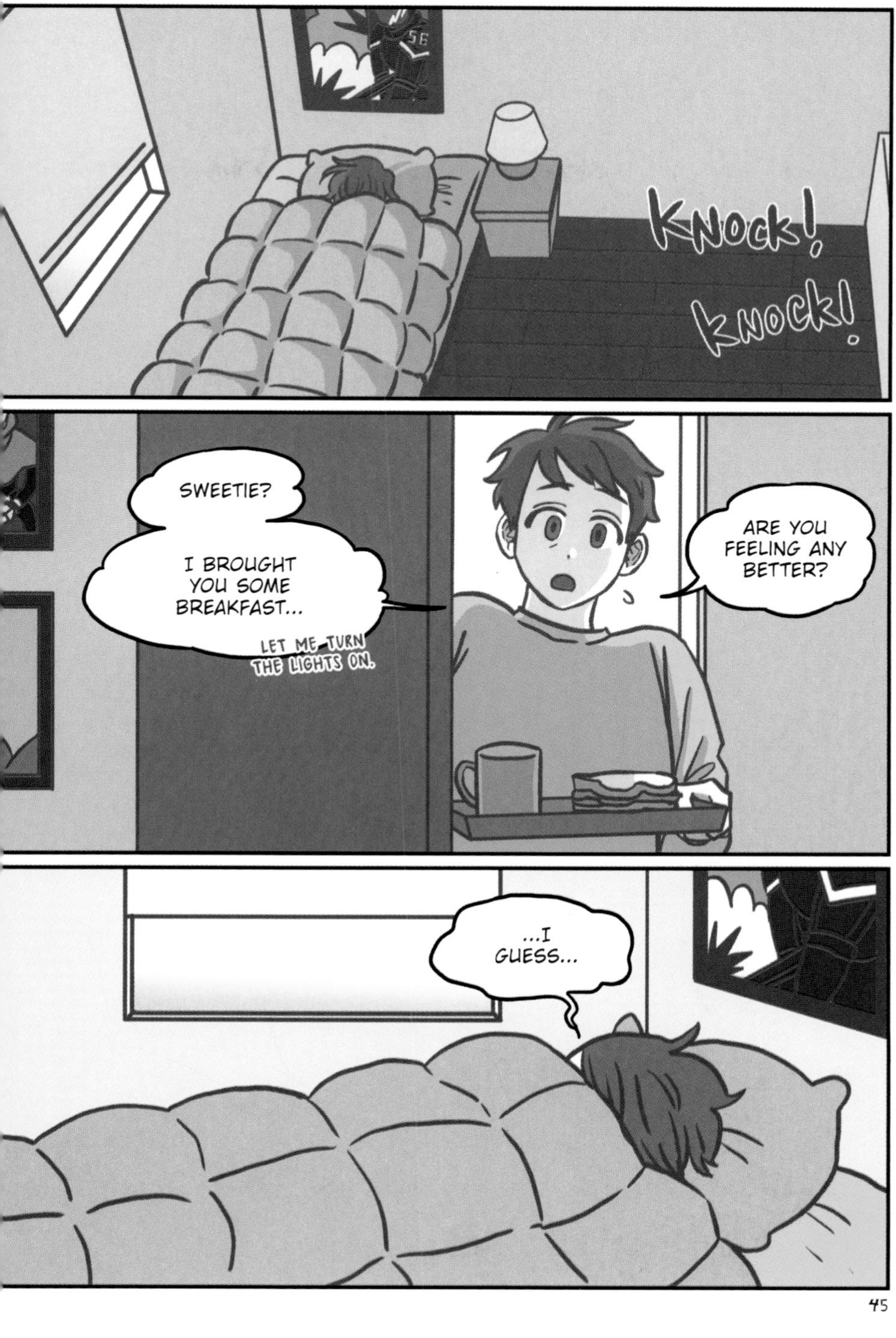
KNOCK! KNOCK!
SWEETIE?
I BROUGHT YOU SOME BREAKFAST...
LET ME TURN THE LIGHTS ON.
ARE YOU FEELING ANY BETTER?
...I GUESS...

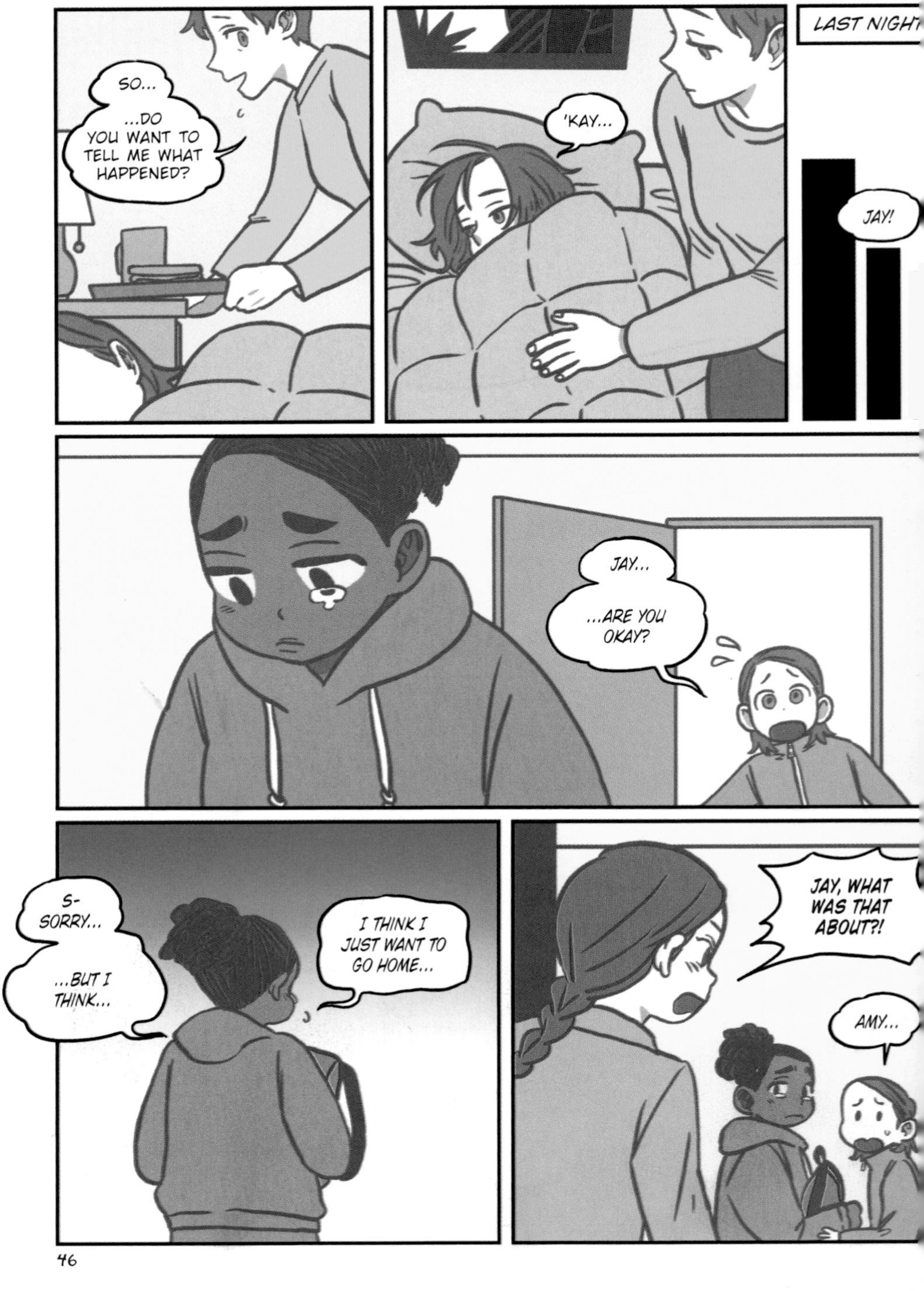
SO...
...DO YOU WANT TO TELL ME WHAT HAPPENED?
'KAY...
LAST NIGHT
JAY!
JAY...
...ARE YOU OKAY?
S-SORRY...
...BUT I THINK...
I THINK I JUST WANT TO GO HOME...
JAY, WHAT WAS THAT ABOUT?!
AMY...

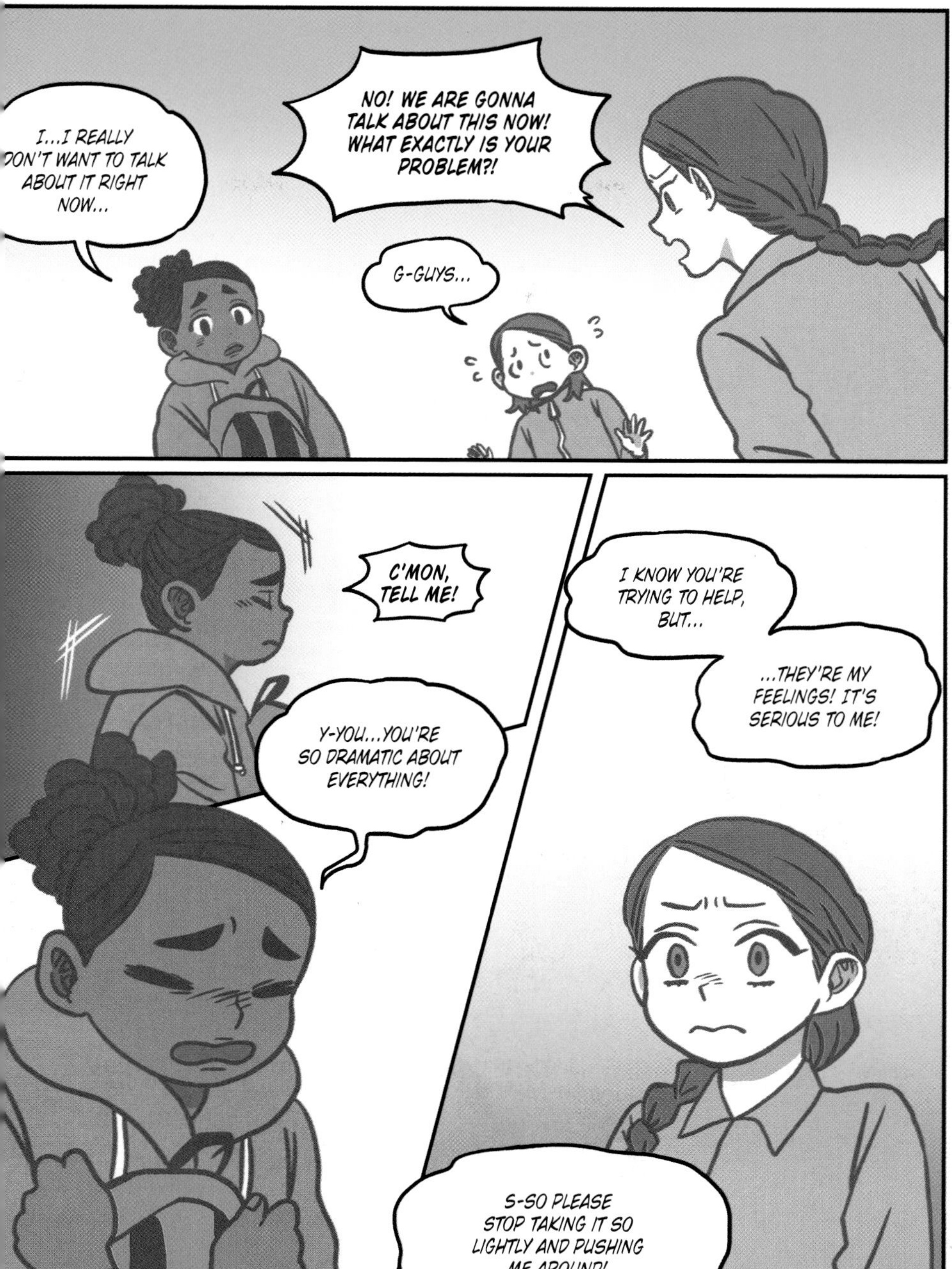
I...I REALLY DON'T WANT TO TALK ABOUT IT RIGHT NOW...
NO! WE ARE GONNA TALK ABOUT THIS NOW! WHAT EXACTLY IS YOUR PROBLEM?!
G-GUYS...
C'MON, TELL ME!
Y-YOU...YOU'RE SO DRAMATIC ABOUT EVERYTHING!
I KNOW YOU'RE TRYING TO HELP, BUT...
...THEY'RE MY FEELINGS! IT'S SERIOUS TO ME!
S-SO PLEASE STOP TAKING IT SO LIGHTLY AND PUSHING ME AROUND!

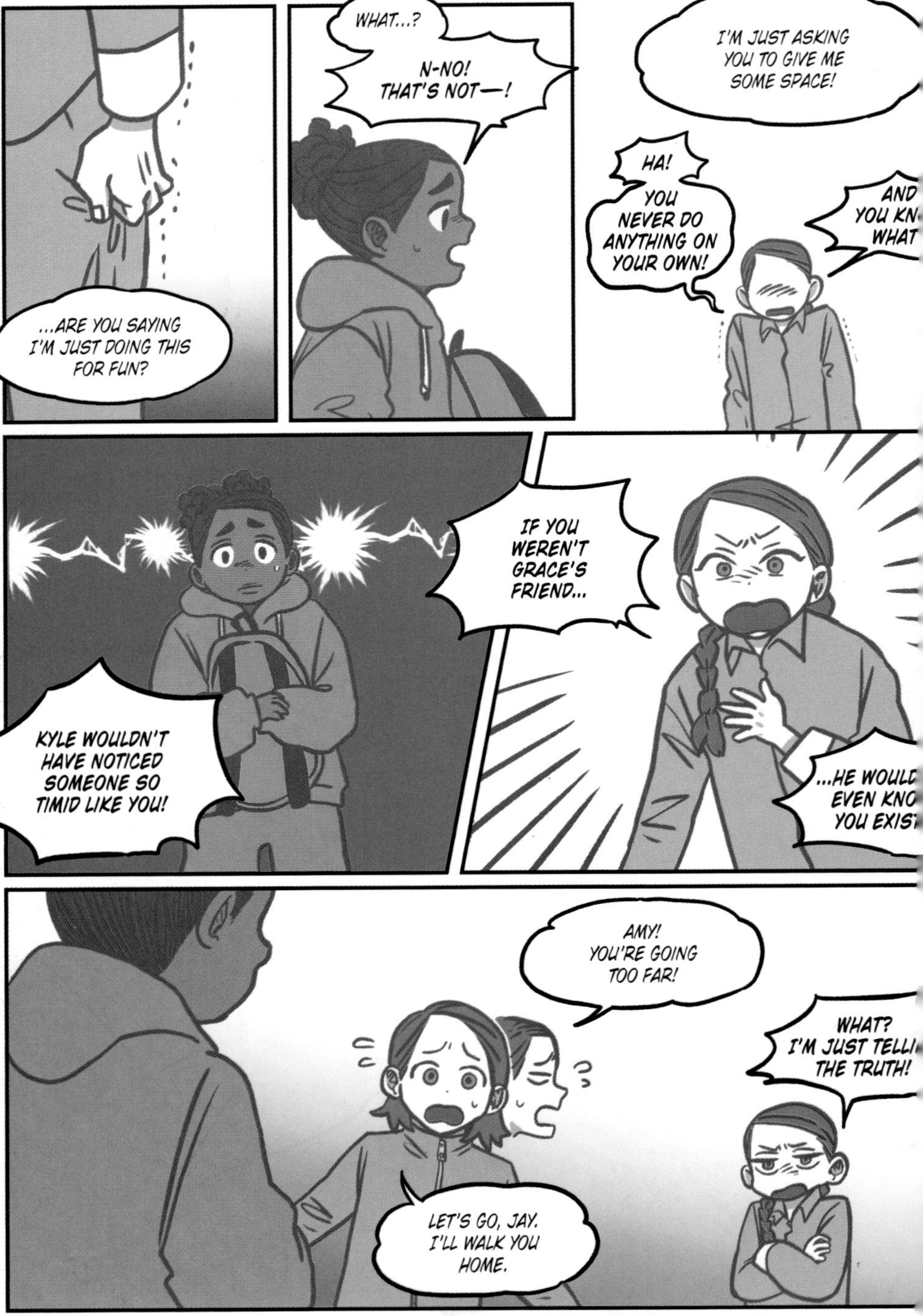
...ARE YOU SAYING I'M JUST DOING THIS FOR FUN?
WHAT...?
N-NO! THAT'S NOT—!
I'M JUST ASKING YOU TO GIVE ME SOME SPACE!
HA!
YOU NEVER DO ANYTHING ON YOUR OWN!
AND YOU KN WHAT
IF YOU WEREN'T GRACE'S FRIEND...
...HE WOULD EVEN KNO YOU EXIST
KYLE WOULDN'T HAVE NOTICED SOMEONE SO TIMID LIKE YOU!
AMY! YOU'RE GOING TOO FAR!
WHAT? I'M JUST TELLI THE TRUTH!
LET'S GO, JAY. I'LL WALK YOU HOME.

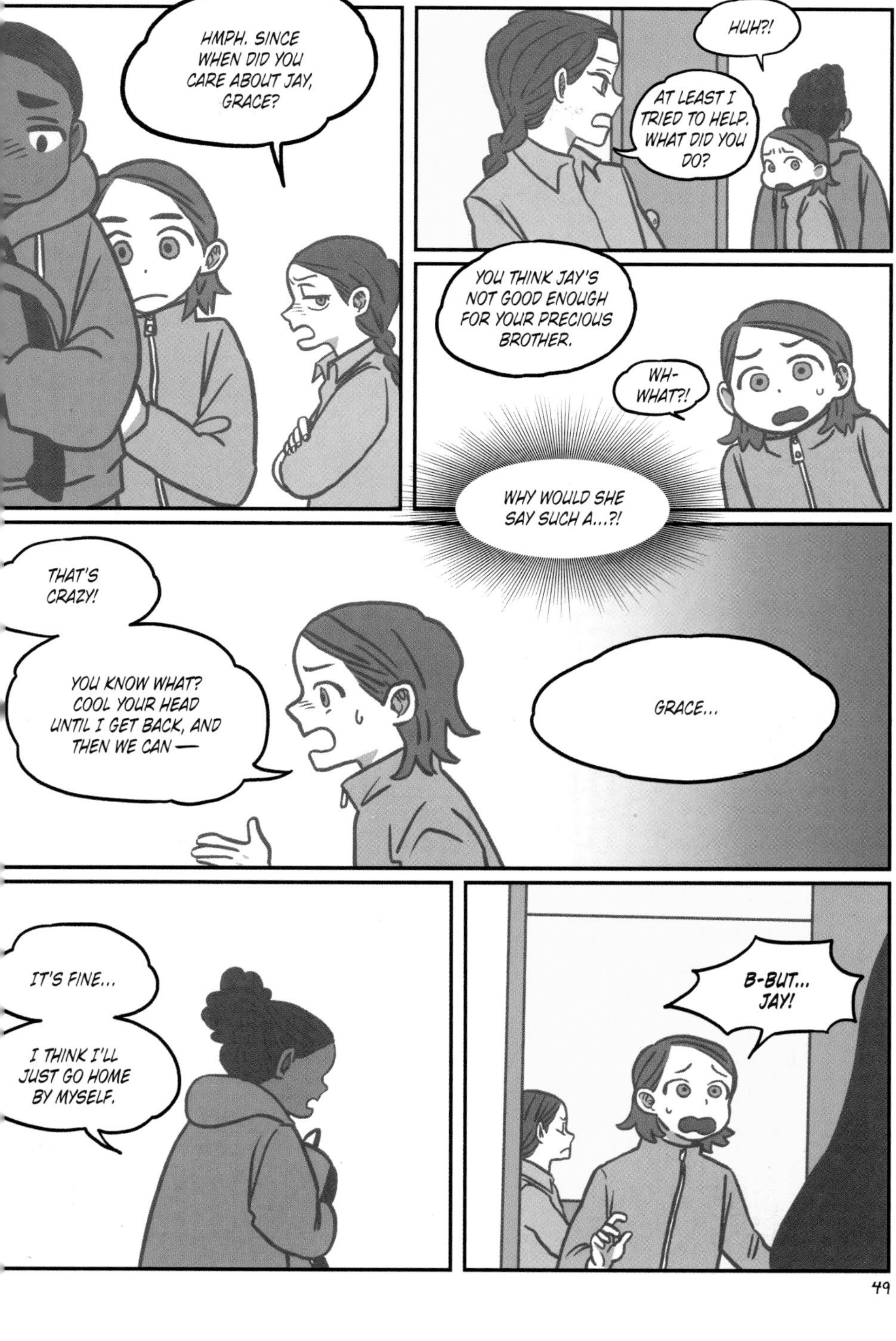

HMPH. SINCE WHEN DID YOU CARE ABOUT JAY, GRACE?
HUH?!
AT LEAST I TRIED TO HELP. WHAT DID YOU DO?
YOU THINK JAY'S NOT GOOD ENOUGH FOR YOUR PRECIOUS BROTHER.
WH- WHAT?!
WHY WOULD SHE SAY SUCH A...?!
THAT'S CRAZY!
YOU KNOW WHAT? COOL YOUR HEAD UNTIL I GET BACK, AND THEN WE CAN—
GRACE...
IT'S FINE...
I THINK I'LL JUST GO HOME BY MYSELF.
B-BUT... JAY!

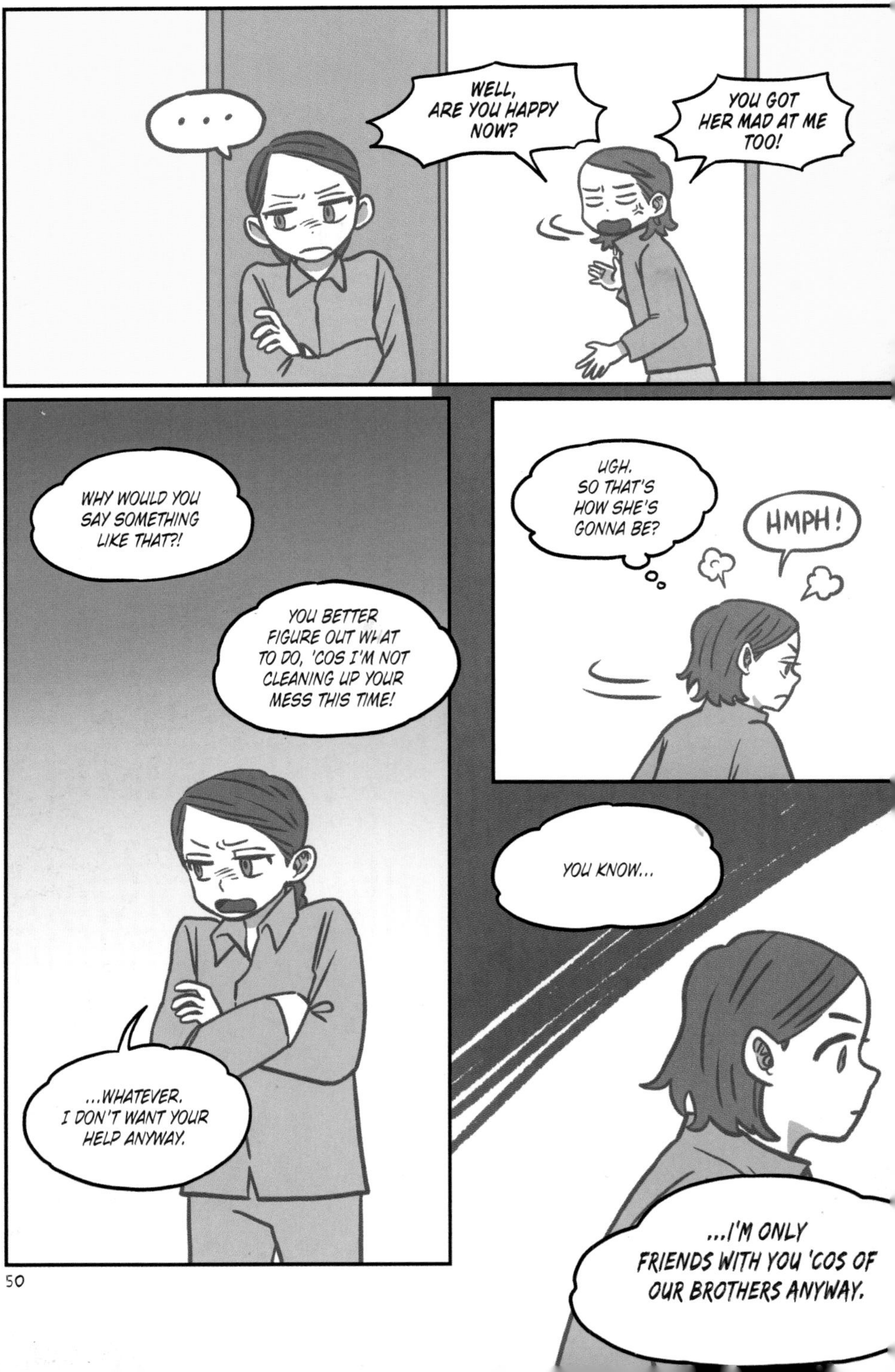
...
WELL, ARE YOU HAPPY NOW?
YOU GOT HER MAD AT ME TOO!
WHY WOULD YOU SAY SOMETHING LIKE THAT?!
YOU BETTER FIGURE OUT WHAT TO DO, 'COS I'M NOT CLEANING UP YOUR MESS THIS TIME!
...WHATEVER. I DON'T WANT YOUR HELP ANYWAY.
UGH. SO THAT'S HOW SHE'S GONNA BE?
HMPH!
YOU KNOW...
...I'M ONLY FRIENDS WITH YOU 'COS OF OUR BROTHERS ANYWAY.

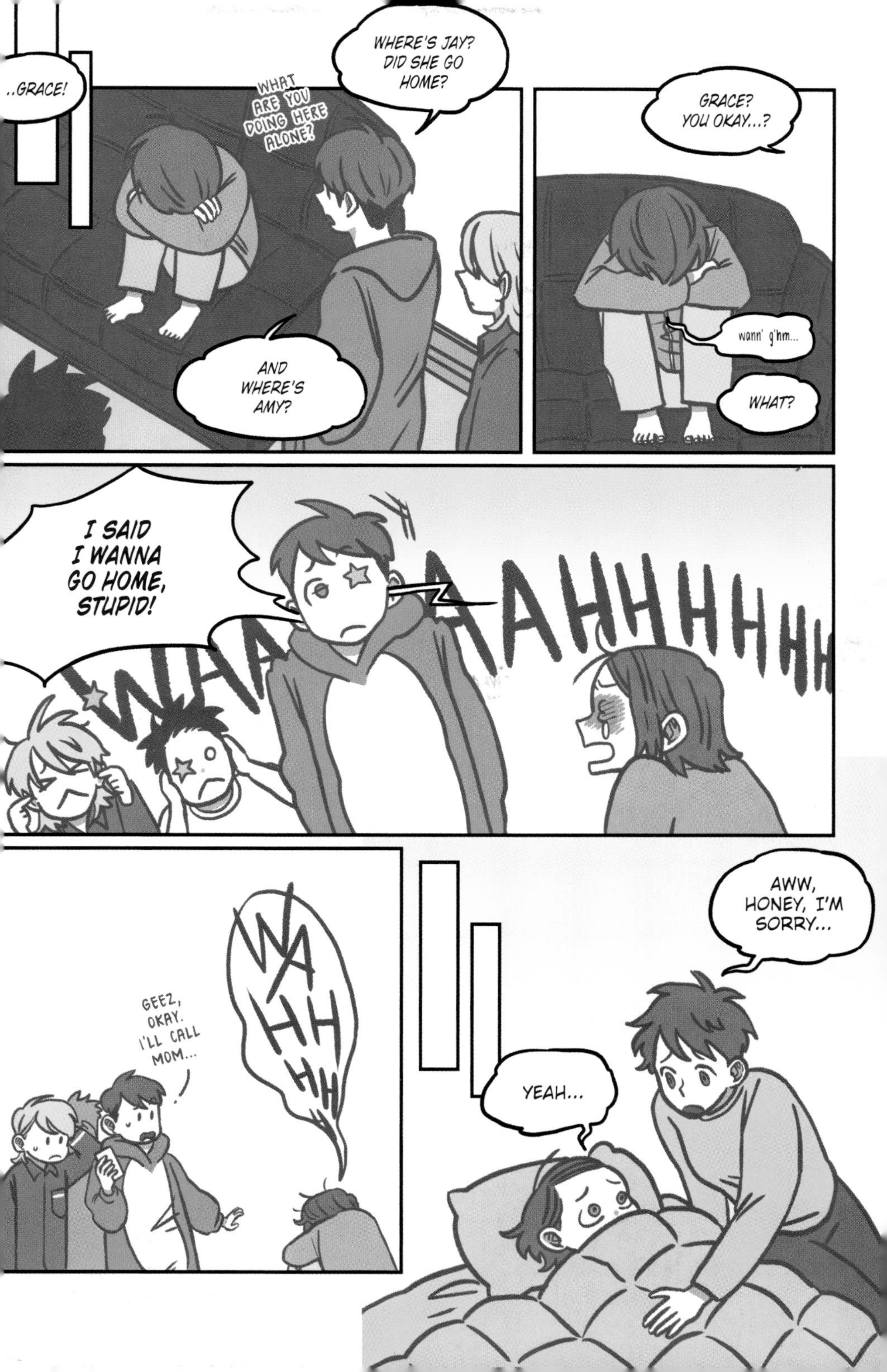
..GRACE!
WHAT ARE YOU DOING HERE ALONE?
WHERE'S JAY? DID SHE GO HOME?
AND WHERE'S AMY?
GRACE? YOU OKAY...?
wann' g'hm...
WHAT?
I SAID I WANNA GO HOME, STUPID!
WHAAAHHHHHHH
GEEZ, OKAY. I'LL CALL MOM...
WAHHHH
AWW, HONEY, I'M SORRY...
YEAH...

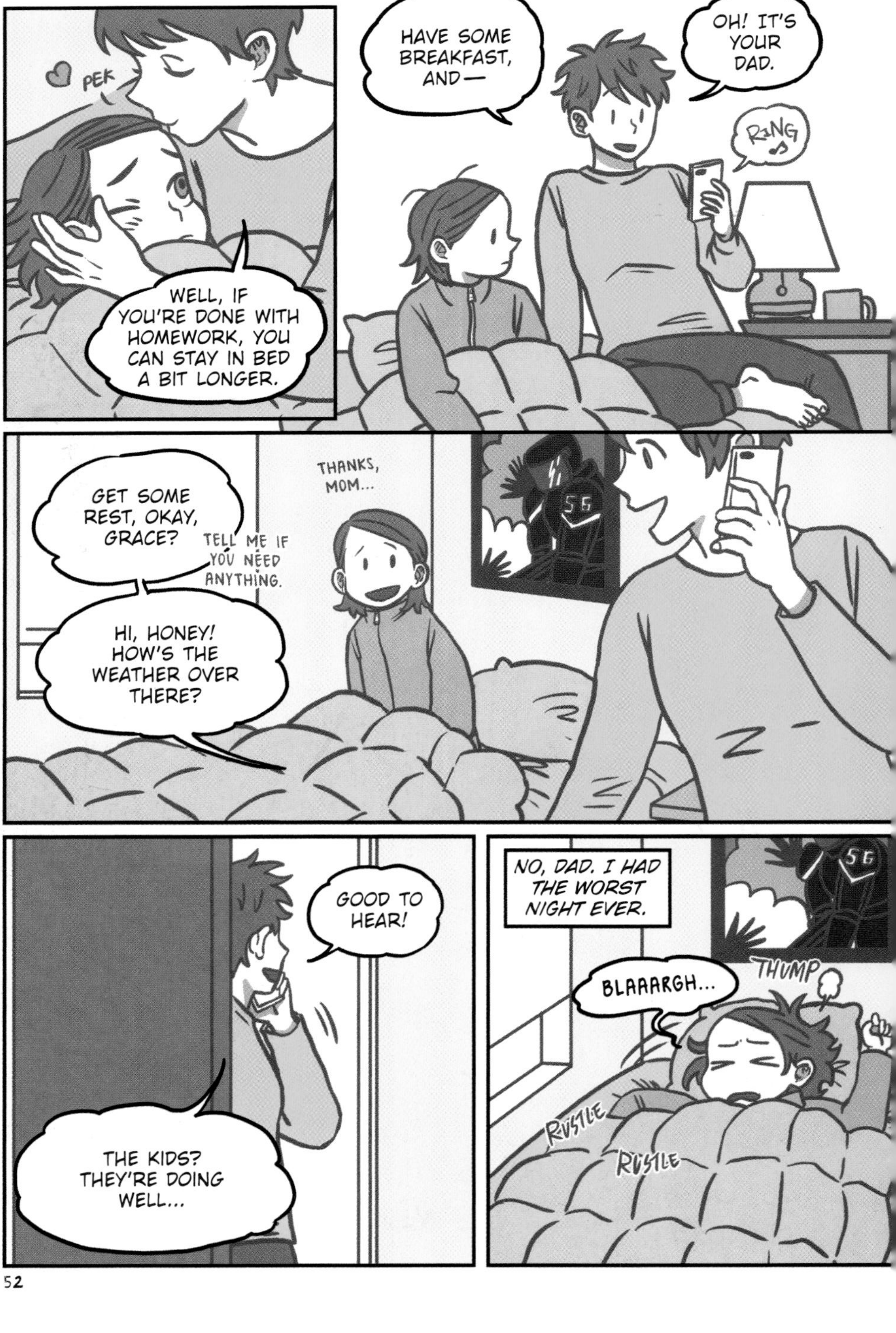
PEK
WELL, IF YOU'RE DONE WITH HOMEWORK, YOU CAN STAY IN BED A BIT LONGER.
HAVE SOME BREAKFAST, AND—
OH! IT'S YOUR DAD.
RING
GET SOME REST, OKAY, GRACE?
TELL ME IF YOU NEED ANYTHING.
THANKS, MOM...
HI, HONEY! HOW'S THE WEATHER OVER THERE?
GOOD TO HEAR!
THE KIDS? THEY'RE DOING WELL...
NO, DAD. I HAD THE WORST NIGHT EVER.
BLAAARGH...
THUMP
RUSTLE
RUSTLE

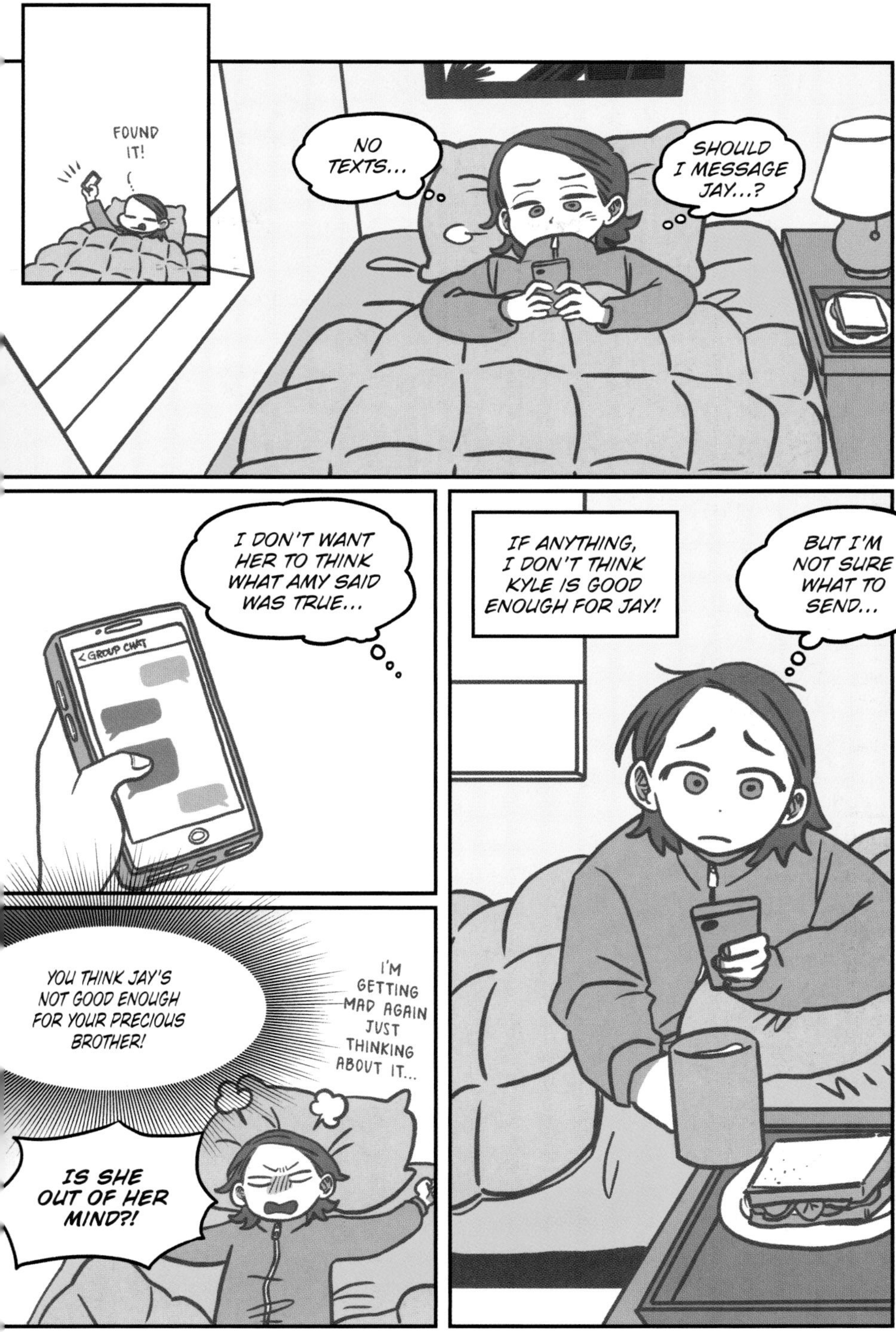
FOUND IT!
NO TEXTS...
SHOULD I MESSAGE JAY...?
I DON'T WANT HER TO THINK WHAT AMY SAID WAS TRUE...
< GROUP CHAT
YOU THINK JAY'S NOT GOOD ENOUGH FOR YOUR PRECIOUS BROTHER!
I'M GETTING MAD AGAIN JUST THINKING ABOUT IT...
IS SHE OUT OF HER MIND?!
IF ANYTHING, I DON'T THINK KYLE IS GOOD ENOUGH FOR JAY!
BUT I'M NOT SURE WHAT TO SEND...

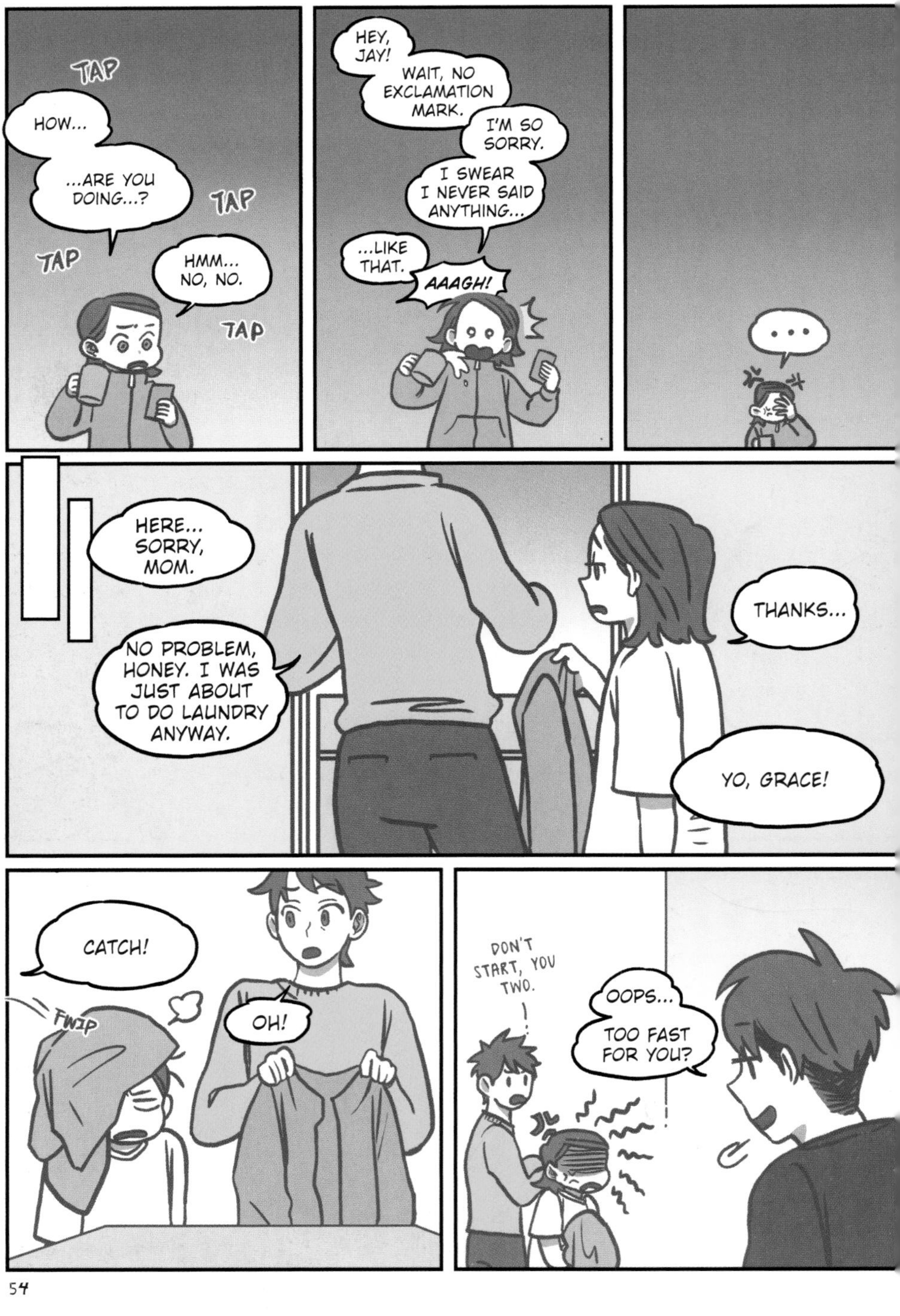
TAP
HOW...
...ARE YOU DOING...?
TAP
TAP
HMM... NO, NO.
TAP
HEY, JAY!
WAIT, NO EXCLAMATION MARK.
I'M SO SORRY.
I SWEAR I NEVER SAID ANYTHING...
...LIKE THAT.
AAAGH!
• • •
HERE... SORRY, MOM.
NO PROBLEM, HONEY. I WAS JUST ABOUT TO DO LAUNDRY ANYWAY.
THANKS...
YO, GRACE!
CATCH!
FWIP
OH!
DON'T START, YOU TWO.
OOPS...
TOO FAST FOR YOU?

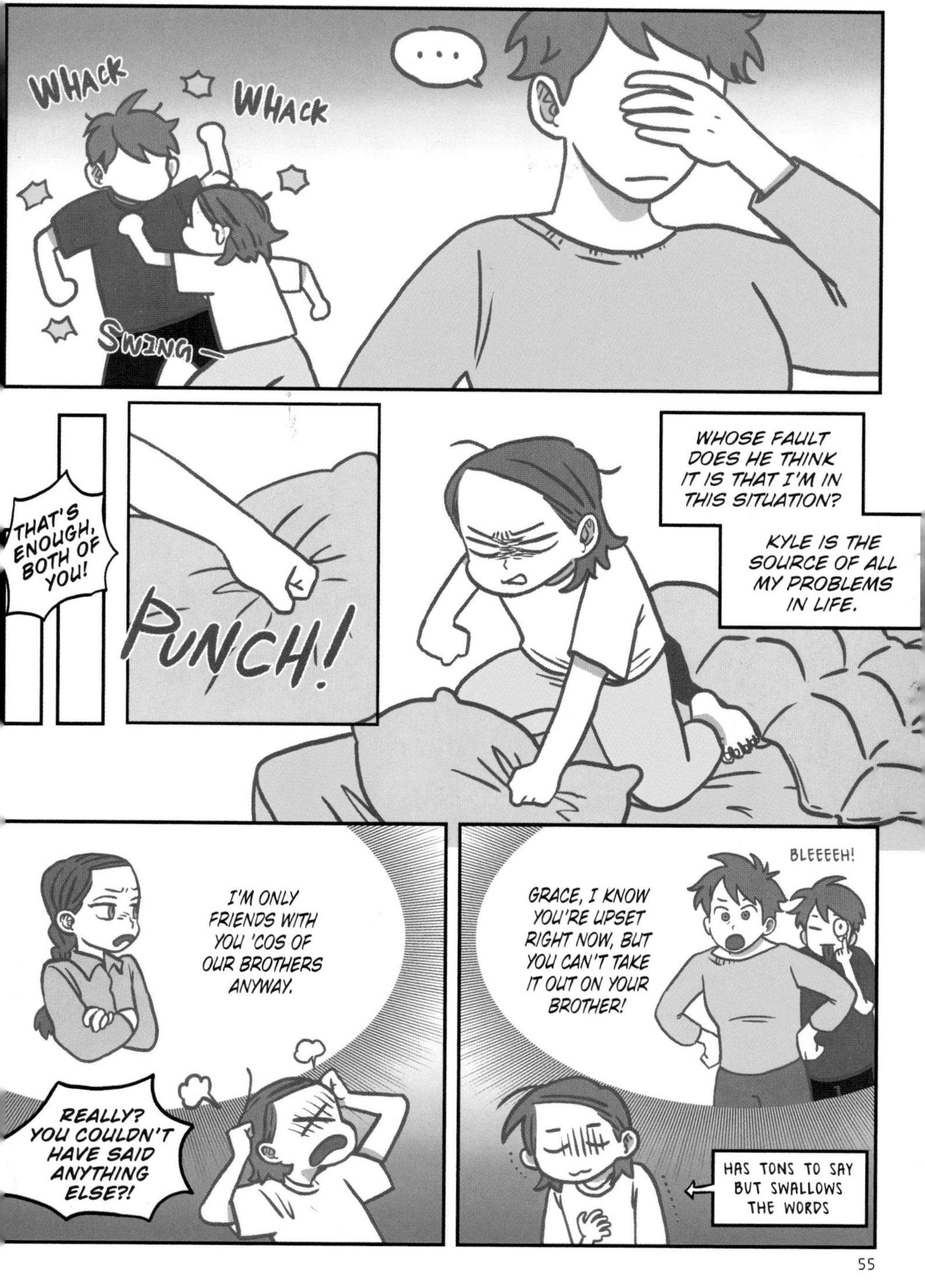
WHACK
WHACK
SWING—
...
THAT'S ENOUGH, BOTH OF YOU!
PUNCH!
WHOSE FAULT DOES HE THINK IT IS THAT I'M IN THIS SITUATION?
KYLE IS THE SOURCE OF ALL MY PROBLEMS IN LIFE.
I'M ONLY FRIENDS WITH YOU 'COS OF OUR BROTHERS ANYWAY.
REALLY? YOU COULDN'T HAVE SAID ANYTHING ELSE?!
BLEEEEH!
GRACE, I KNOW YOU'RE UPSET RIGHT NOW, BUT YOU CAN'T TAKE IT OUT ON YOUR BROTHER!
HAS TONS TO SAY BUT SWALLOWS THE WORDS

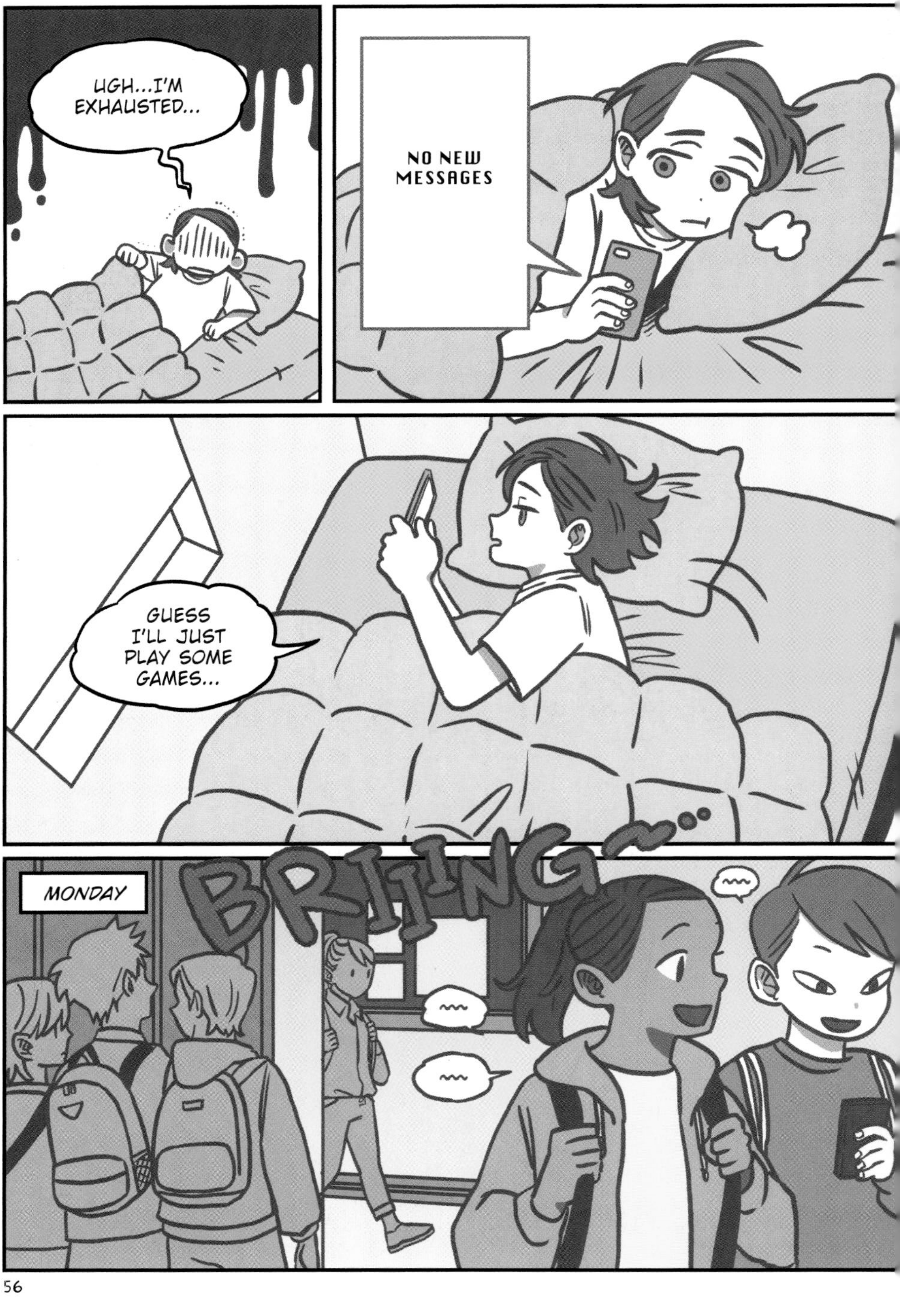

UGH...I'M EXHAUSTED...
NO NEW MESSAGES
GUESS I'LL JUST PLAY SOME GAMES...
BRIIING~...
MONDAY

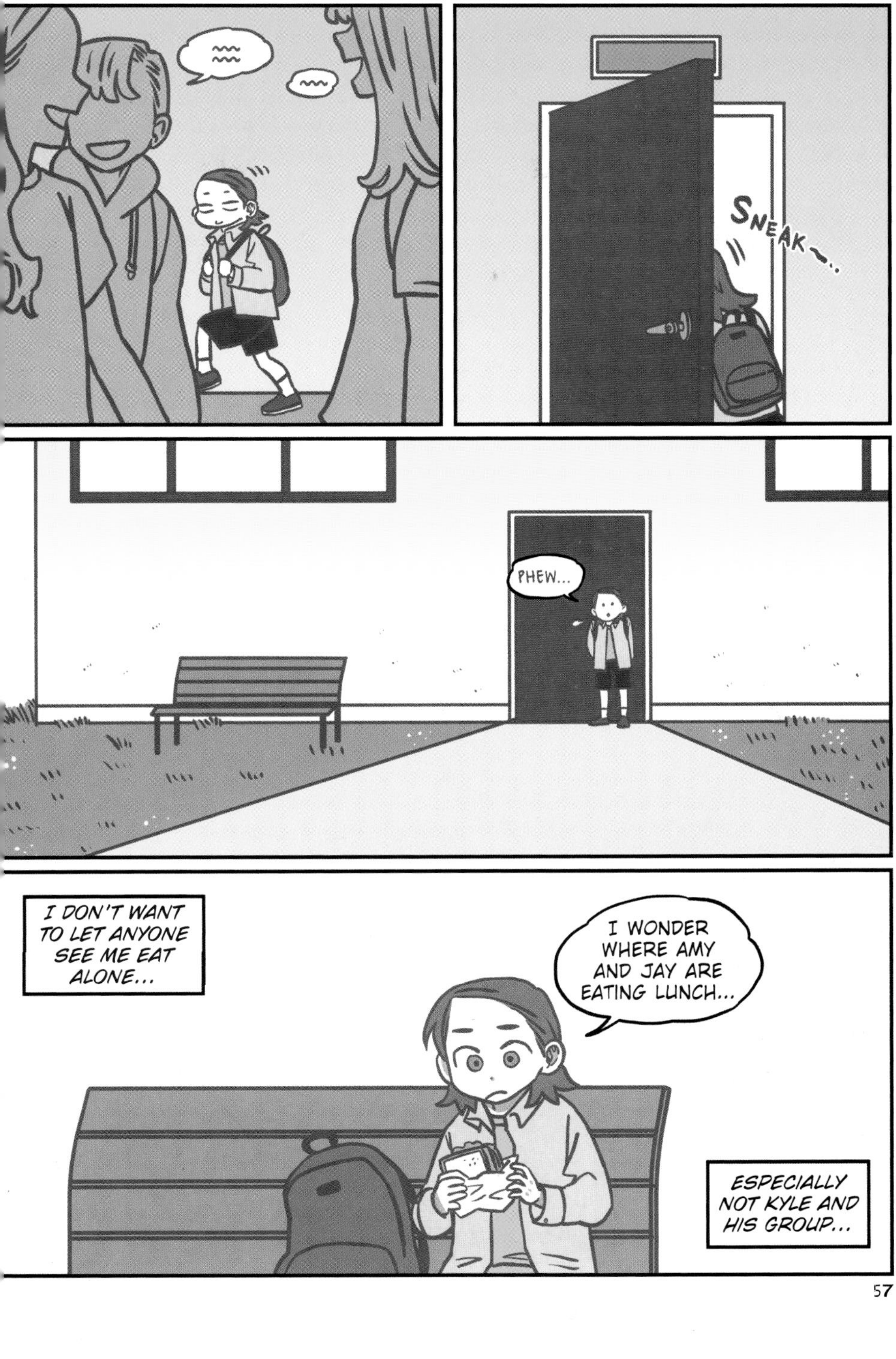
SNEAK~..
PHEW...
I DON'T WANT TO LET ANYONE SEE ME EAT ALONE...
I WONDER WHERE AMY AND JAY ARE EATING LUNCH...
ESPECIALLY NOT KYLE AND HIS GROUP...

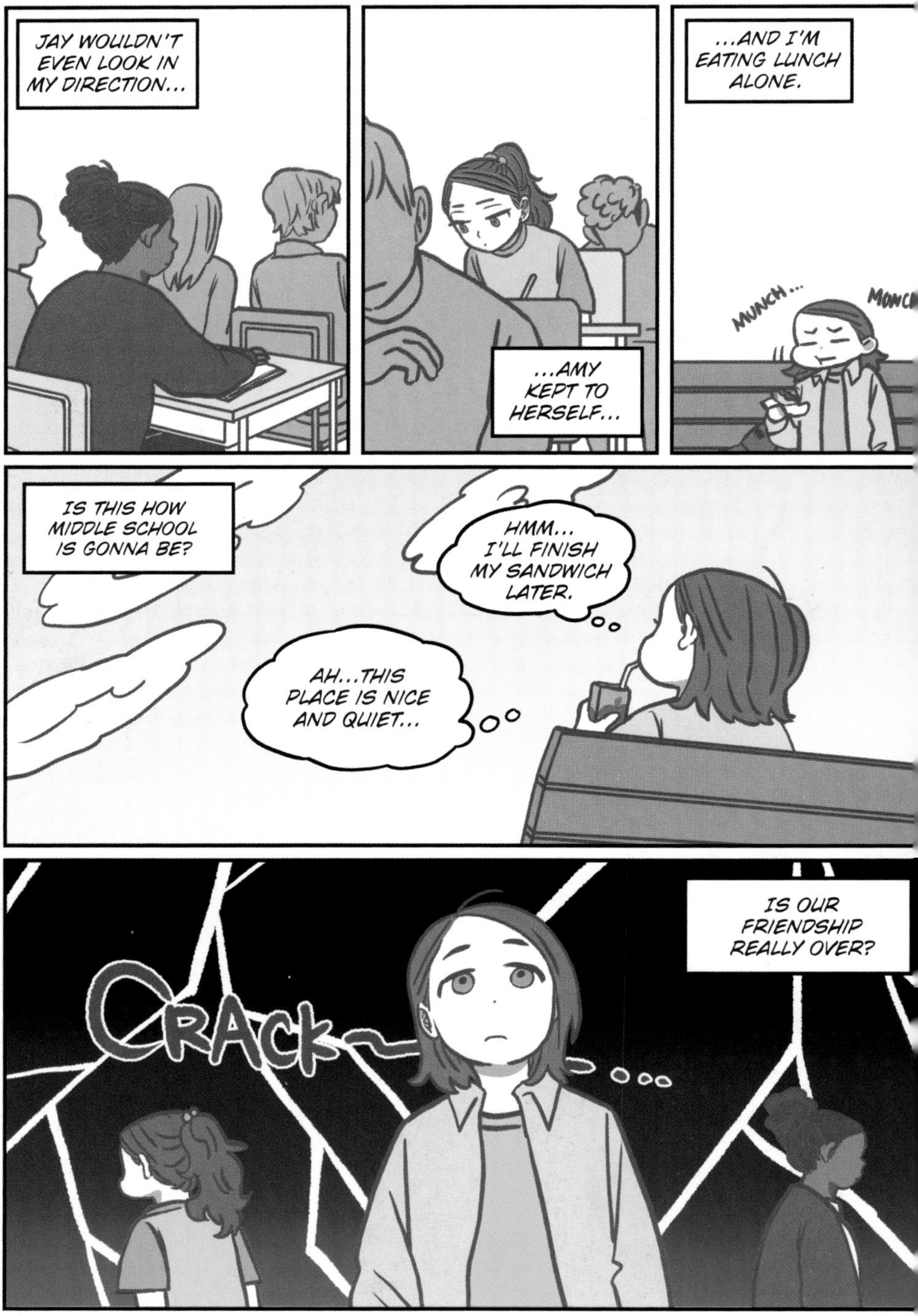
JAY WOULDN'T EVEN LOOK IN MY DIRECTION...
...AMY KEPT TO HERSELF...
...AND I'M EATING LUNCH ALONE.
MUNCH...
IS THIS HOW MIDDLE SCHOOL IS GONNA BE?
HMM... I'LL FINISH MY SANDWICH LATER.
AH...THIS PLACE IS NICE AND QUIET...
IS OUR FRIENDSHIP REALLY OVER?
CRACK

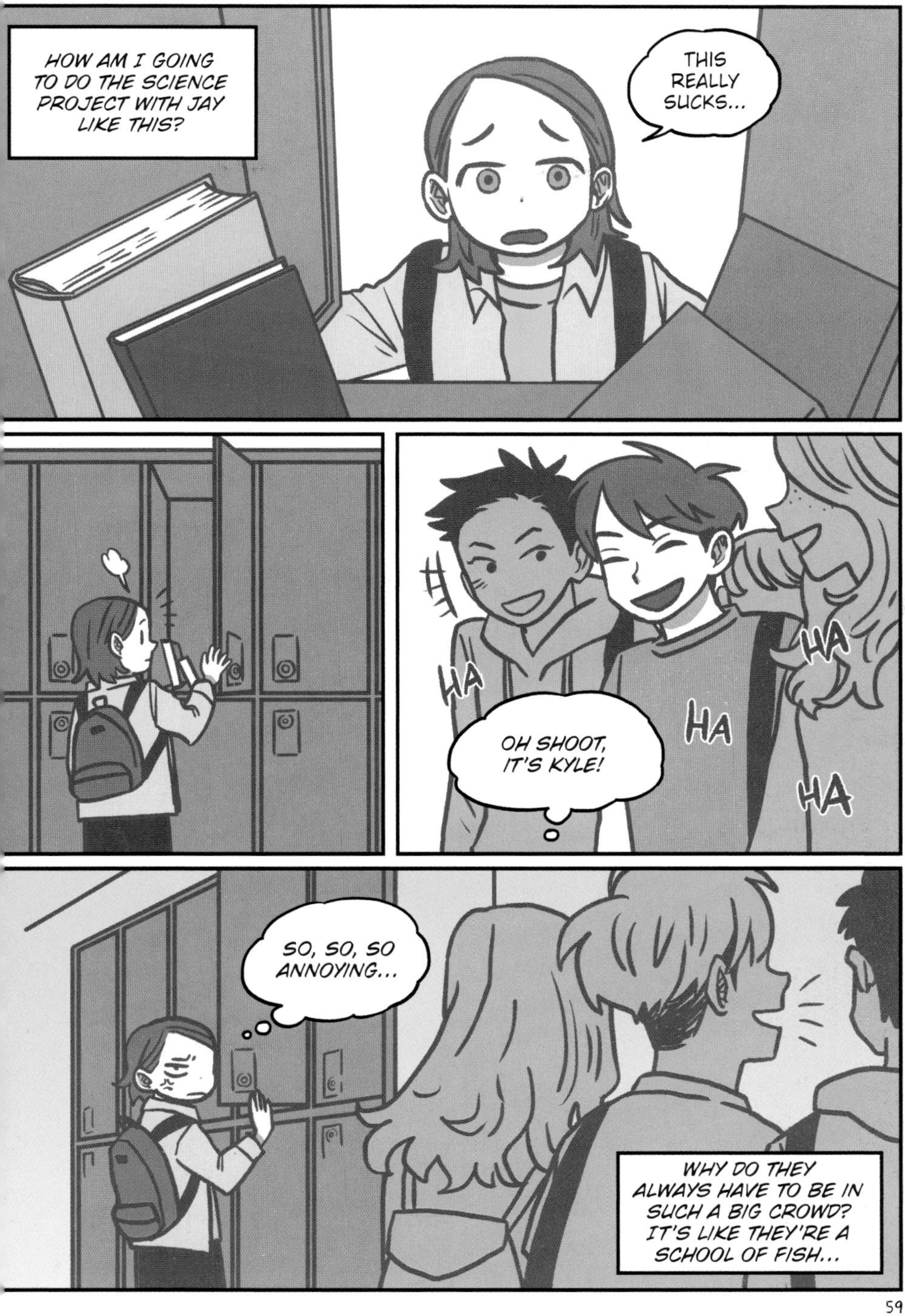
HOW AM I GOING TO DO THE SCIENCE PROJECT WITH JAY LIKE THIS?
THIS REALLY SUCKS...
HA
HA
HA
HA
OH SHOOT, IT'S KYLE!
SO, SO, SO ANNOYING...
WHY DO THEY ALWAYS HAVE TO BE IN SUCH A BIG CROWD? IT'S LIKE THEY'RE A SCHOOL OF FISH...

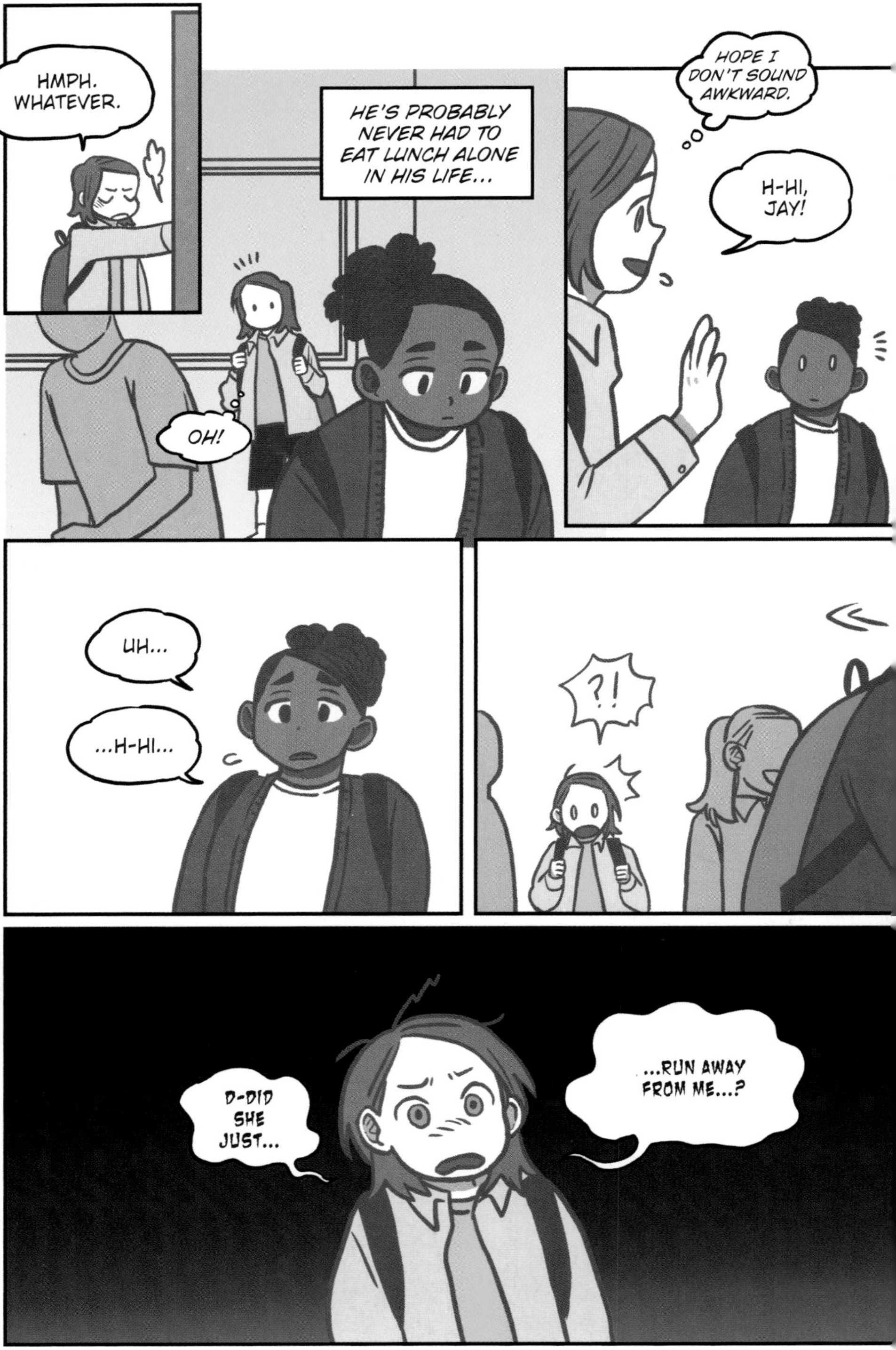
HMPH. WHATEVER.
HE'S PROBABLY NEVER HAD TO EAT LUNCH ALONE IN HIS LIFE...
OH!
HOPE I DON'T SOUND AWKWARD.
H-HI, JAY!
UH...
...H-HI...
?!
D-DID SHE JUST...
...RUN AWAY FROM ME...?

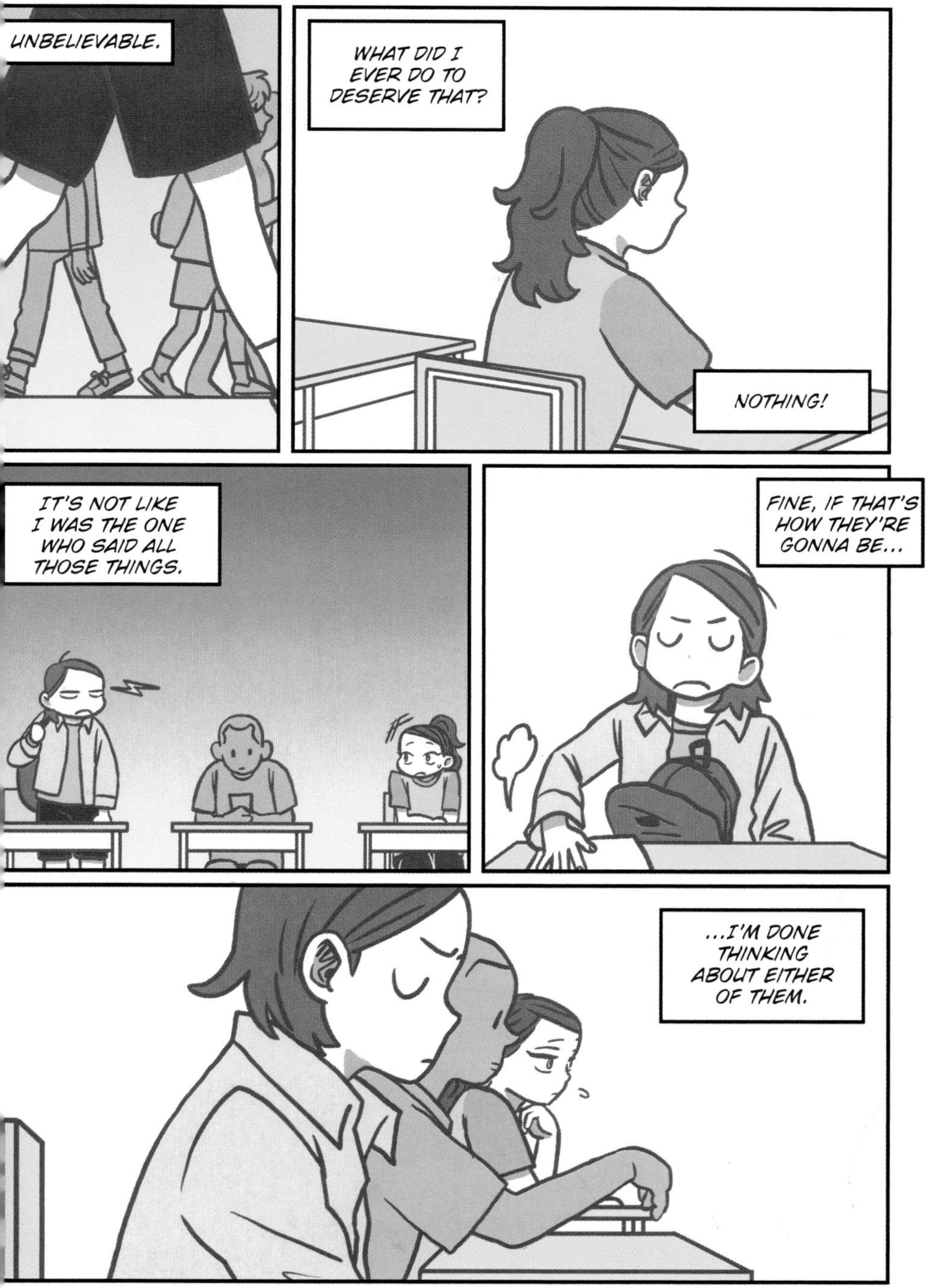
UNBELIEVABLE.
WHAT DID I EVER DO TO DESERVE THAT?
NOTHING!
IT'S NOT LIKE I WAS THE ONE WHO SAID ALL THOSE THINGS.
FINE, IF THAT'S HOW THEY'RE GONNA BE...
...I'M DONE THINKING ABOUT EITHER OF THEM.

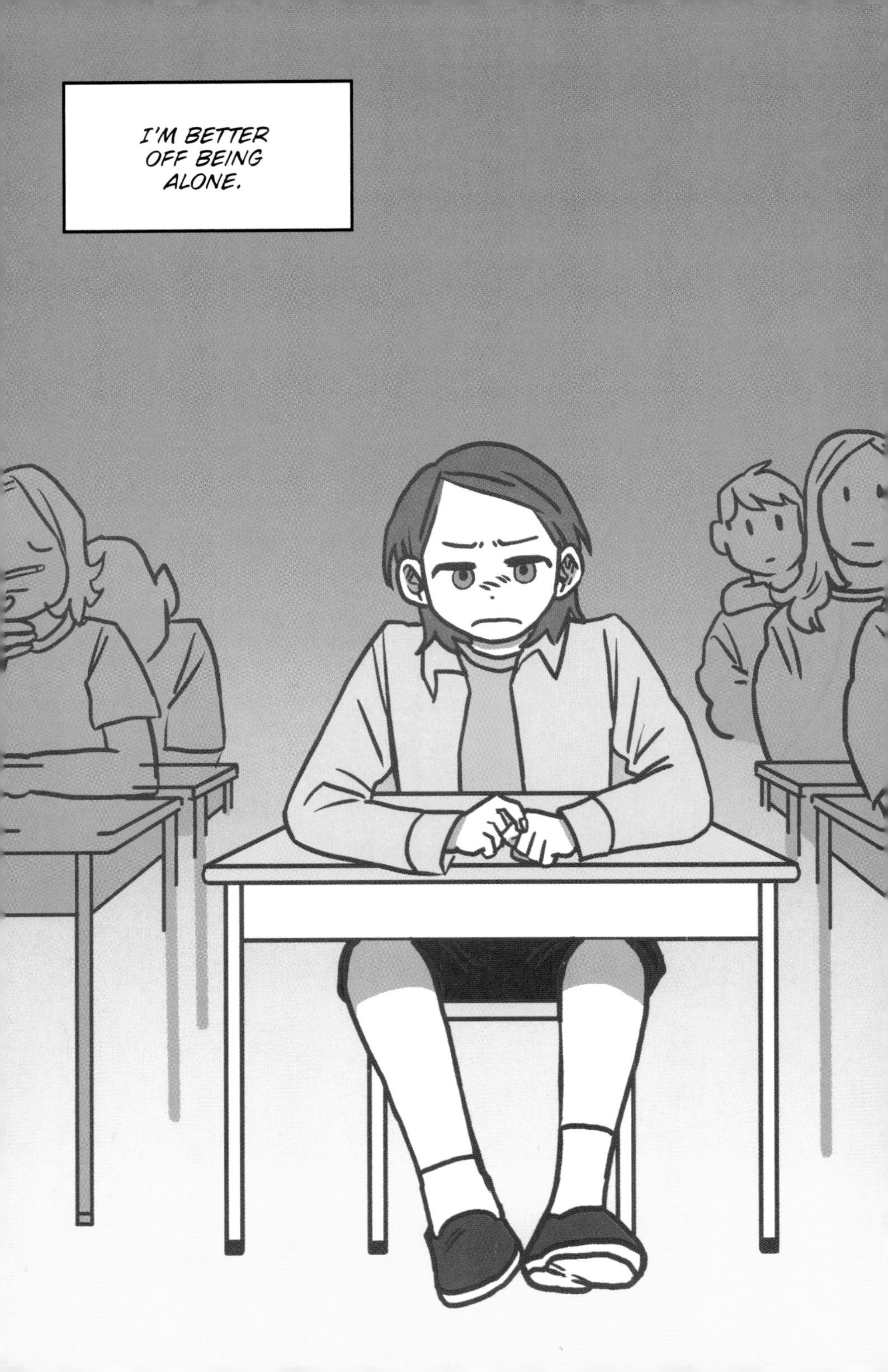
I'M BETTER OFF BEING ALONE.

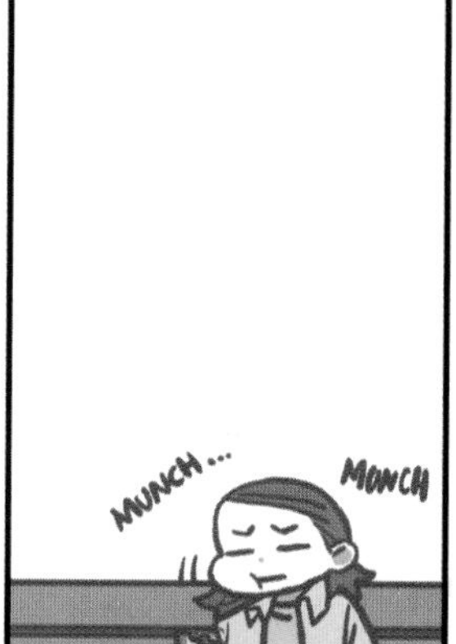
MUNCH...
MONCH

CHAPTER 4

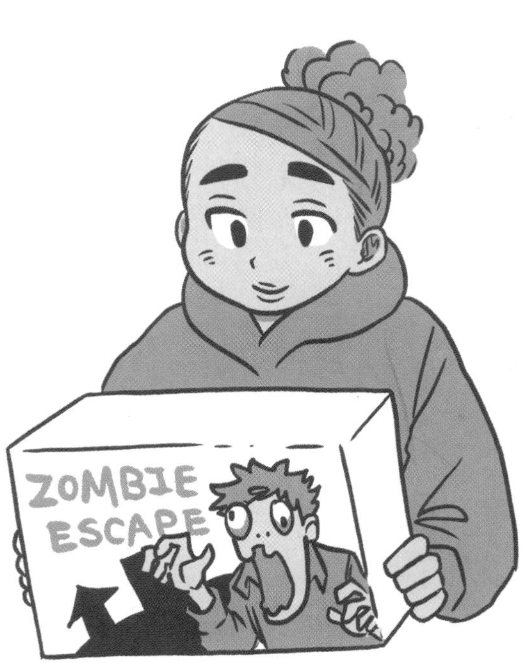
ZOMBIE
ESCAPE

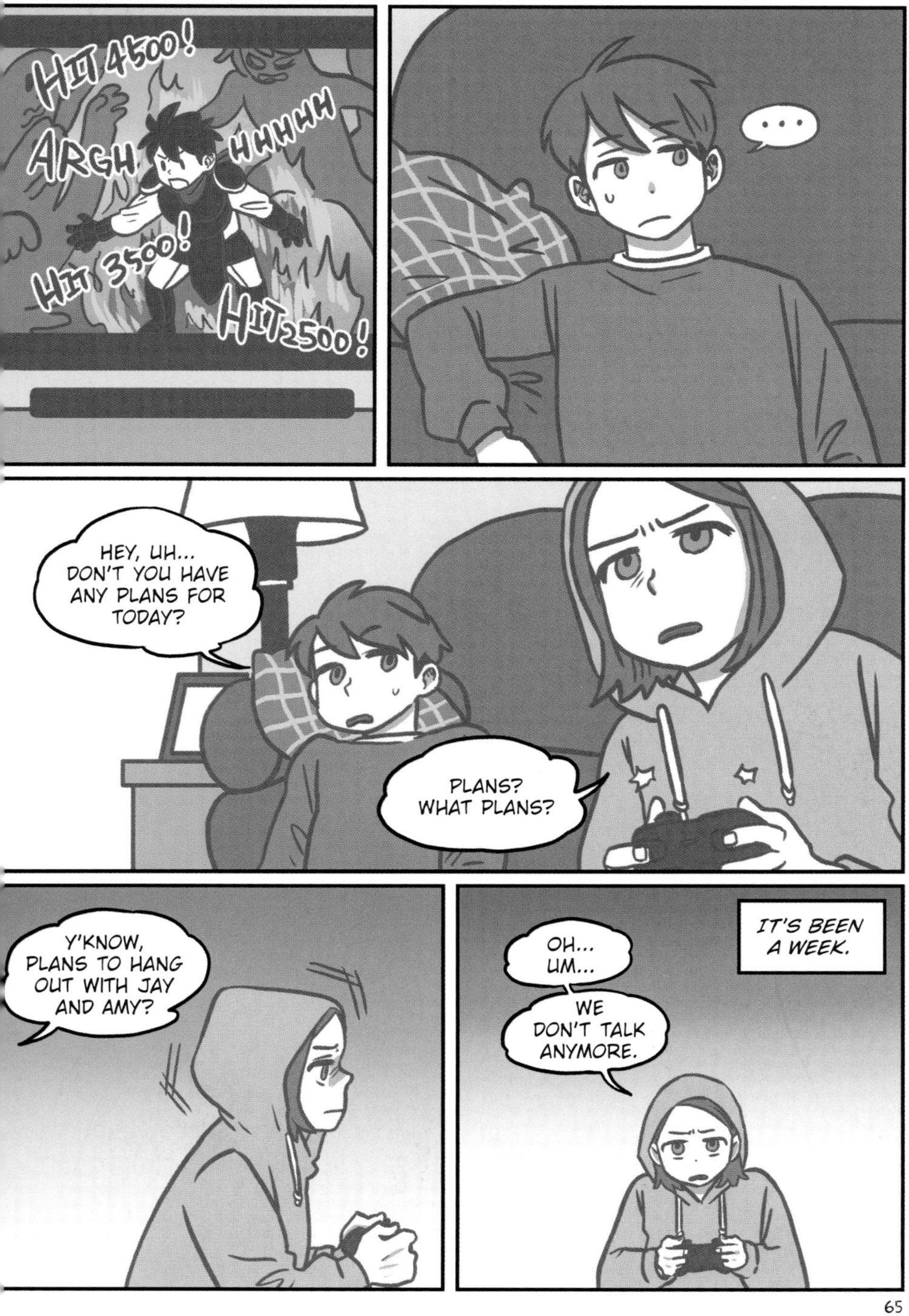
HIT 4500!
ARGH HHHHH
HIT 3500!
HIT 2500!
...
HEY, UH... DON'T YOU HAVE ANY PLANS FOR TODAY?
PLANS? WHAT PLANS?
Y'KNOW, PLANS TO HANG OUT WITH JAY AND AMY?
IT'S BEEN A WEEK.
OH... UM...
WE DON'T TALK ANYMORE.

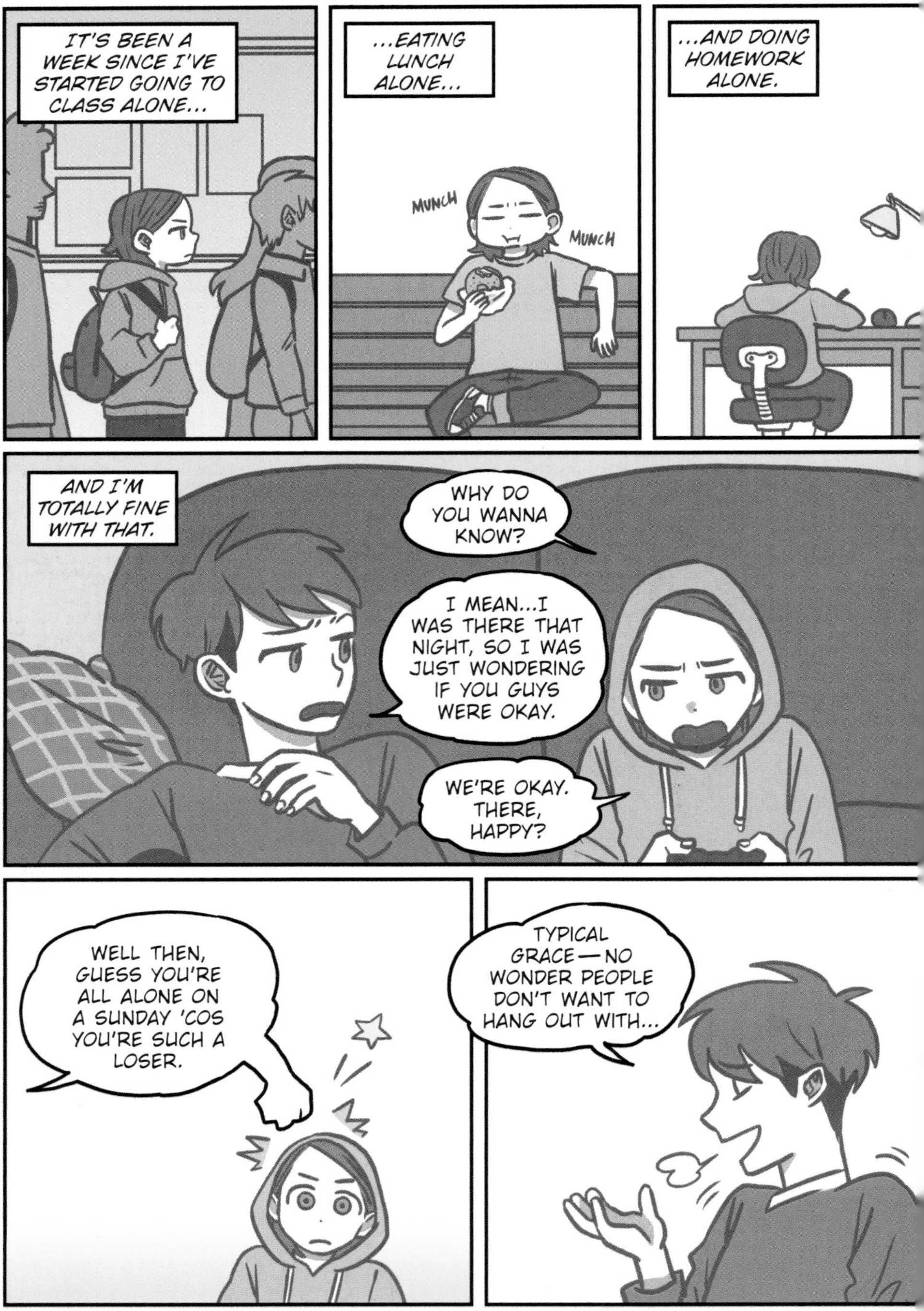
IT'S BEEN A WEEK SINCE I'VE STARTED GOING TO CLASS ALONE...
...EATING LUNCH ALONE...
MUNCH
MUNCH
...AND DOING HOMEWORK ALONE.
AND I'M TOTALLY FINE WITH THAT.
WHY DO YOU WANNA KNOW?
I MEAN...I WAS THERE THAT NIGHT, SO I WAS JUST WONDERING IF YOU GUYS WERE OKAY.
WE'RE OKAY. THERE, HAPPY?
WELL THEN, GUESS YOU'RE ALL ALONE ON A SUNDAY 'COS YOU'RE SUCH A LOSER.
TYPICAL GRACE—NO WONDER PEOPLE DON'T WANT TO HANG OUT WITH...

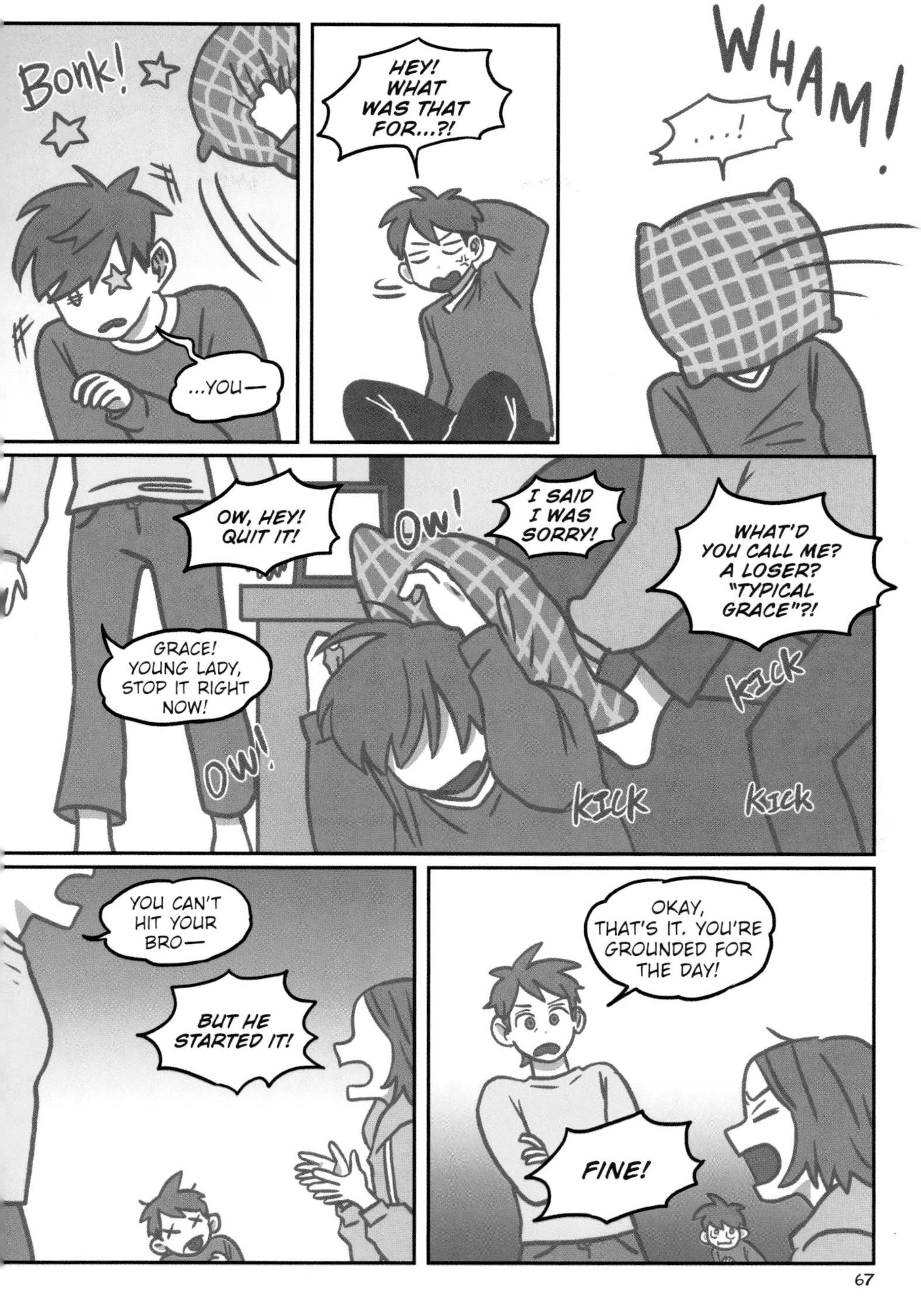
Bonk!
...YOU—
HEY! WHAT WAS THAT FOR...?!
WHAM!
...!
OW, HEY! QUIT IT!
OW!
I SAID I WAS SORRY!
WHAT'D YOU CALL ME? A LOSER? "TYPICAL GRACE"?!
GRACE! YOUNG LADY, STOP IT RIGHT NOW!
OW!
KICK
KICK
KICK
YOU CAN'T HIT YOUR BRO—
BUT HE STARTED IT!
OKAY, THAT'S IT. YOU'RE GROUNDED FOR THE DAY!
FINE!

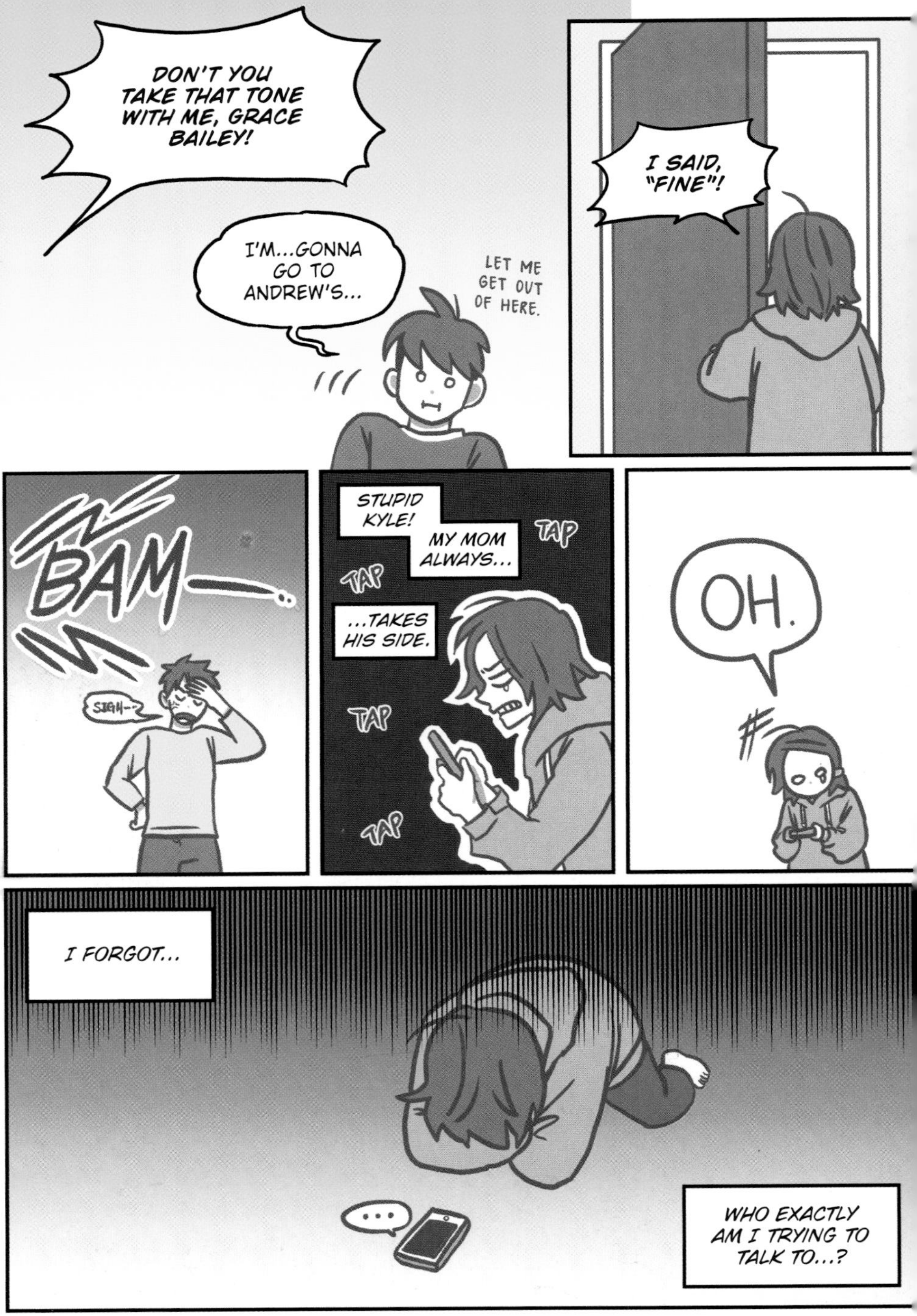
DON'T YOU TAKE THAT TONE WITH ME, GRACE BAILEY!
I'M...GONNA GO TO ANDREW'S...
LET ME GET OUT OF HERE.
I SAID, "FINE"!
BAM
SIGH
STUPID KYLE!
MY MOM ALWAYS...
...TAKES HIS SIDE.
TAP
TAP
TAP
TAP
OH.
I FORGOT...
...
WHO EXACTLY AM I TRYING TO TALK TO...?

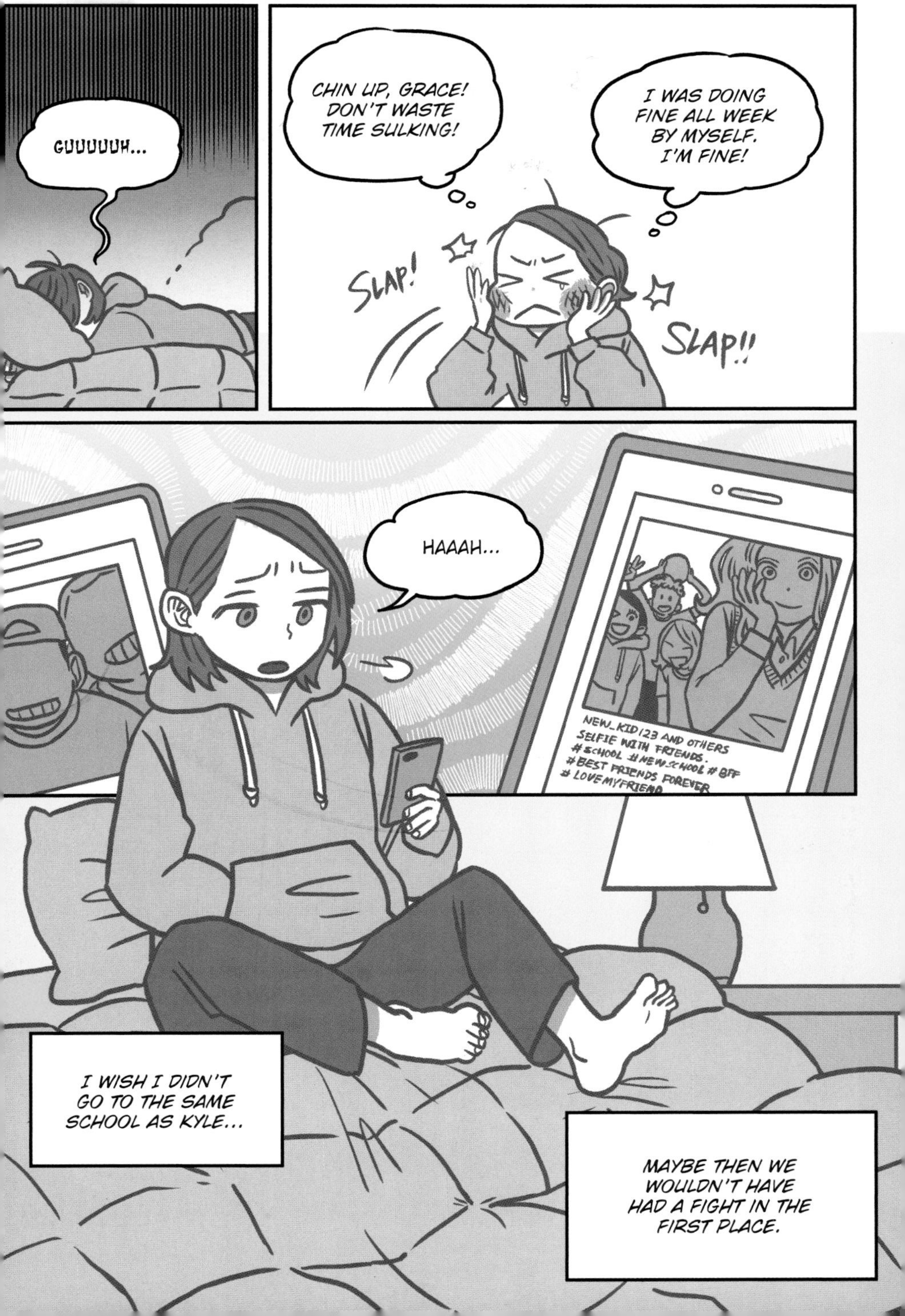
GUUUUUH...
CHIN UP, GRACE! DON'T WASTE TIME SULKING!
I WAS DOING FINE ALL WEEK BY MYSELF. I'M FINE!
SLAP!
SLAP!!
HAAAH...
NEW_KID123 AND OTHERS
SELFIE WITH FRIENDS.
#SCHOOL #NEWSCHOOL #BFF
#BEST FRIENDS FOREVER
#LOVEMYFRIEND
I WISH I DIDN'T GO TO THE SAME SCHOOL AS KYLE...
MAYBE THEN WE WOULDN'T HAVE HAD A FIGHT IN THE FIRST PLACE.

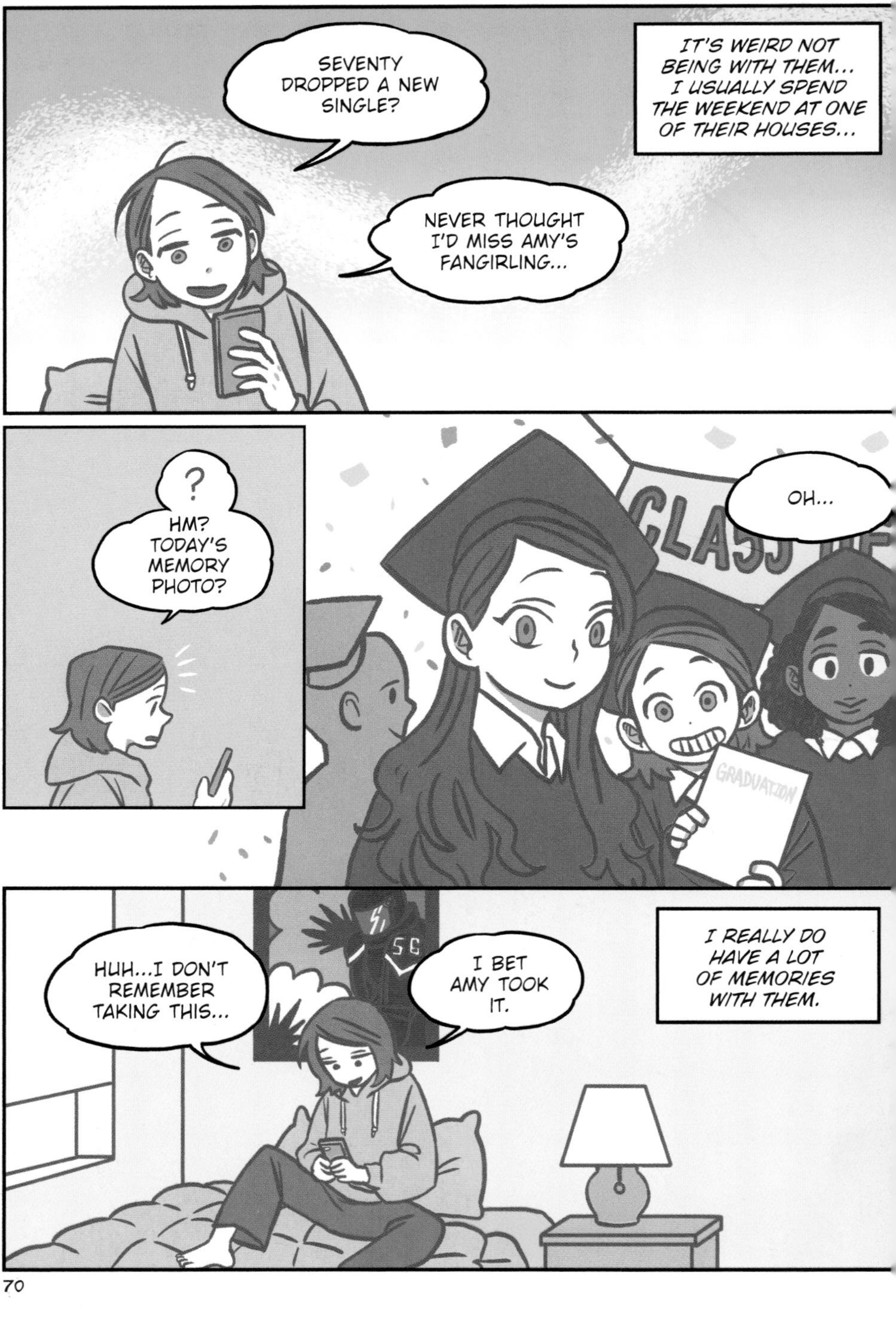
IT'S WEIRD NOT BEING WITH THEM... I USUALLY SPEND THE WEEKEND AT ONE OF THEIR HOUSES...
SEVENTY DROPPED A NEW SINGLE?
NEVER THOUGHT I'D MISS AMY'S FANGIRLING...
?
HM? TODAY'S MEMORY PHOTO?
OH...
GRADUATION
HUH...I DON'T REMEMBER TAKING THIS...
I BET AMY TOOK IT.
I REALLY DO HAVE A LOT OF MEMORIES WITH THEM.

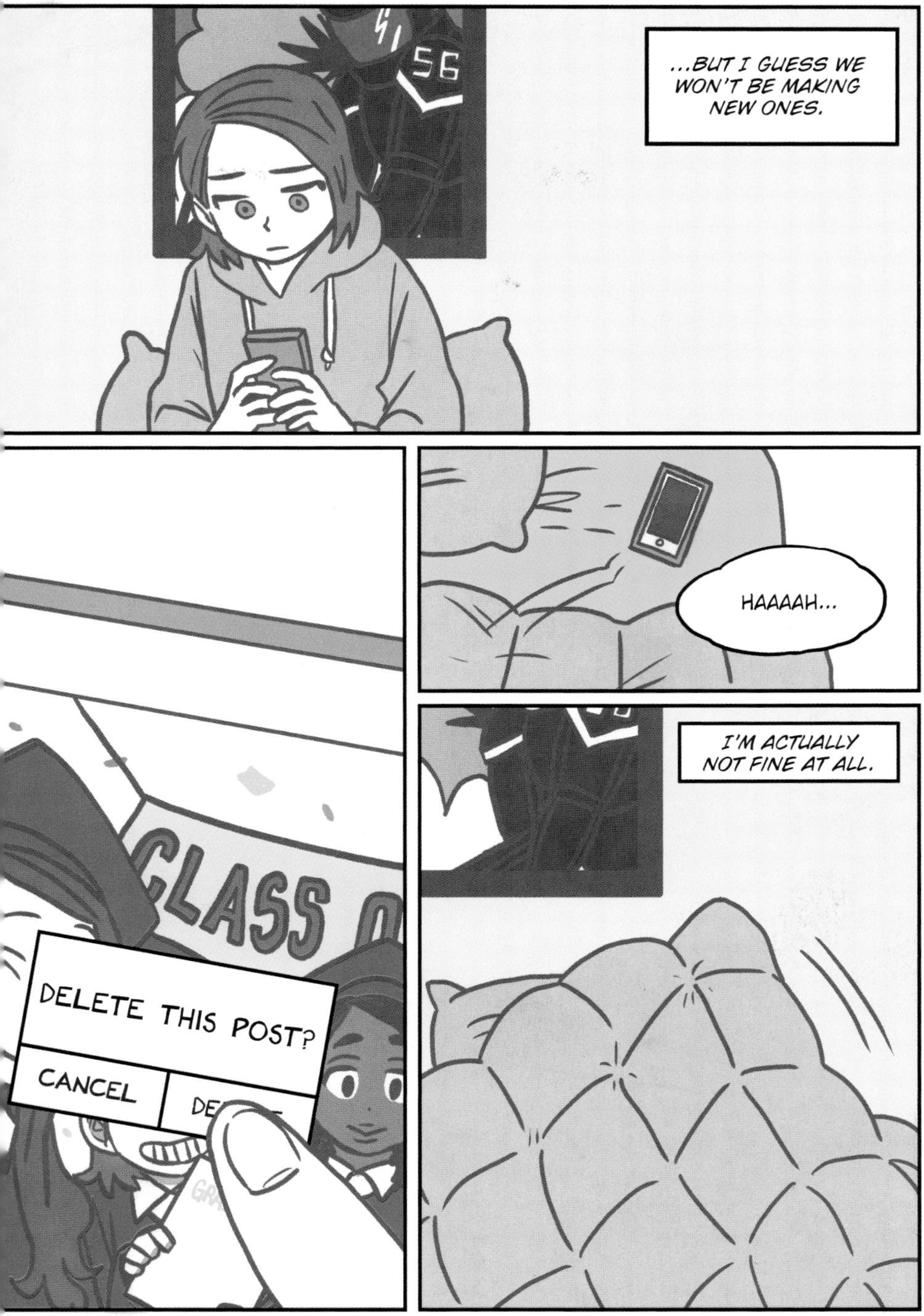
...BUT I GUESS WE WON'T BE MAKING NEW ONES.
CLASS O
DELETE THIS POST?
CANCEL
HAAAAH...
I'M ACTUALLY NOT FINE AT ALL.

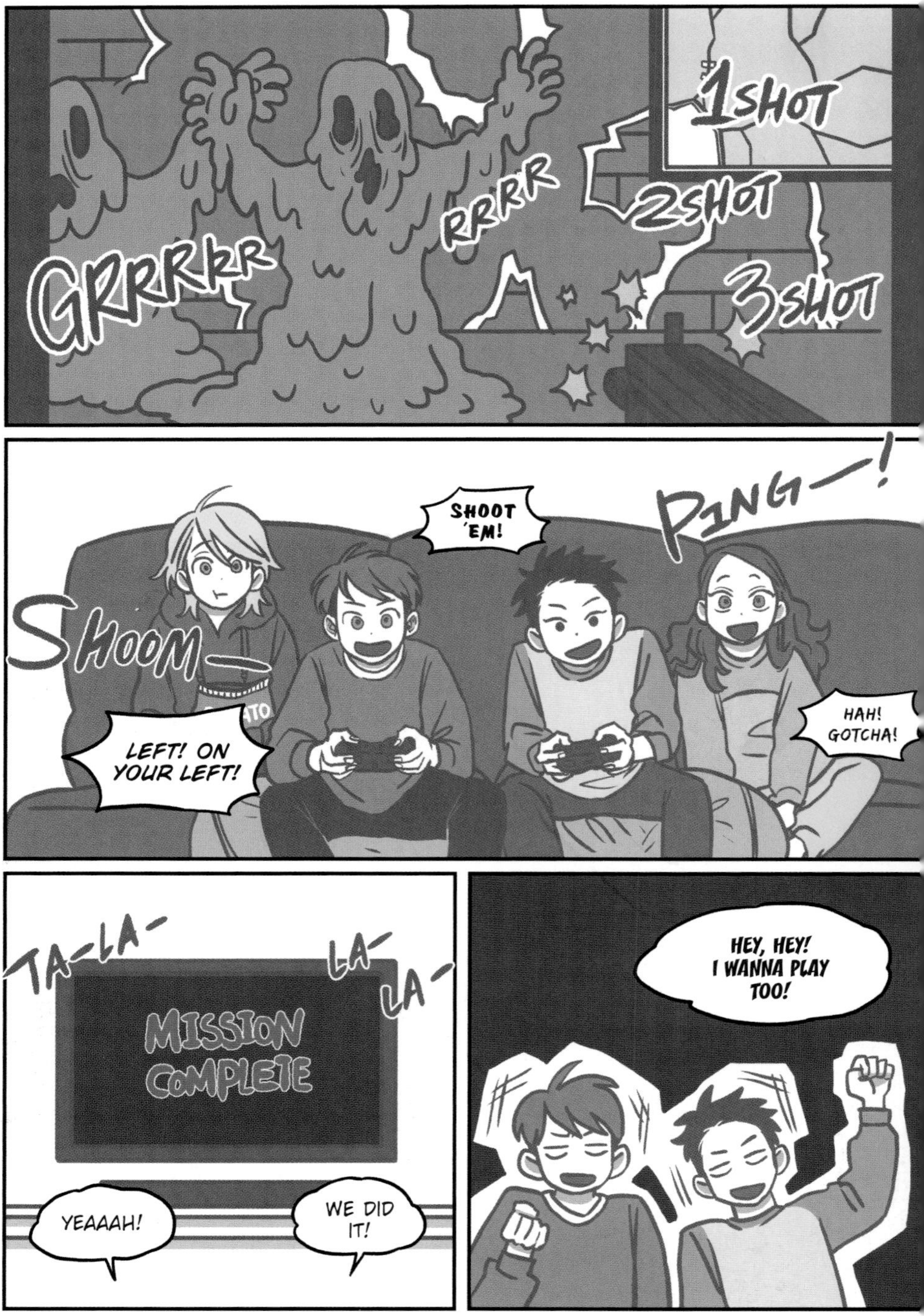
GRRRRR
RRRR
1SHOT
2SHOT
3SHOT
SHOOM—
LEFT! ON YOUR LEFT!
SHOOT 'EM!
PING—!
HAH! GOTCHA!
TA-LA-LA-LA-
MISSION COMPLETE
YEAAAH!
WE DID IT!
HEY, HEY! I WANNA PLAY TOO!

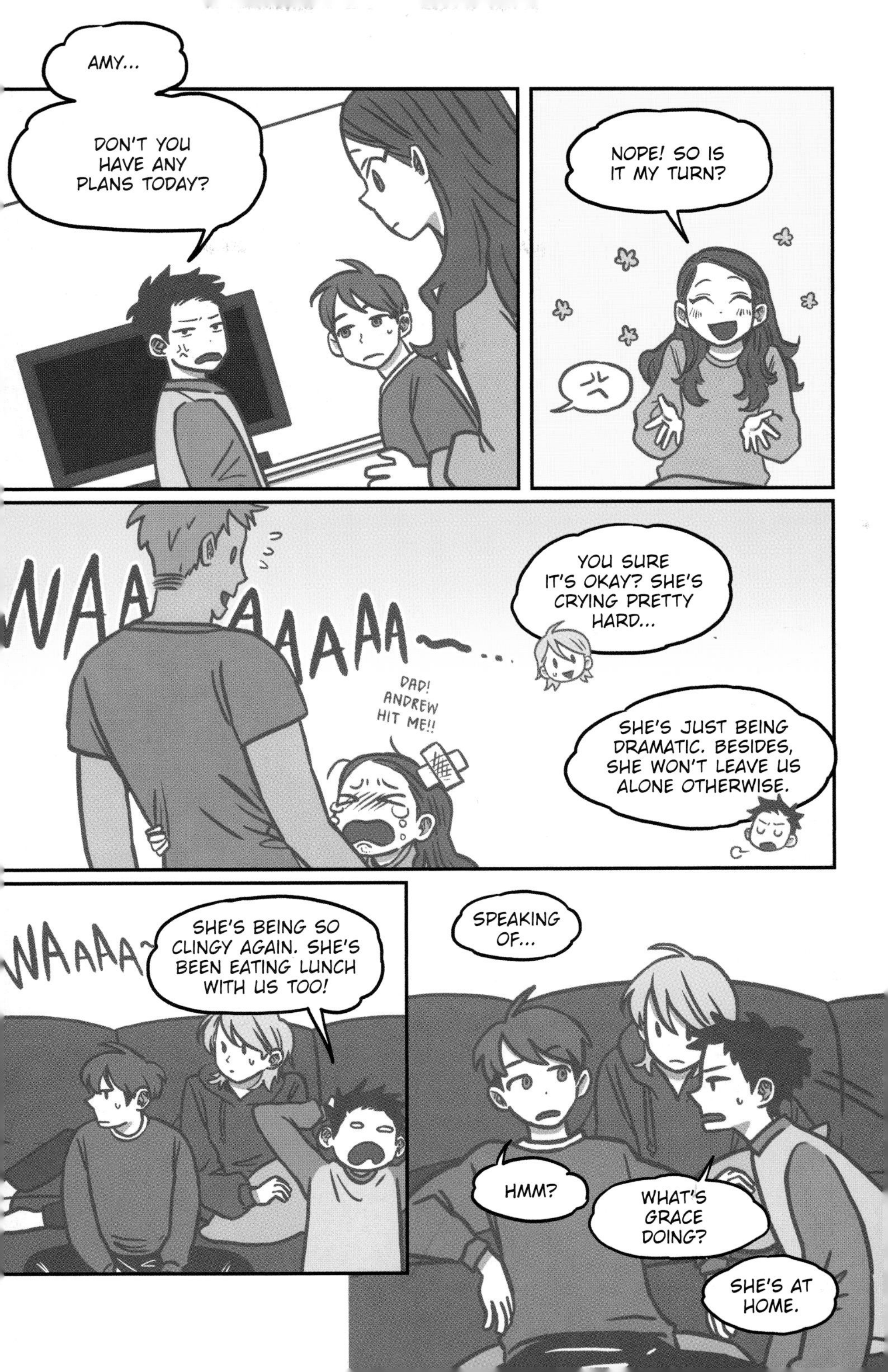
AMY...
DON'T YOU HAVE ANY PLANS TODAY?
NOPE! SO IS IT MY TURN?
WAAAAAAAA~...
YOU SURE IT'S OKAY? SHE'S CRYING PRETTY HARD...
DAD! ANDREW HIT ME!!
SHE'S JUST BEING DRAMATIC. BESIDES, SHE WON'T LEAVE US ALONE OTHERWISE.
WAAAA~
SHE'S BEING SO CLINGY AGAIN. SHE'S BEEN EATING LUNCH WITH US TOO!
SPEAKING OF...
HMM?
WHAT'S GRACE DOING?
SHE'S AT HOME.

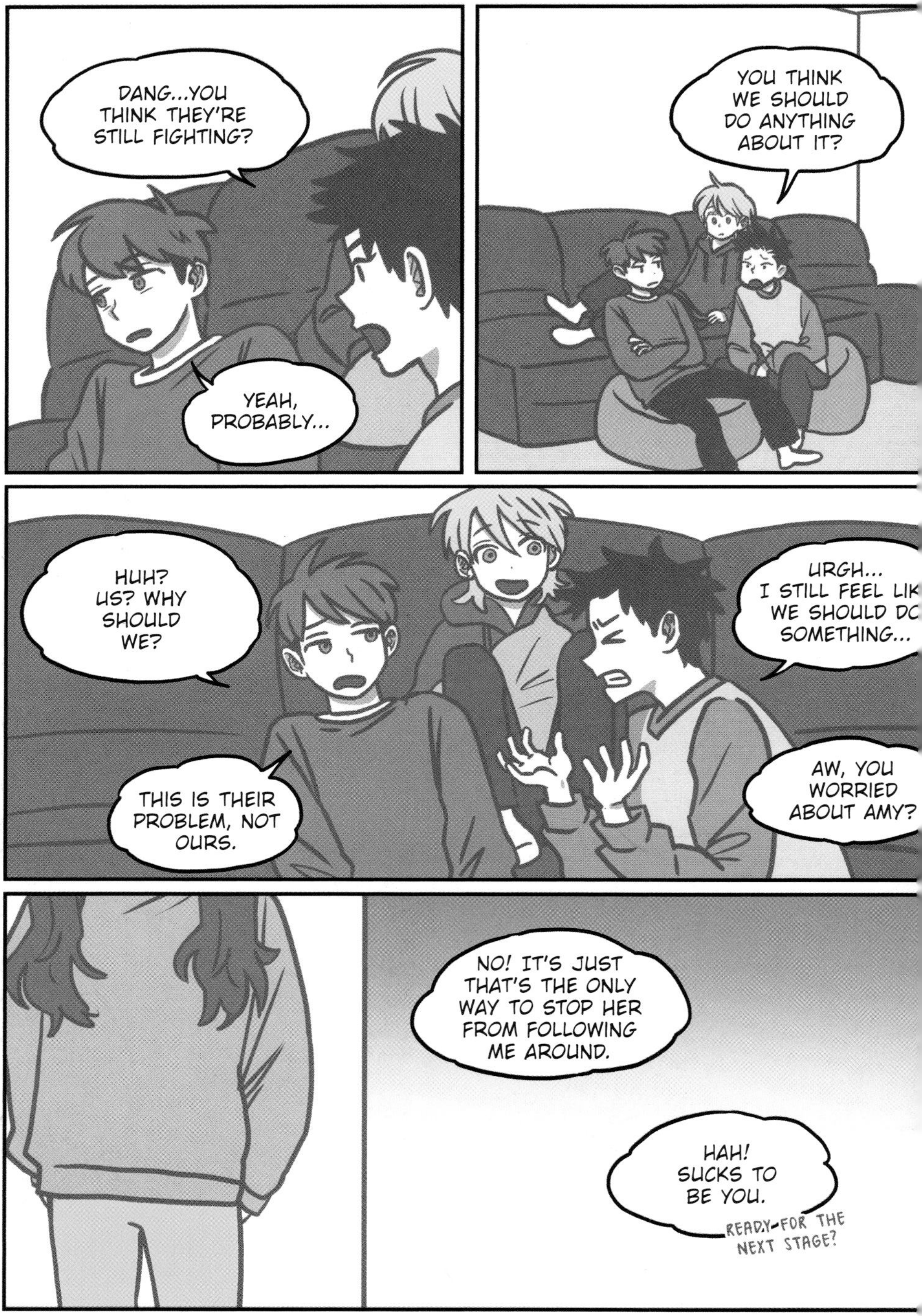
DANG...YOU THINK THEY'RE STILL FIGHTING?
YEAH, PROBABLY...
YOU THINK WE SHOULD DO ANYTHING ABOUT IT?
HUH? US? WHY SHOULD WE?
THIS IS THEIR PROBLEM, NOT OURS.
URGH... I STILL FEEL LIK WE SHOULD DO SOMETHING...
AW, YOU WORRIED ABOUT AMY?
NO! IT'S JUST THAT'S THE ONLY WAY TO STOP HER FROM FOLLOWING ME AROUND.
HAH! SUCKS TO BE YOU.
READY FOR THE NEXT STAGE?

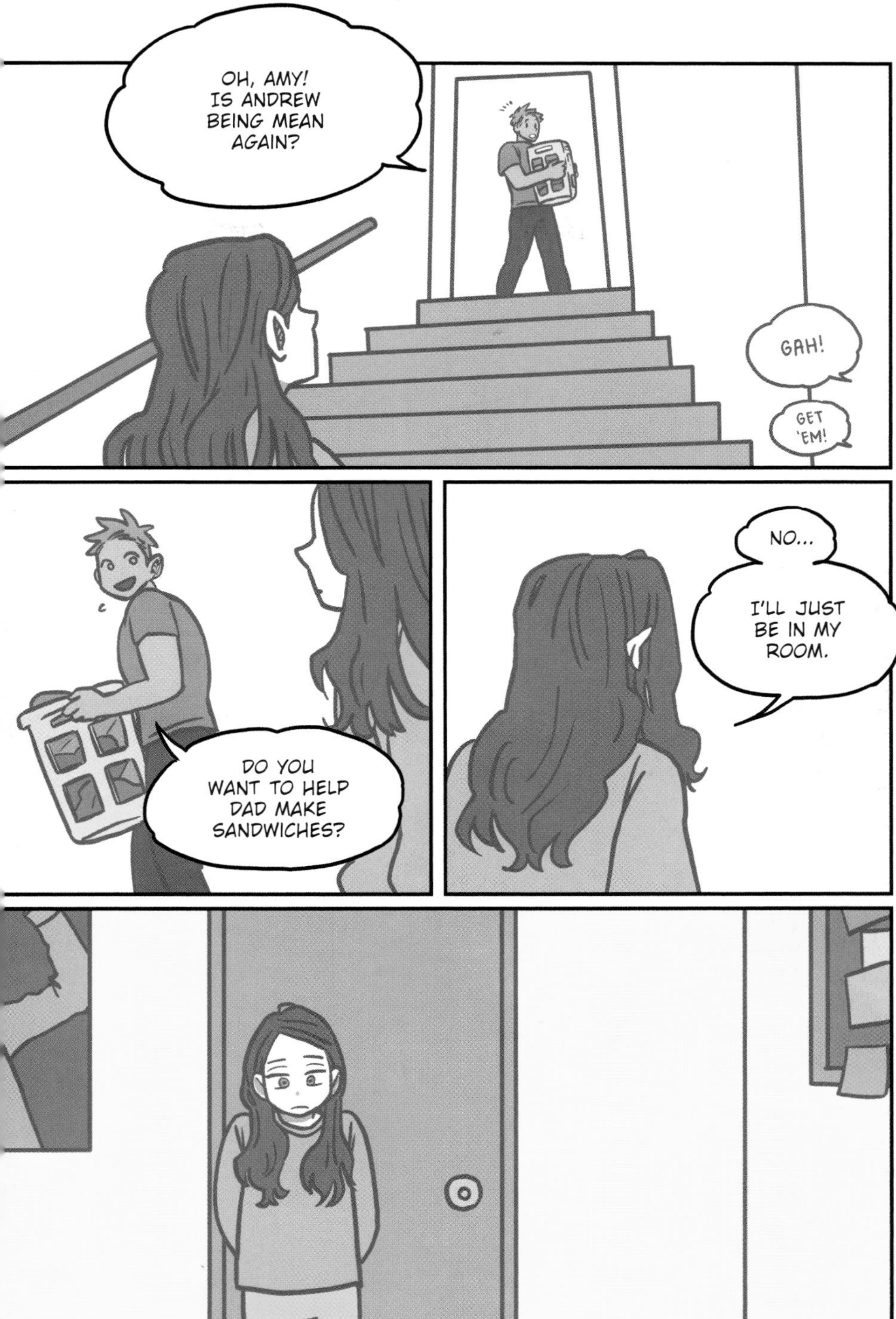
OH, AMY! IS ANDREW BEING MEAN AGAIN?
GAH!
GET 'EM!
DO YOU WANT TO HELP DAD MAKE SANDWICHES?
NO...
I'LL JUST BE IN MY ROOM.

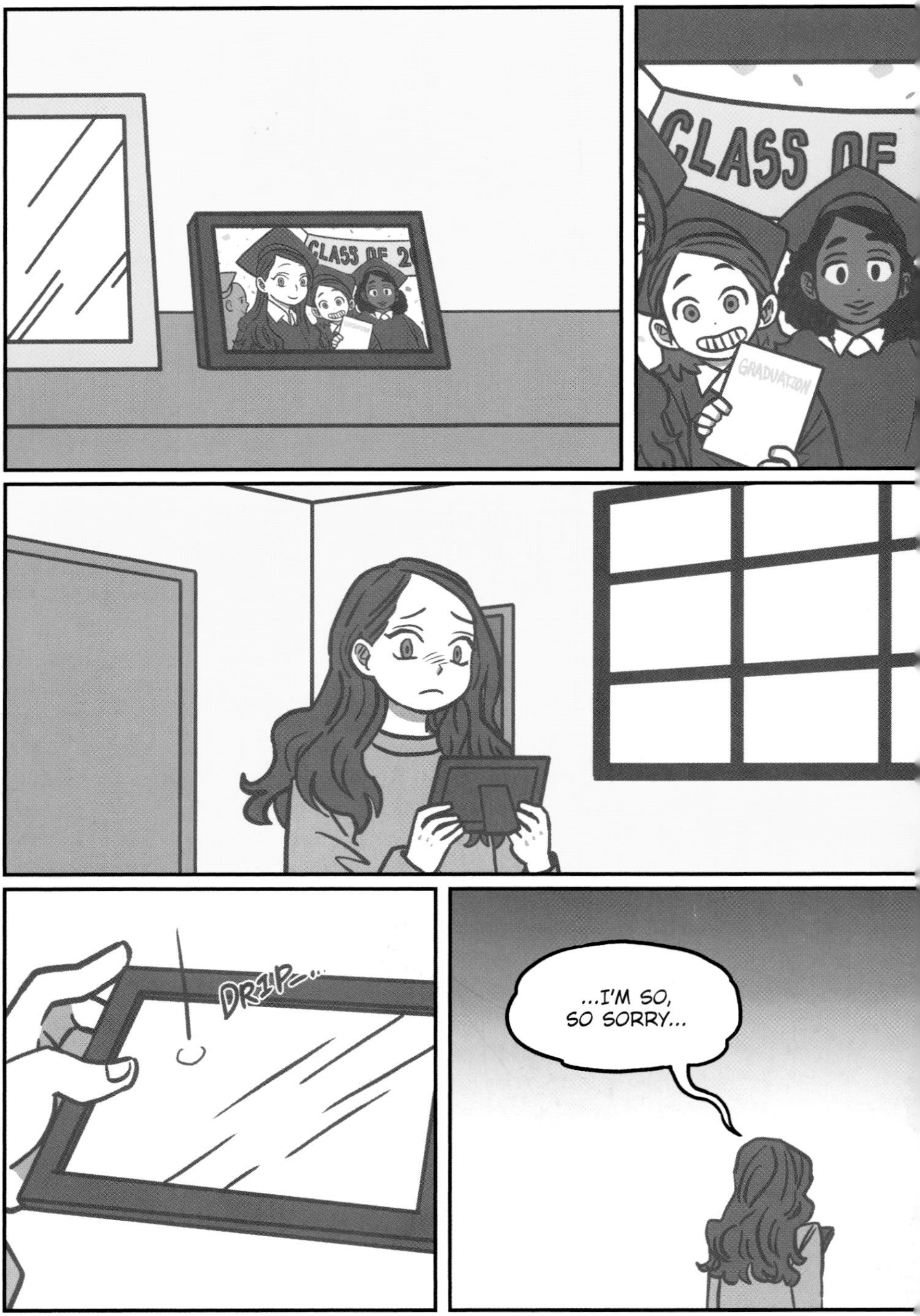
CLASS OF 2
GRADUATION
CLASS OF
GRADUATION
DRIP...
...I'M SO,
SO SORRY...

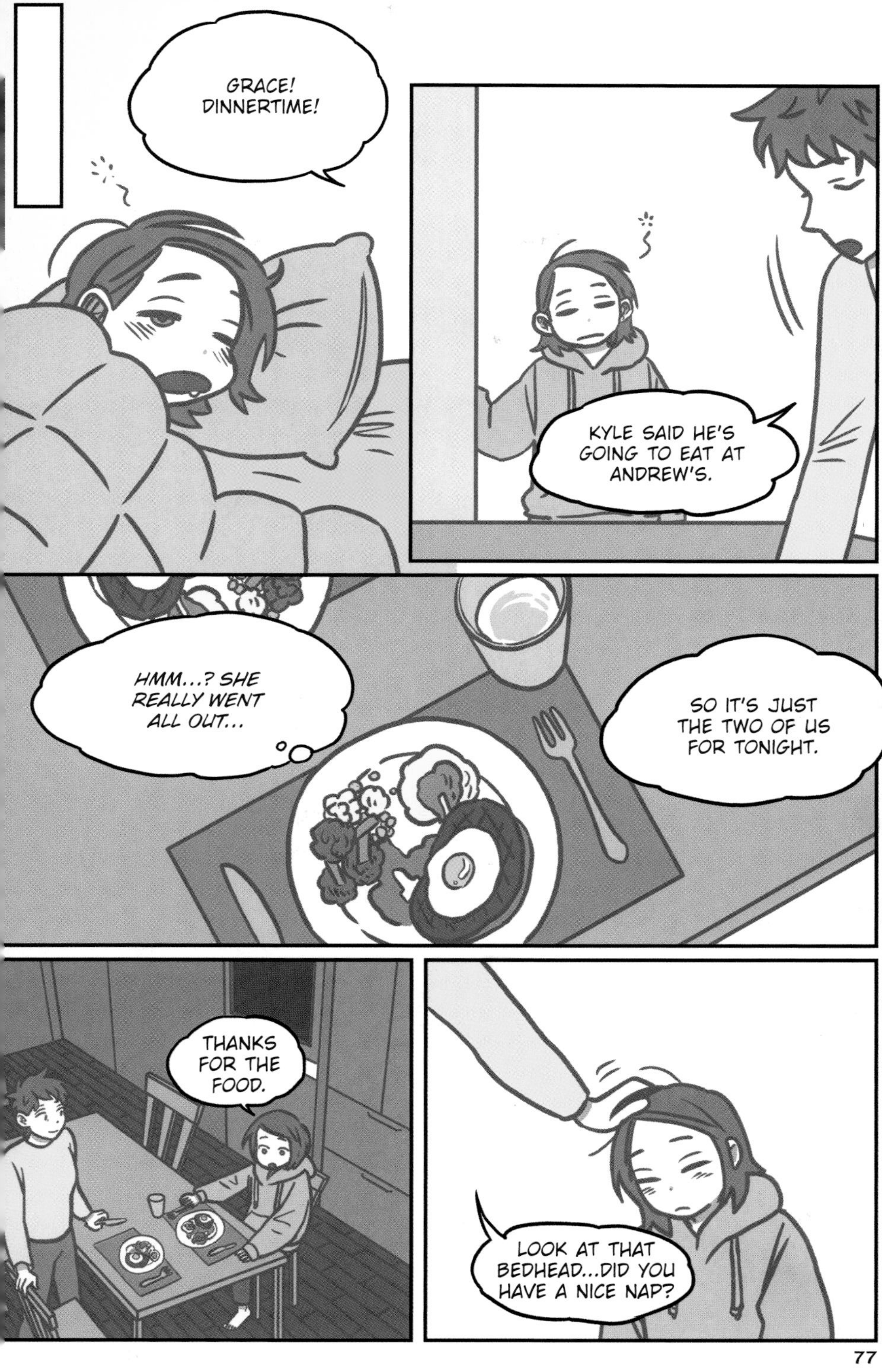
GRACE! DINNERTIME!
KYLE SAID HE'S GOING TO EAT AT ANDREW'S.
HMM...? SHE REALLY WENT ALL OUT...
SO IT'S JUST THE TWO OF US FOR TONIGHT.
THANKS FOR THE FOOD.
LOOK AT THAT BEDHEAD...DID YOU HAVE A NICE NAP?

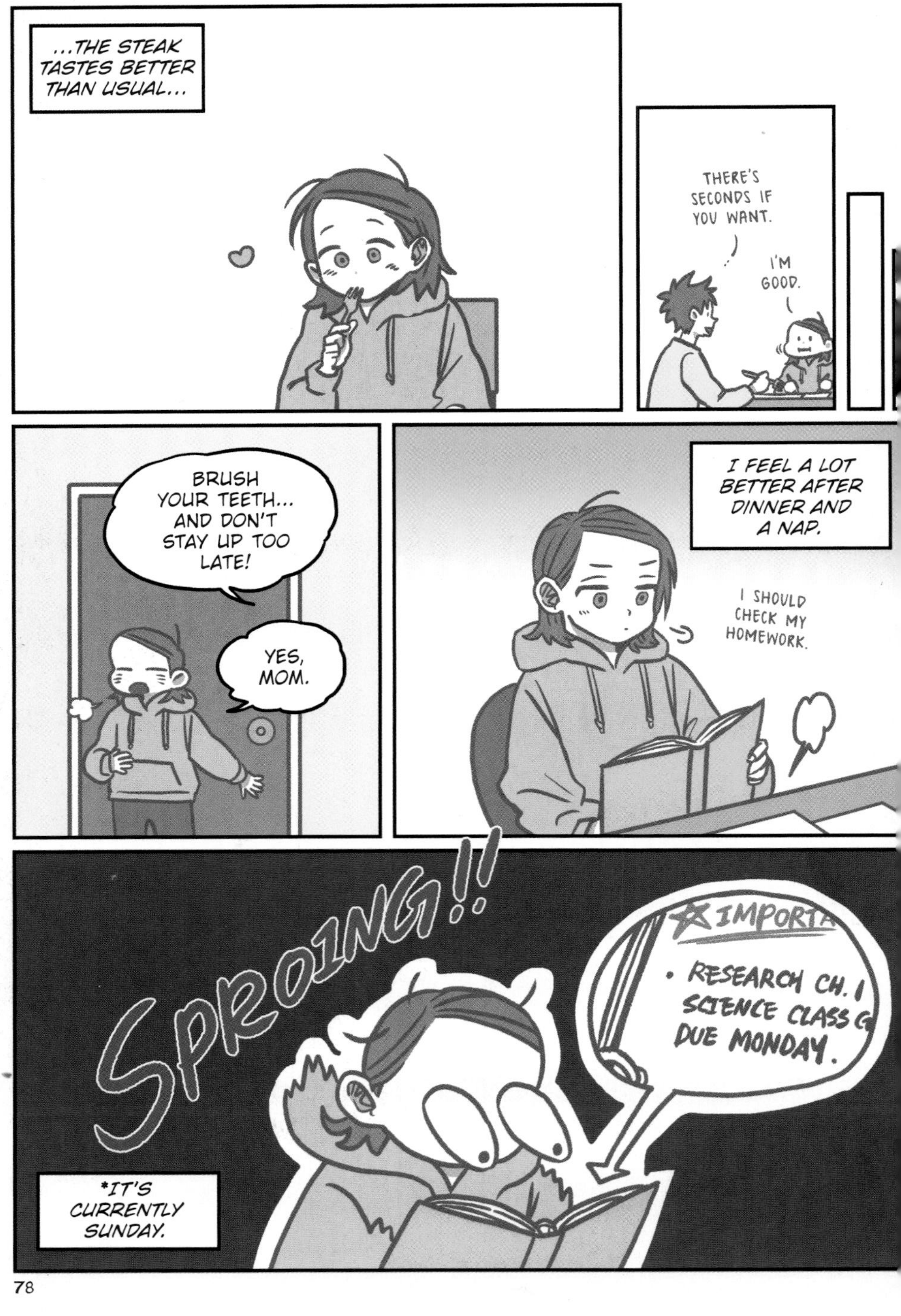
...THE STEAK TASTES BETTER THAN USUAL...
THERE'S SECONDS IF YOU WANT.
I'M GOOD.
BRUSH YOUR TEETH... AND DON'T STAY UP TOO LATE!
YES, MOM.
I FEEL A LOT BETTER AFTER DINNER AND A NAP.
I SHOULD CHECK MY HOMEWORK.
SPROING!!
IMPORTA
• RESEARCH CH. I SCIENCE CLASS DUE MONDAY.
*IT'S CURRENTLY SUNDAY.

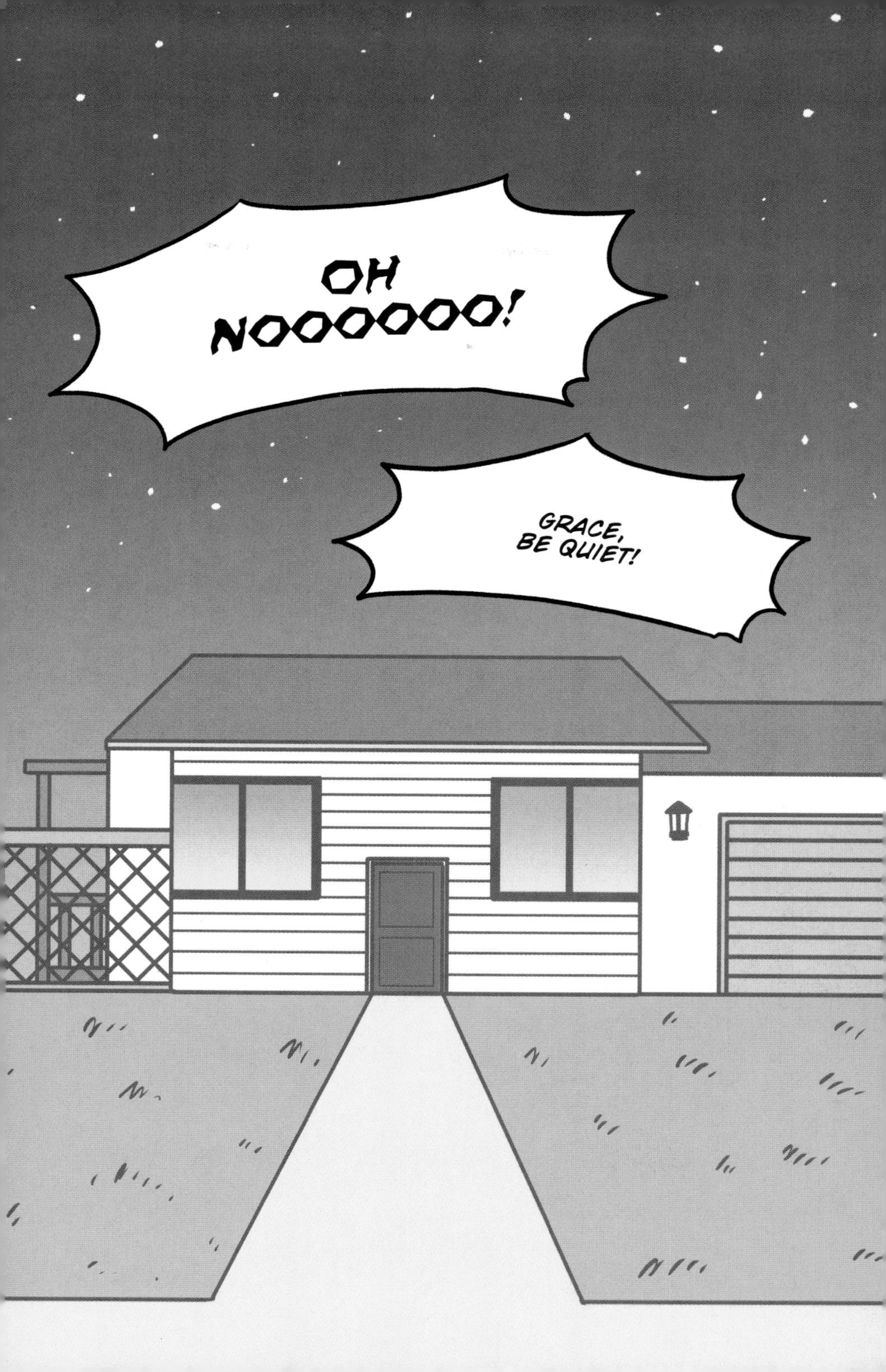
OH NOOOOOOO!
GRACE, BE QUIET!

CHAPTER 5

ESE

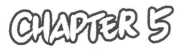

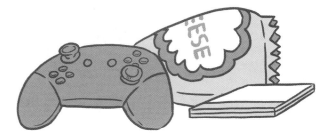

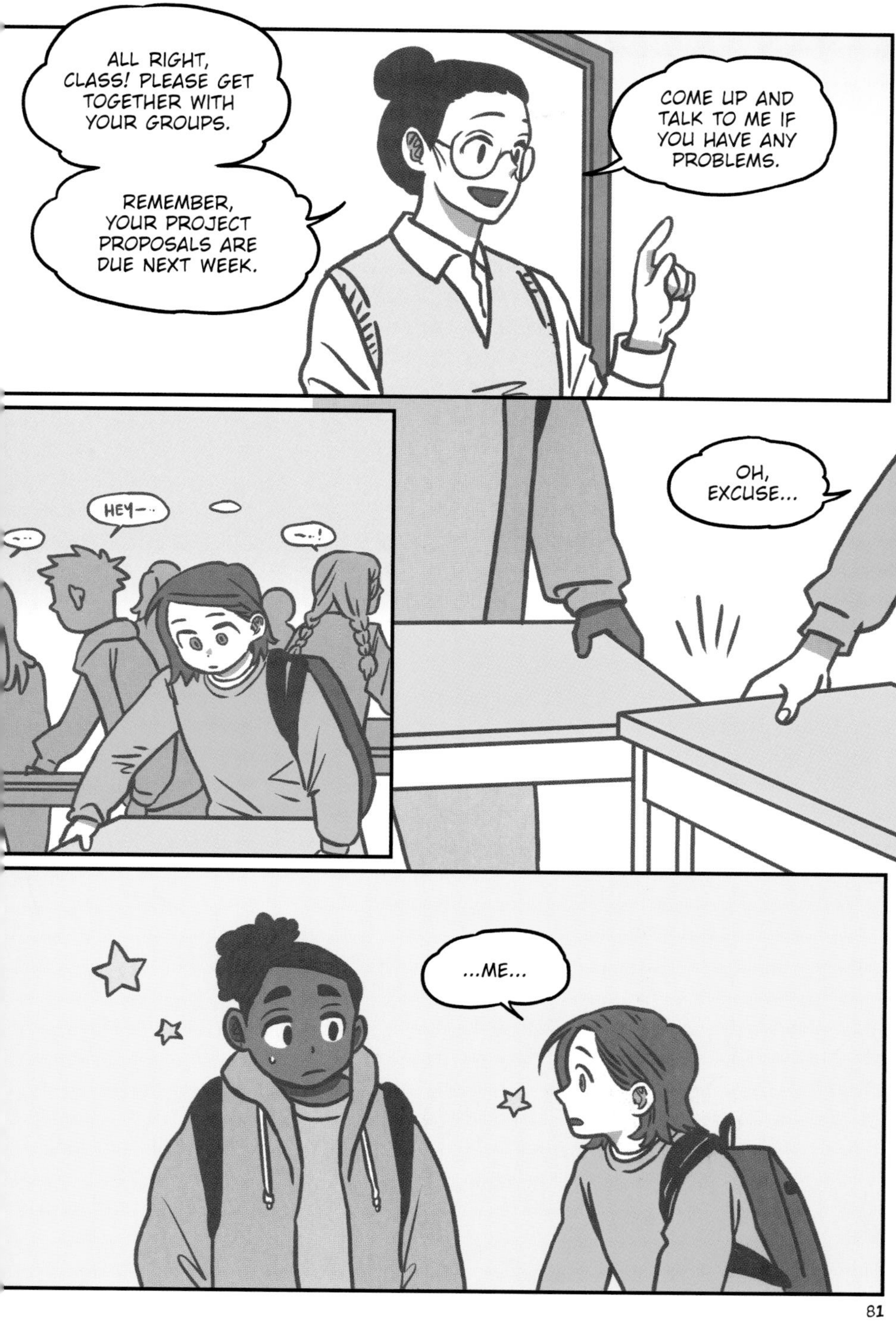
ALL RIGHT, CLASS! PLEASE GET TOGETHER WITH YOUR GROUPS.
REMEMBER, YOUR PROJECT PROPOSALS ARE DUE NEXT WEEK.
COME UP AND TALK TO ME IF YOU HAVE ANY PROBLEMS.
HEY—..
OH, EXCUSE...
...ME...

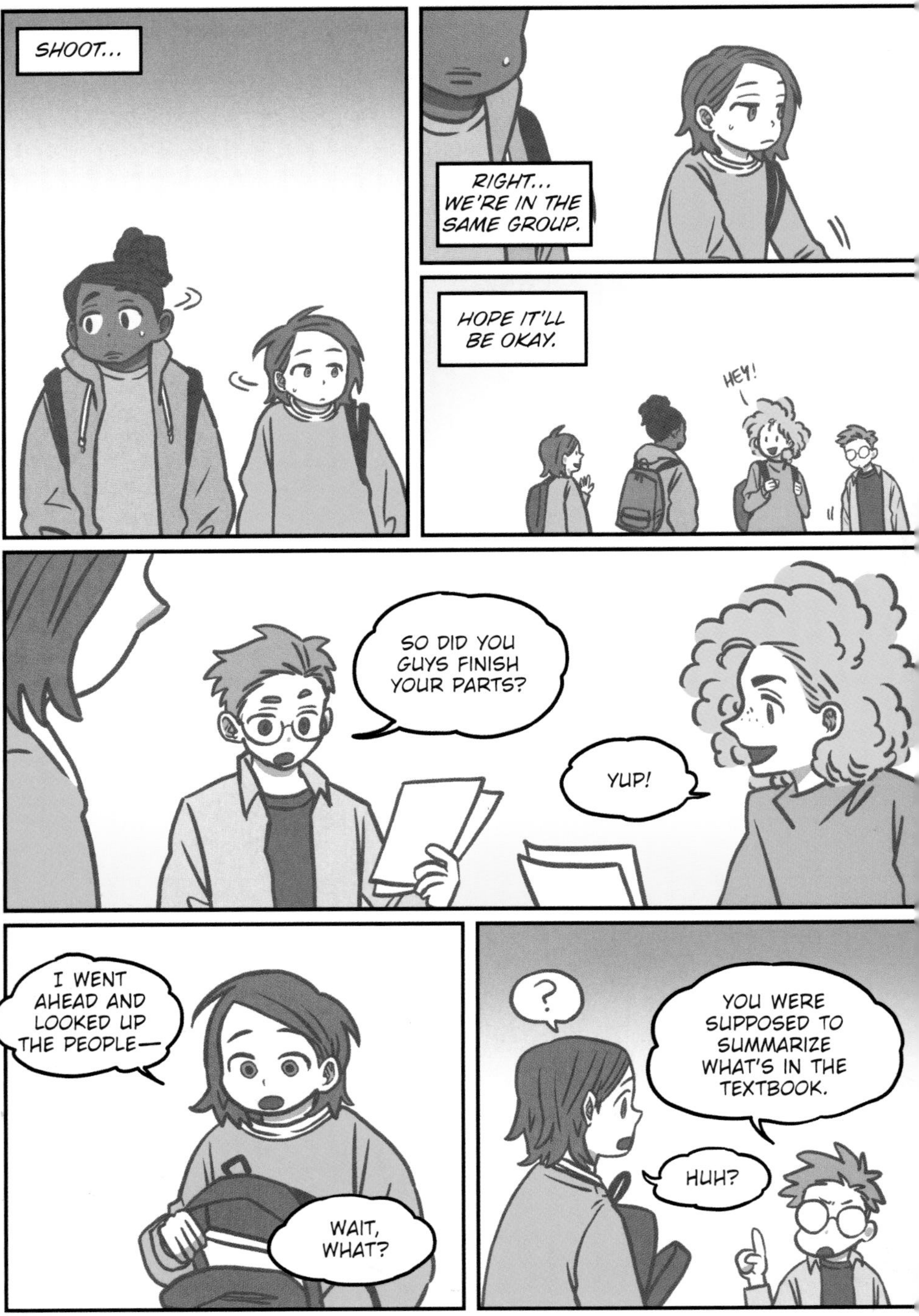
SHOOT...
RIGHT... WE'RE IN THE SAME GROUP.
HOPE IT'LL BE OKAY.
HEY!
SO DID YOU GUYS FINISH YOUR PARTS?
YUP!
I WENT AHEAD AND LOOKED UP THE PEOPLE—
WAIT, WHAT?
?
YOU WERE SUPPOSED TO SUMMARIZE WHAT'S IN THE TEXTBOOK.
HUH?

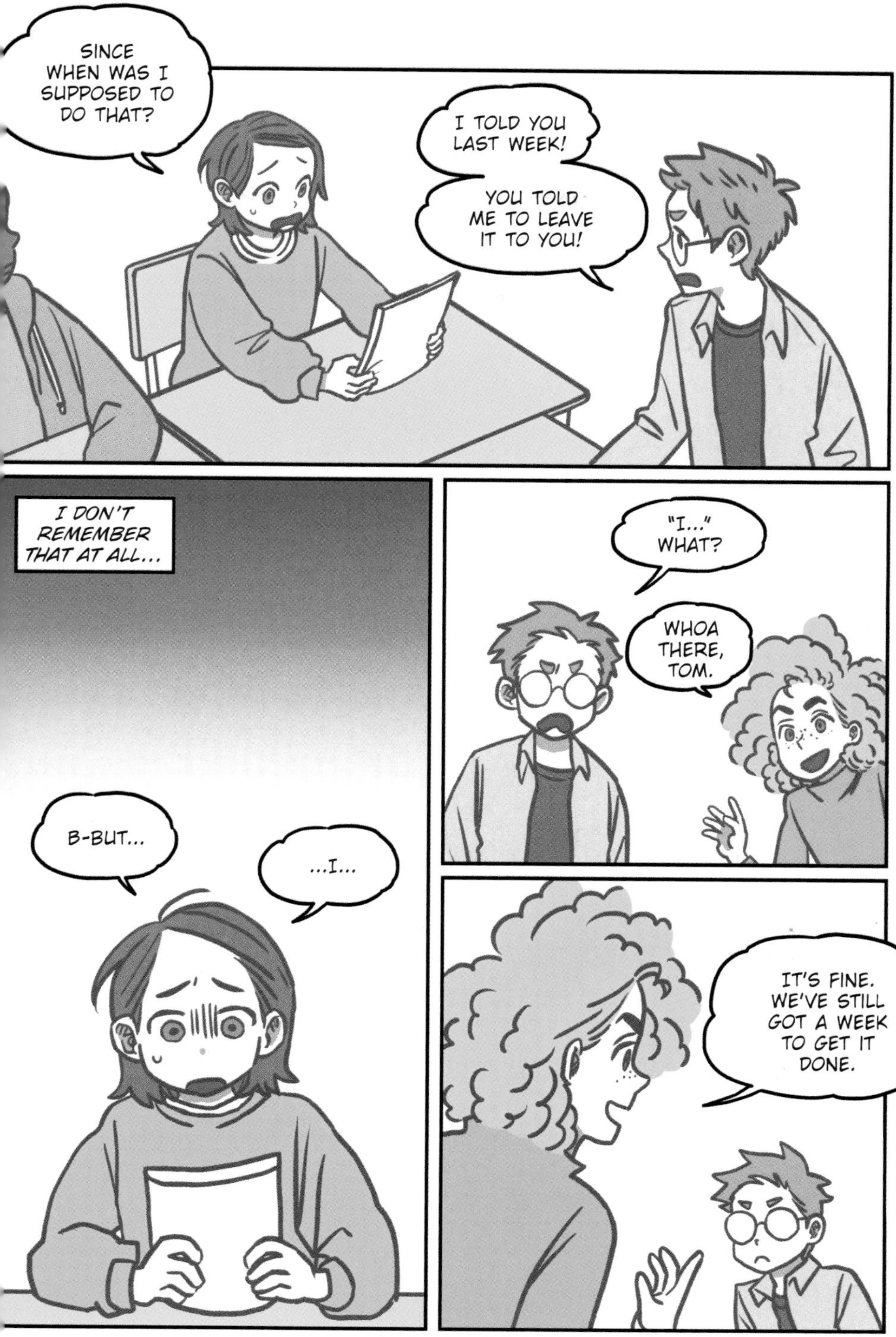
SINCE WHEN WAS I SUPPOSED TO DO THAT?
I TOLD YOU LAST WEEK!
YOU TOLD ME TO LEAVE IT TO YOU!
I DON'T REMEMBER THAT AT ALL...
B-BUT...
...I...
"I..." WHAT?
WHOA THERE, TOM.
IT'S FINE. WE'VE STILL GOT A WEEK TO GET IT DONE.

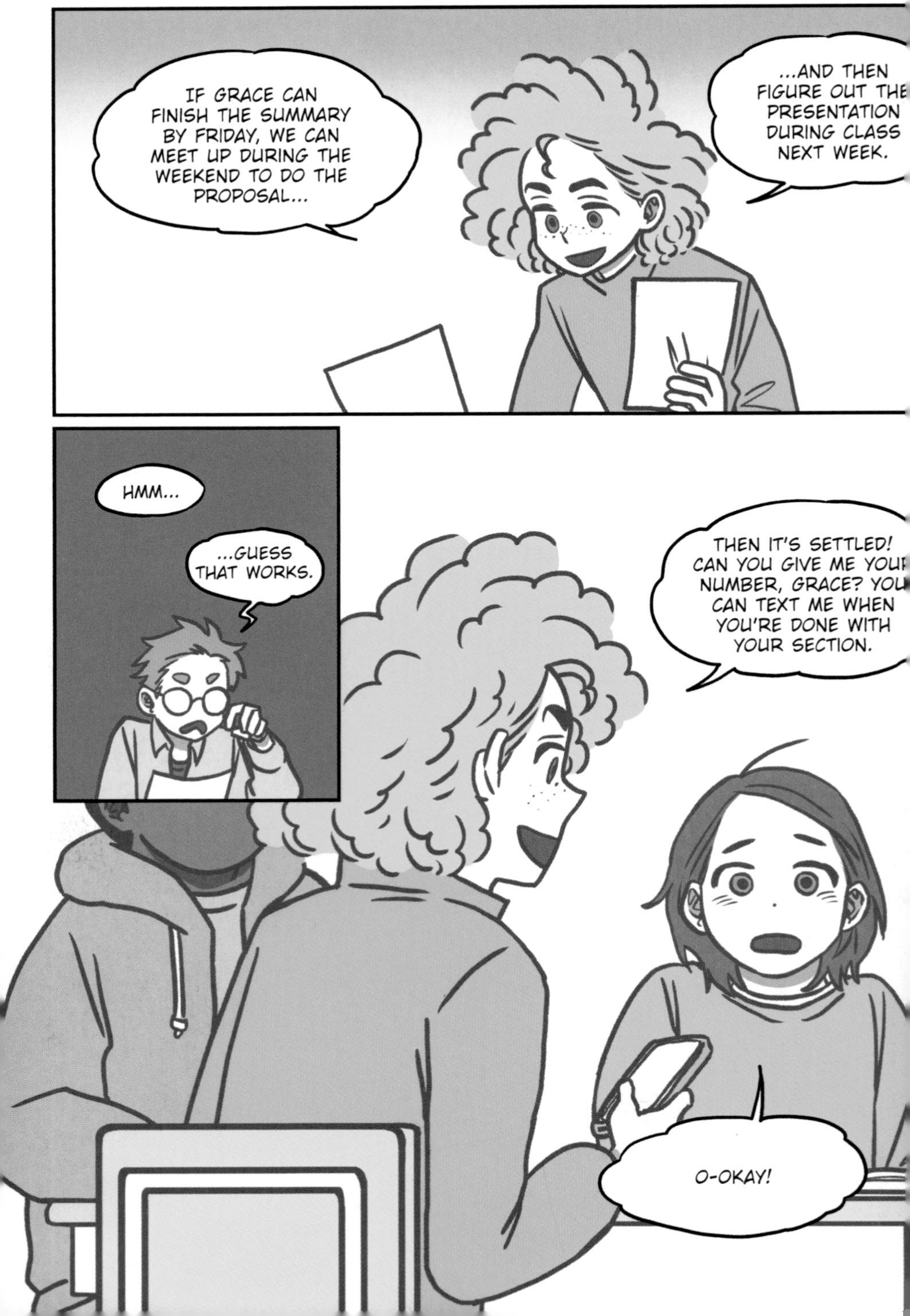
IF GRACE CAN FINISH THE SUMMARY BY FRIDAY, WE CAN MEET UP DURING THE WEEKEND TO DO THE PROPOSAL...
...AND THEN FIGURE OUT THE PRESENTATION DURING CLASS NEXT WEEK.
HMM...
...GUESS THAT WORKS.
THEN IT'S SETTLED! CAN YOU GIVE ME YOUR NUMBER, GRACE? YOU CAN TEXT ME WHEN YOU'RE DONE WITH YOUR SECTION.
O-OKAY!

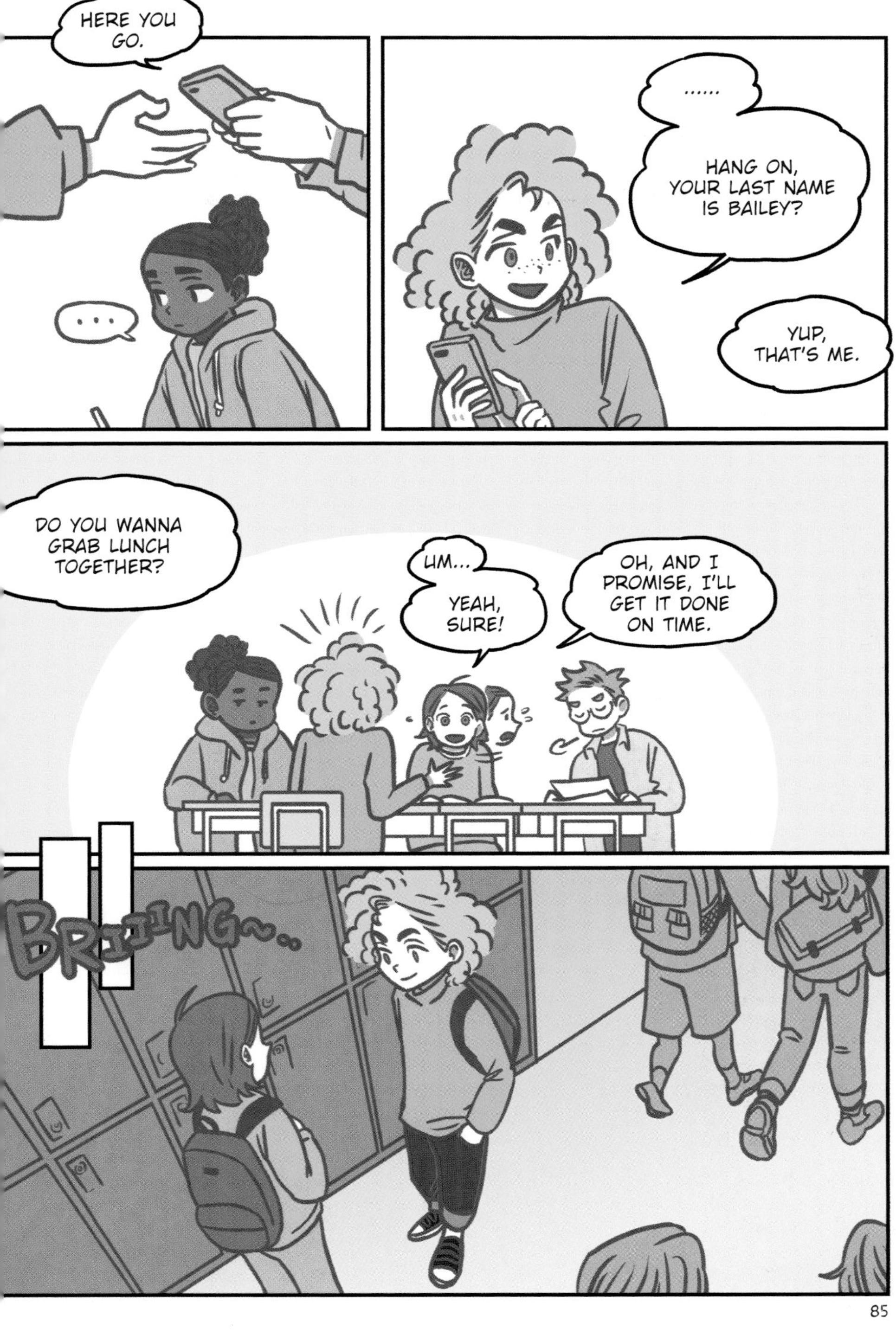
HERE YOU GO.
...
......
HANG ON, YOUR LAST NAME IS BAILEY?
YUP, THAT'S ME.
DO YOU WANNA GRAB LUNCH TOGETHER?
UM...
YEAH, SURE!
OH, AND I PROMISE, I'LL GET IT DONE ON TIME.
BRIIIING~..

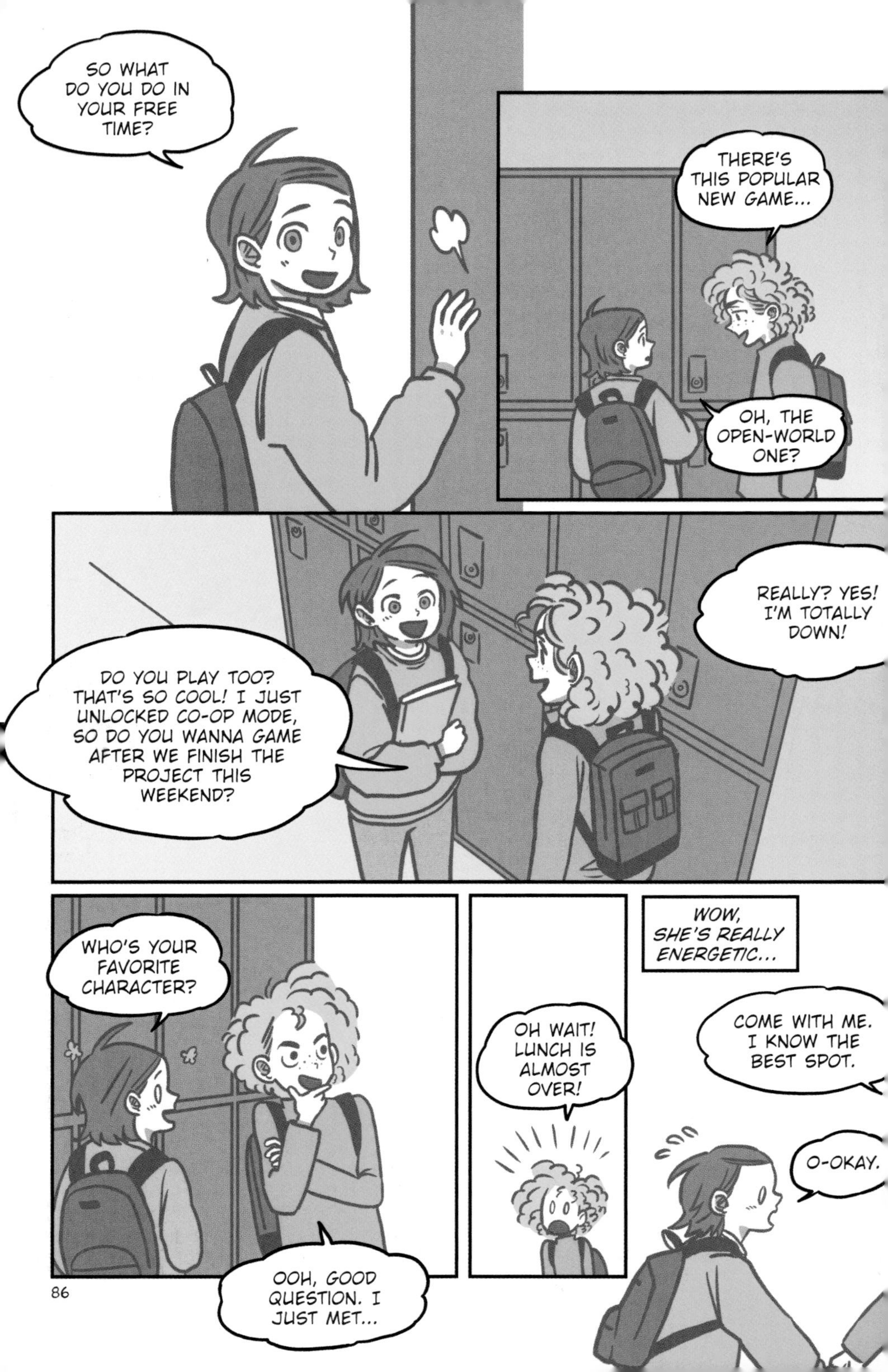
SO WHAT DO YOU DO IN YOUR FREE TIME?
THERE'S THIS POPULAR NEW GAME...
OH, THE OPEN-WORLD ONE?
REALLY? YES! I'M TOTALLY DOWN!
DO YOU PLAY TOO? THAT'S SO COOL! I JUST UNLOCKED CO-OP MODE, SO DO YOU WANNA GAME AFTER WE FINISH THE PROJECT THIS WEEKEND?
WHO'S YOUR FAVORITE CHARACTER?
OOH, GOOD QUESTION. I JUST MET...
OH WAIT! LUNCH IS ALMOST OVER!
WOW, SHE'S REALLY ENERGETIC...
COME WITH ME. I KNOW THE BEST SPOT.
O-OKAY.

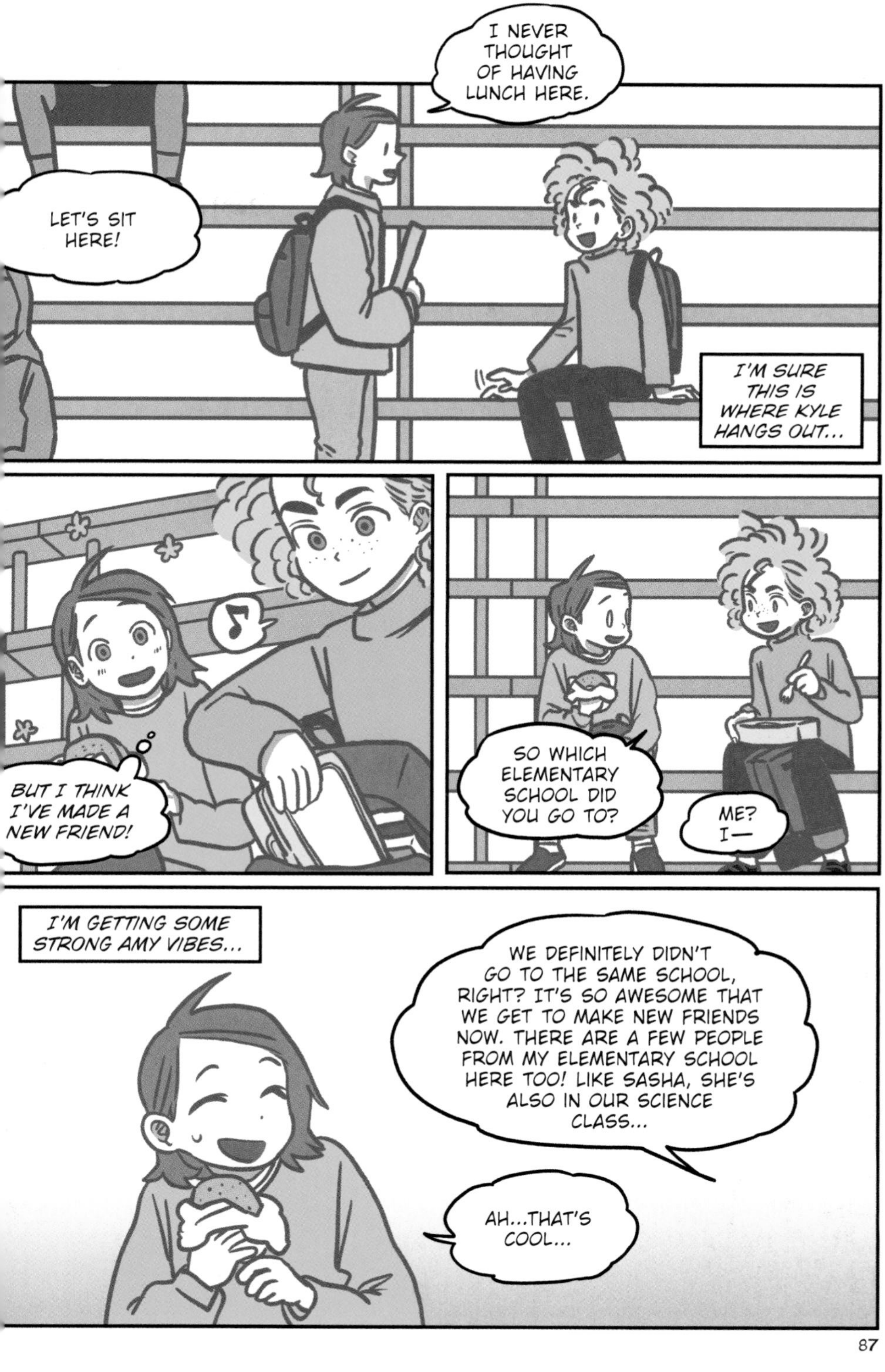

I NEVER THOUGHT OF HAVING LUNCH HERE.
LET'S SIT HERE!
I'M SURE THIS IS WHERE KYLE HANGS OUT...
BUT I THINK I'VE MADE A NEW FRIEND!
SO WHICH ELEMENTARY SCHOOL DID YOU GO TO?
ME? I—
I'M GETTING SOME STRONG AMY VIBES...
WE DEFINITELY DIDN'T GO TO THE SAME SCHOOL, RIGHT? IT'S SO AWESOME THAT WE GET TO MAKE NEW FRIENDS NOW. THERE ARE A FEW PEOPLE FROM MY ELEMENTARY SCHOOL HERE TOO! LIKE SASHA, SHE'S ALSO IN OUR SCIENCE CLASS...
AH...THAT'S COOL...

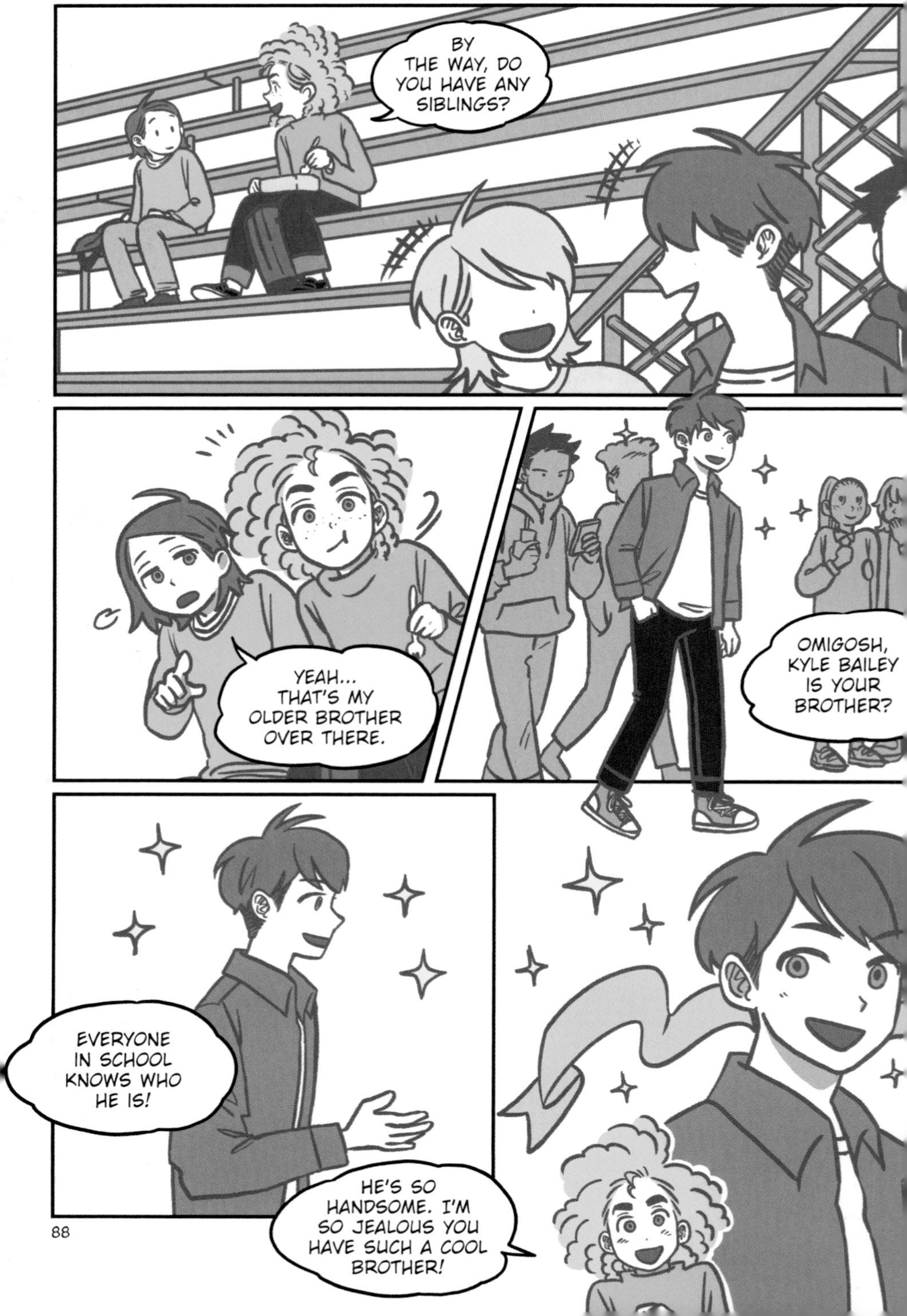
BY THE WAY, DO YOU HAVE ANY SIBLINGS?
YEAH... THAT'S MY OLDER BROTHER OVER THERE.
OMIGOSH, KYLE BAILEY IS YOUR BROTHER?
EVERYONE IN SCHOOL KNOWS WHO HE IS!
HE'S SO HANDSOME. I'M SO JEALOUS YOU HAVE SUCH A COOL BROTHER!

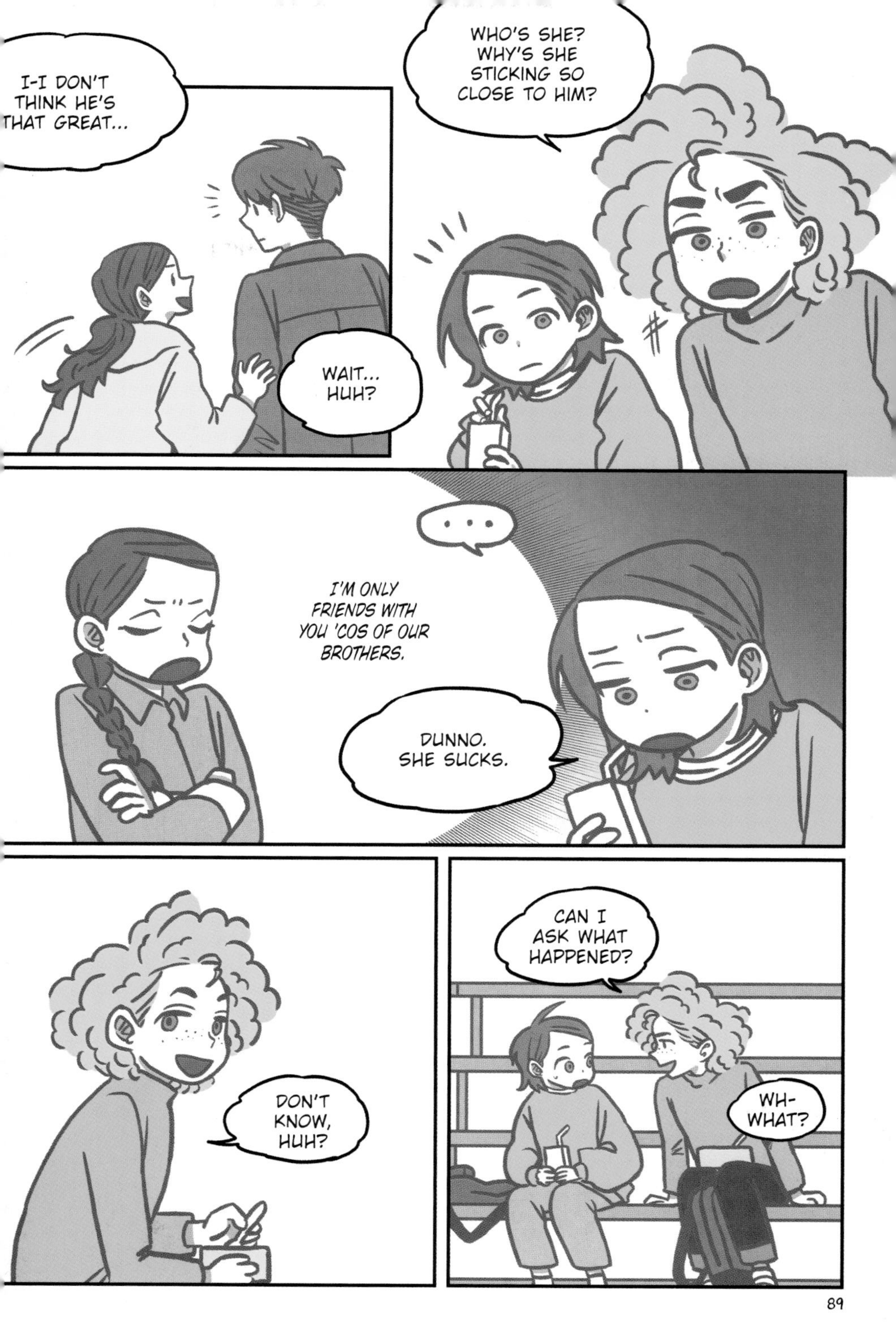
I-I DON'T THINK HE'S THAT GREAT...
WHO'S SHE? WHY'S SHE STICKING SO CLOSE TO HIM?
WAIT... HUH?
...
I'M ONLY FRIENDS WITH YOU 'COS OF OUR BROTHERS.
DUNNO. SHE SUCKS.
DON'T KNOW, HUH?
CAN I ASK WHAT HAPPENED?
WH- WHAT?

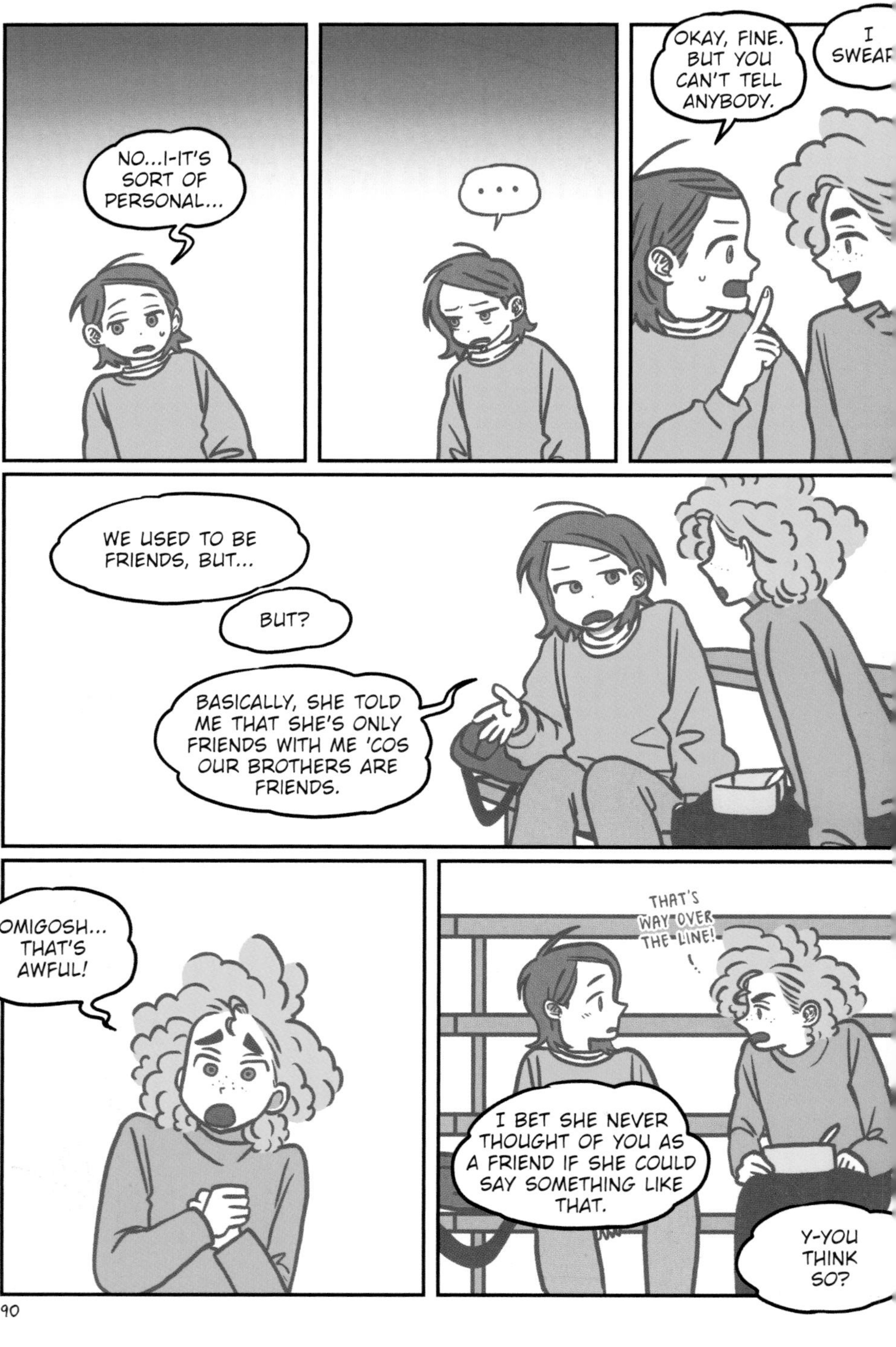
NO...I-IT'S SORT OF PERSONAL...
...
OKAY, FINE. BUT YOU CAN'T TELL ANYBODY.
I SWEAR
WE USED TO BE FRIENDS, BUT...
BUT?
BASICALLY, SHE TOLD ME THAT SHE'S ONLY FRIENDS WITH ME 'COS OUR BROTHERS ARE FRIENDS.
OMIGOSH... THAT'S AWFUL!
THAT'S WAY OVER THE LINE!
I BET SHE NEVER THOUGHT OF YOU AS A FRIEND IF SHE COULD SAY SOMETHING LIKE THAT.
Y-YOU THINK SO?

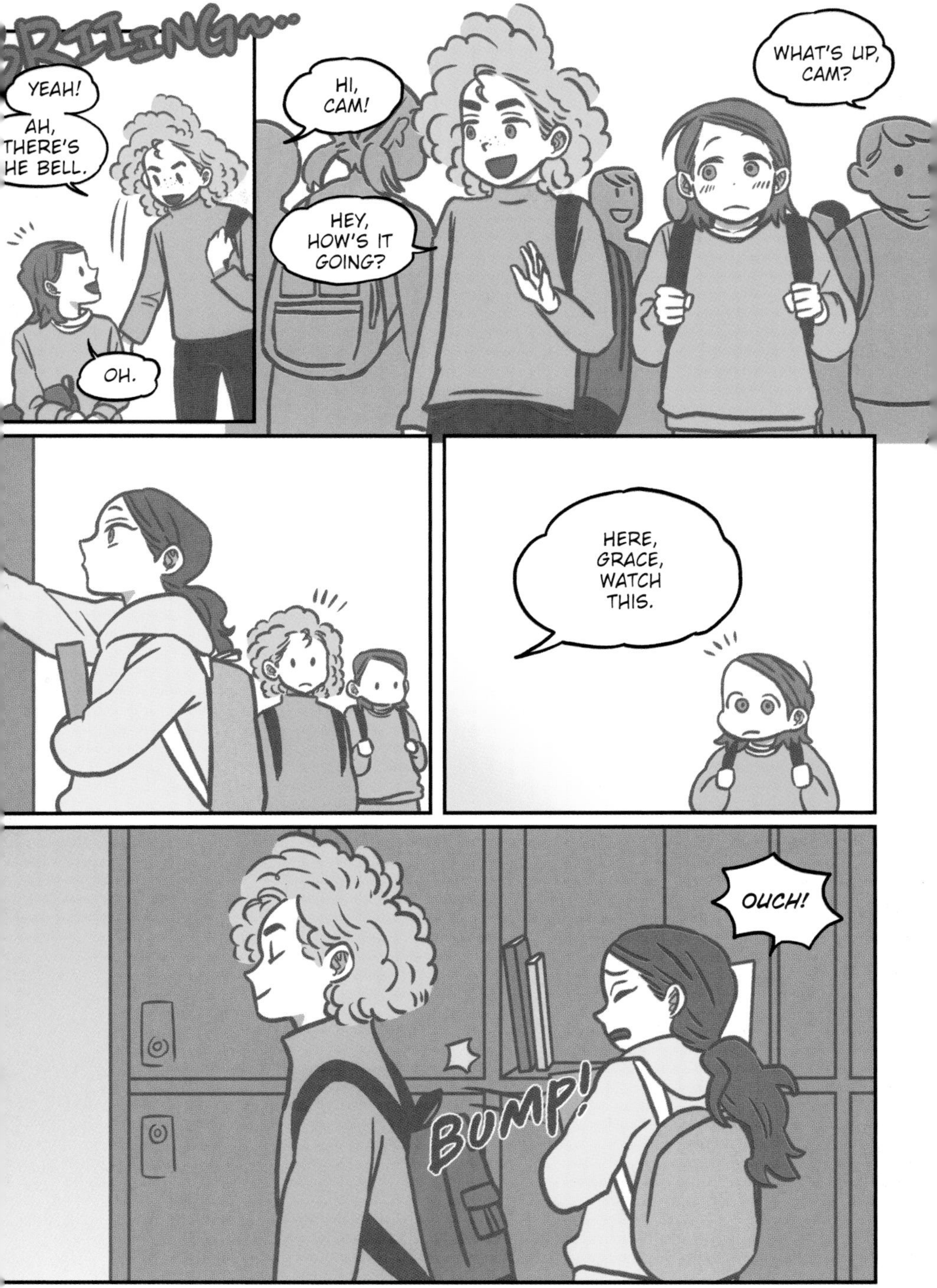
SRIIING~~
YEAH!
AH, THERE'S HE BELL.
OH.
HI, CAM!
HEY, HOW'S IT GOING?
WHAT'S UP, CAM?
HERE, GRACE, WATCH THIS.
BUMP!
OUCH!

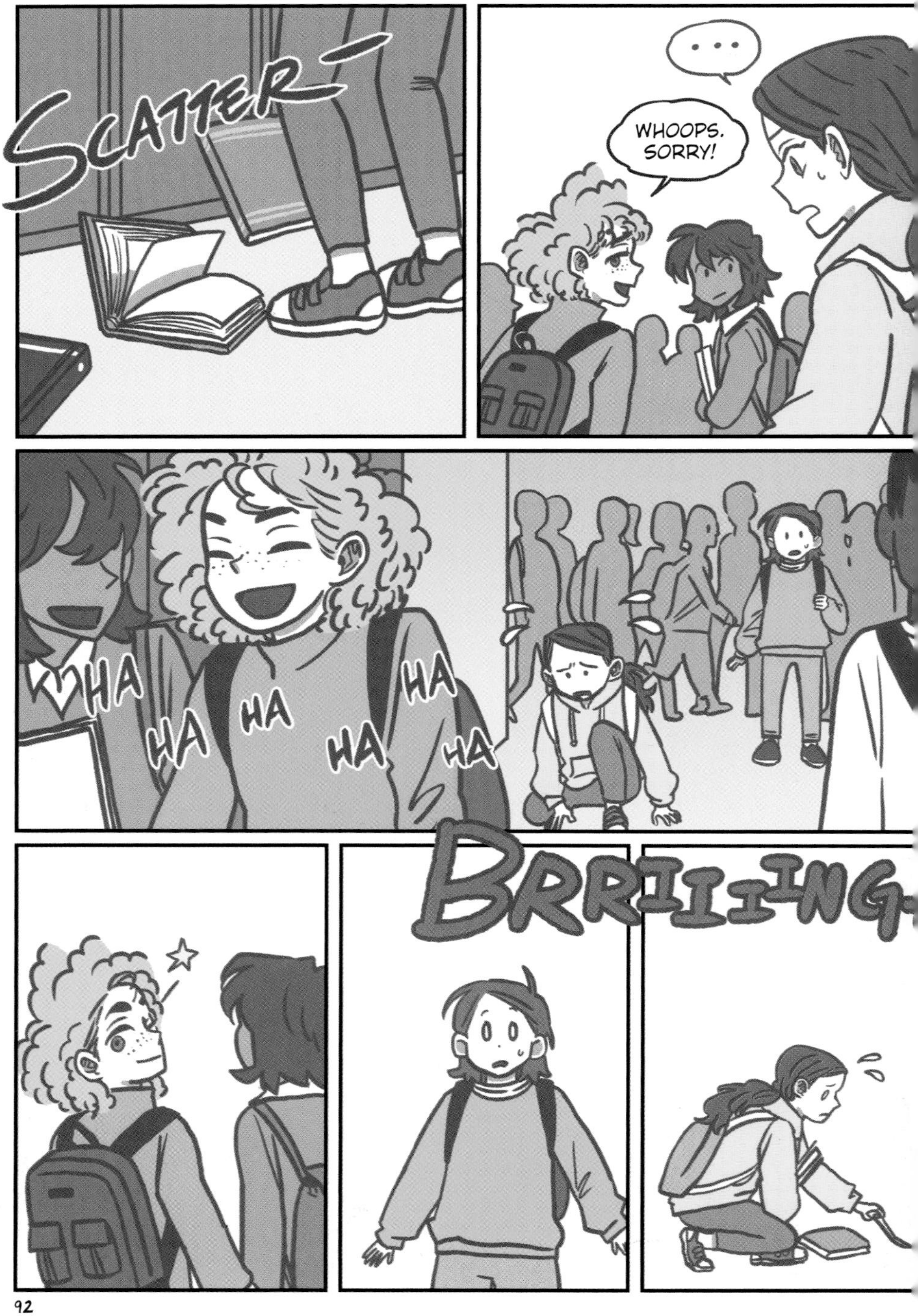
SCATTER–
...
WHOOPS. SORRY!
HA HA HA HA HA HA
BRRIIING–

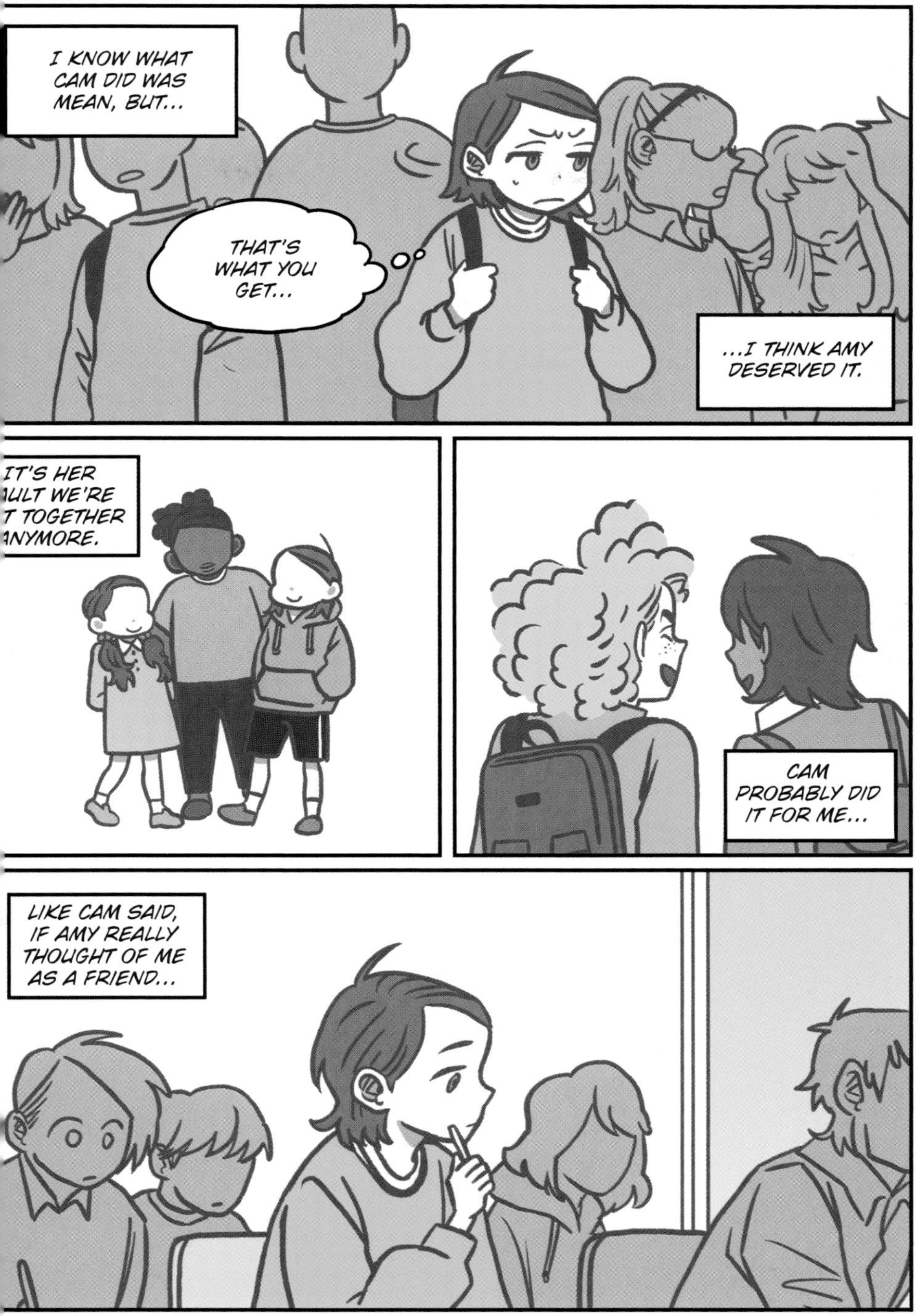
I KNOW WHAT CAM DID WAS MEAN, BUT...
THAT'S WHAT YOU GET...
...I THINK AMY DESERVED IT.
IT'S HER ULT WE'RE T TOGETHER ANYMORE.
CAM PROBABLY DID IT FOR ME...
LIKE CAM SAID, IF AMY REALLY THOUGHT OF ME AS A FRIEND...

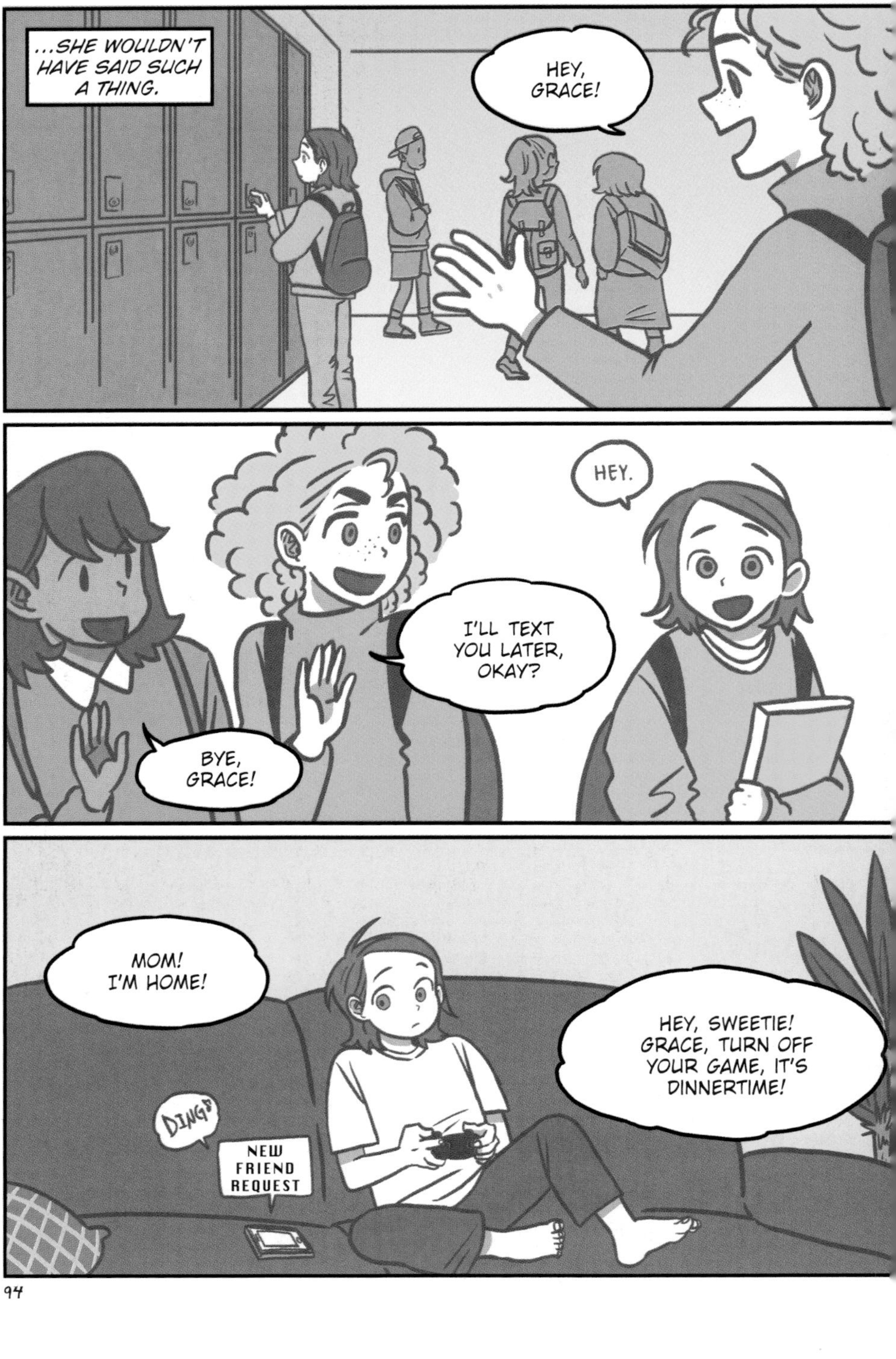
...SHE WOULDN'T HAVE SAID SUCH A THING.
HEY, GRACE!
HEY.
I'LL TEXT YOU LATER, OKAY?
BYE, GRACE!
MOM! I'M HOME!
HEY, SWEETIE! GRACE, TURN OFF YOUR GAME, IT'S DINNERTIME!
DING!
NEW FRIEND REQUEST

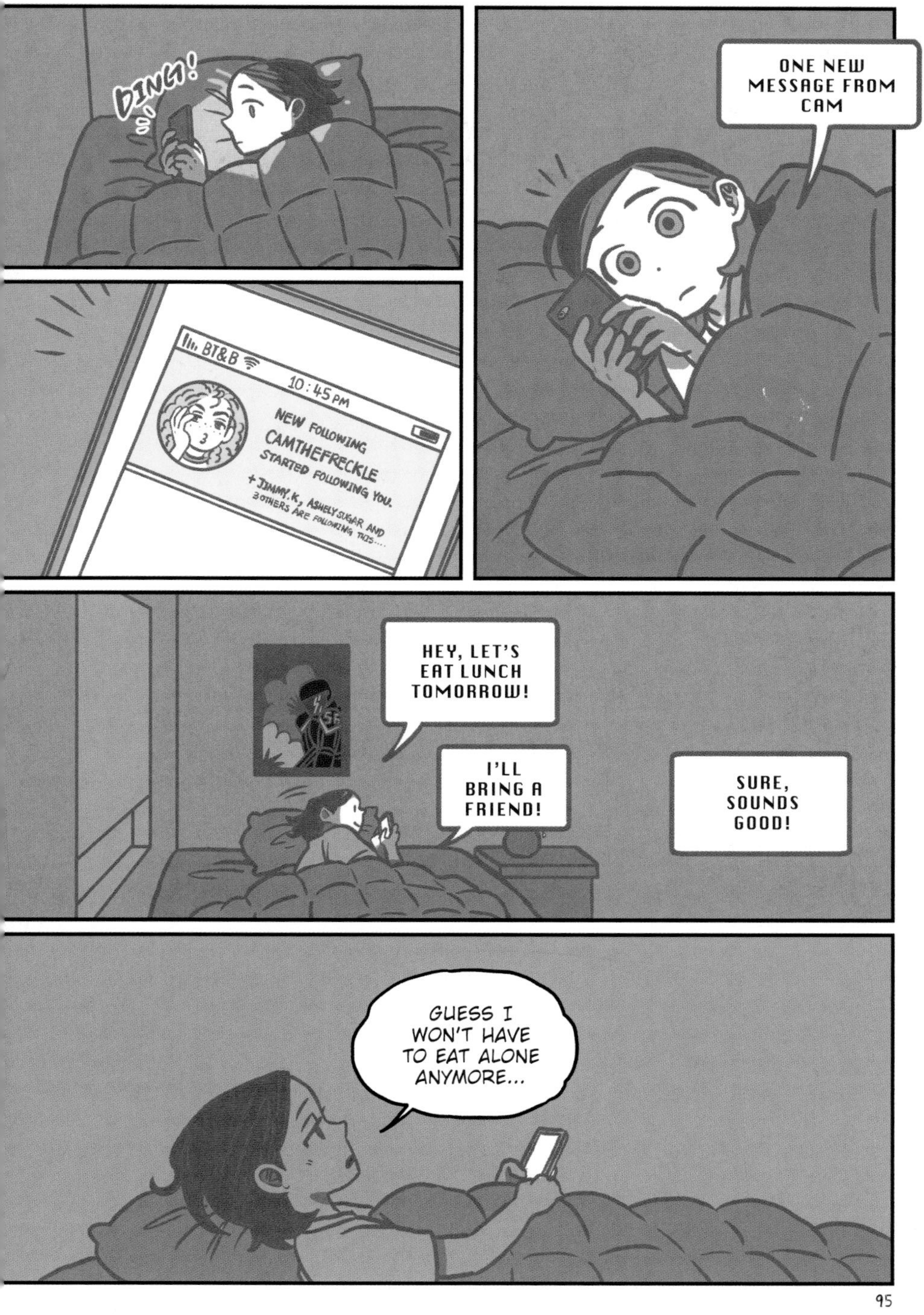
DING!
ONE NEW MESSAGE FROM CAM
BT&B
10:45 PM
NEW FOLLOWING
CAMTHEFRECKLE
STARTED FOLLOWING YOU.
+ JIMMY.K, ASHELY.SUGAR AND 3OTHERS ARE FOLLOWING THIS...
HEY, LET'S EAT LUNCH TOMORROW!
I'LL BRING A FRIEND!
SURE, SOUNDS GOOD!
GUESS I WON'T HAVE TO EAT ALONE ANYMORE...

CHAPTER 6

99

105

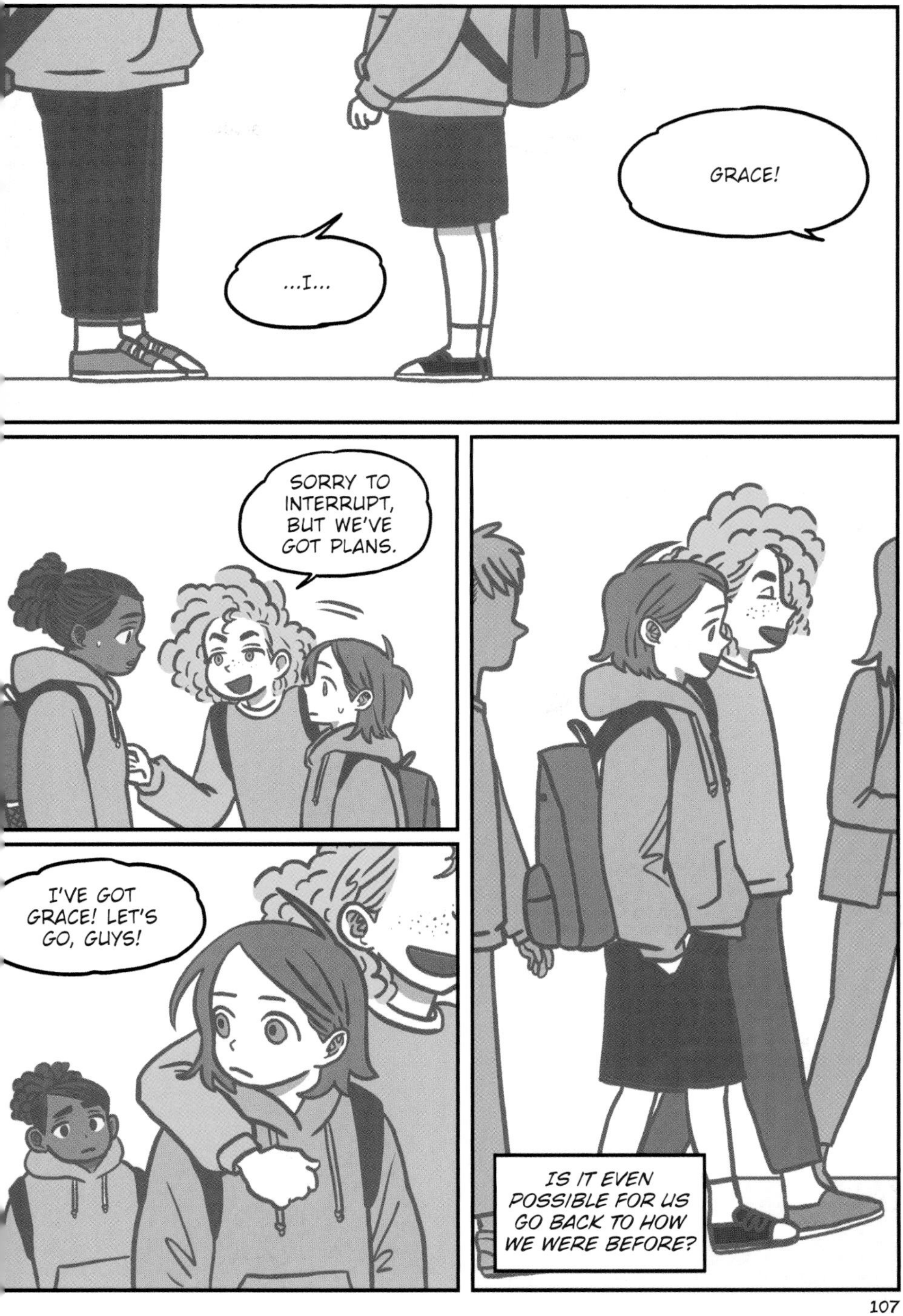
...I...
GRACE!
SORRY TO INTERRUPT, BUT WE'VE GOT PLANS.
I'VE GOT GRACE! LET'S GO, GUYS!
IS IT EVEN POSSIBLE FOR US GO BACK TO HOW WE WERE BEFORE?

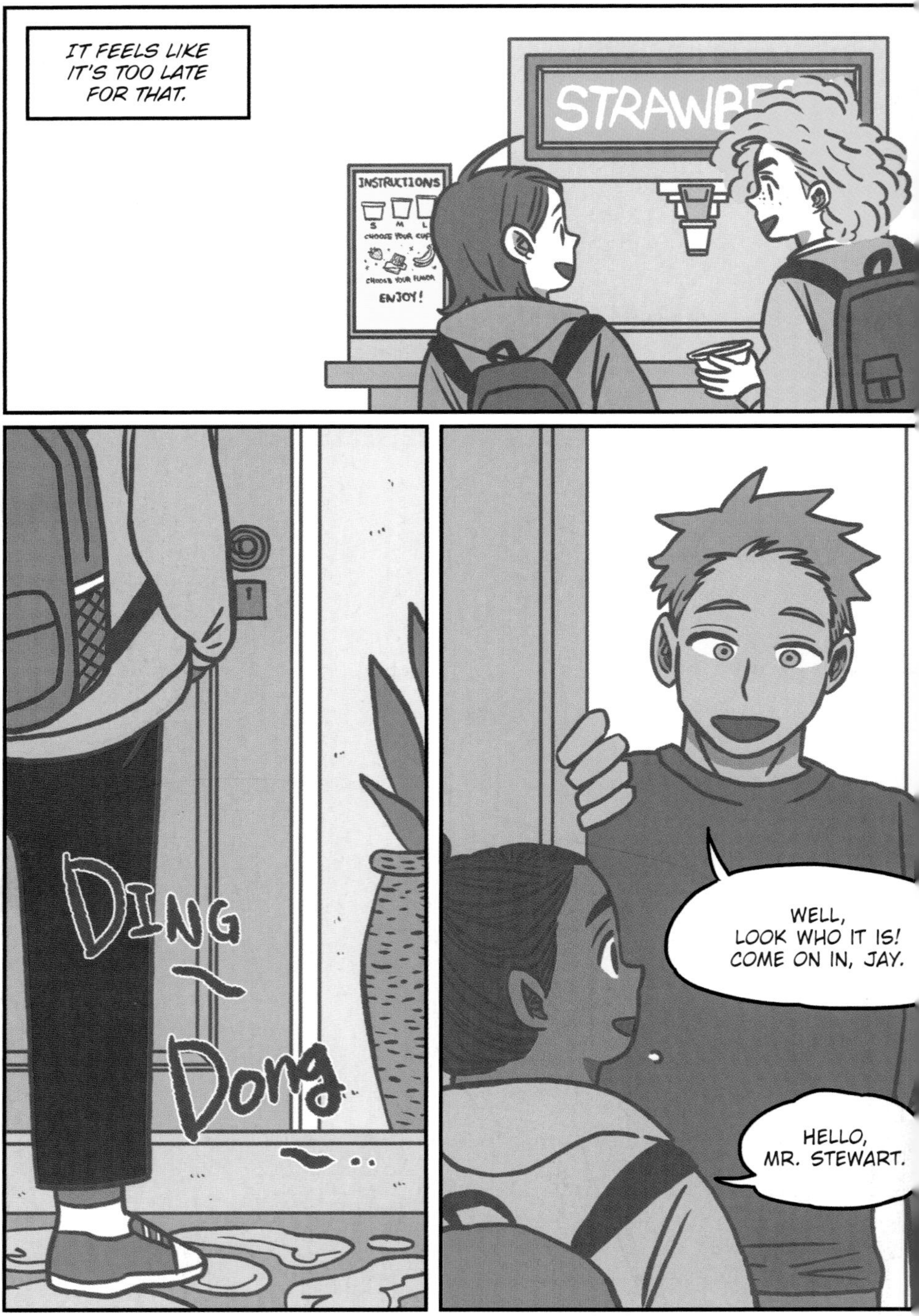
IT FEELS LIKE IT'S TOO LATE FOR THAT.
INSTRUCTIONS
S M L
CHOOSE YOUR CUP
CHOOSE YOUR FLAVOR
ENJOY!
STRAWB
DING ~ DONG ~ ..
WELL, LOOK WHO IT IS! COME ON IN, JAY.
HELLO, MR. STEWART.

CHAPTER 1

113

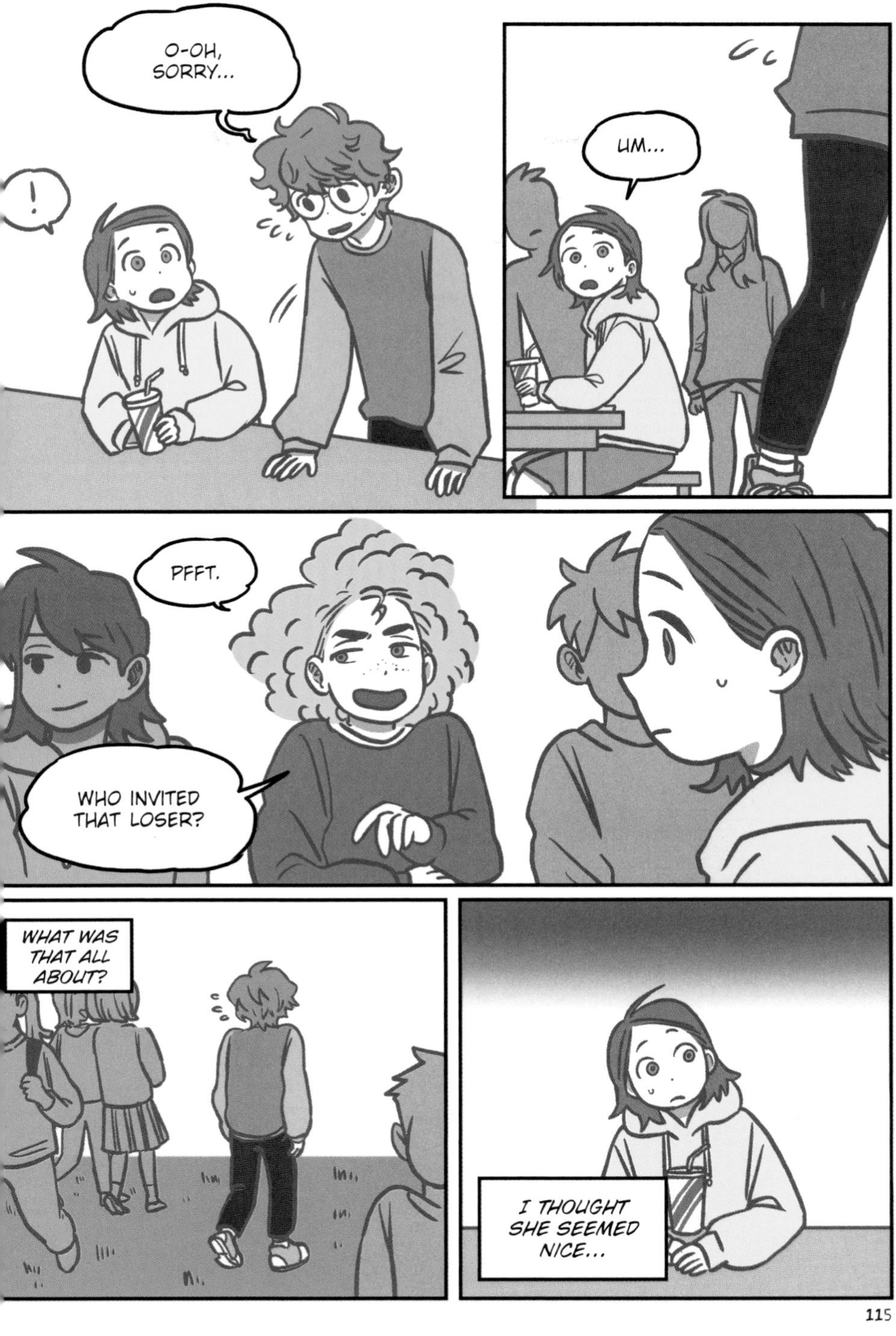
O-OH, SORRY...
!
UM...
PFFT.
WHO INVITED THAT LOSER?
WHAT WAS THAT ALL ABOUT?
I THOUGHT SHE SEEMED NICE...

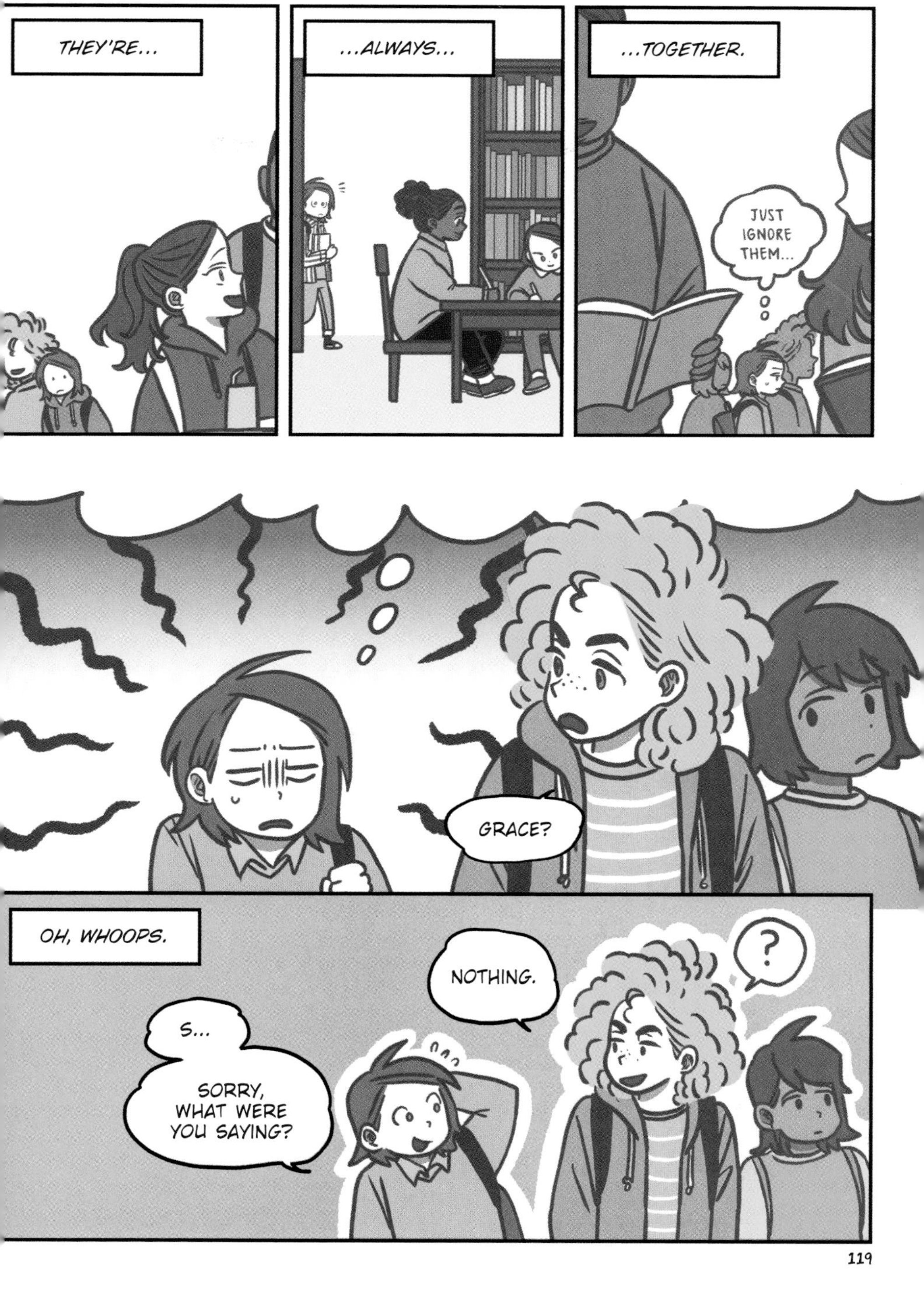

THEY'RE...
...ALWAYS...
...TOGETHER.
JUST IGNORE THEM...
GRACE?
OH, WHOOPS.
NOTHING.
?
S...
SORRY, WHAT WERE YOU SAYING?

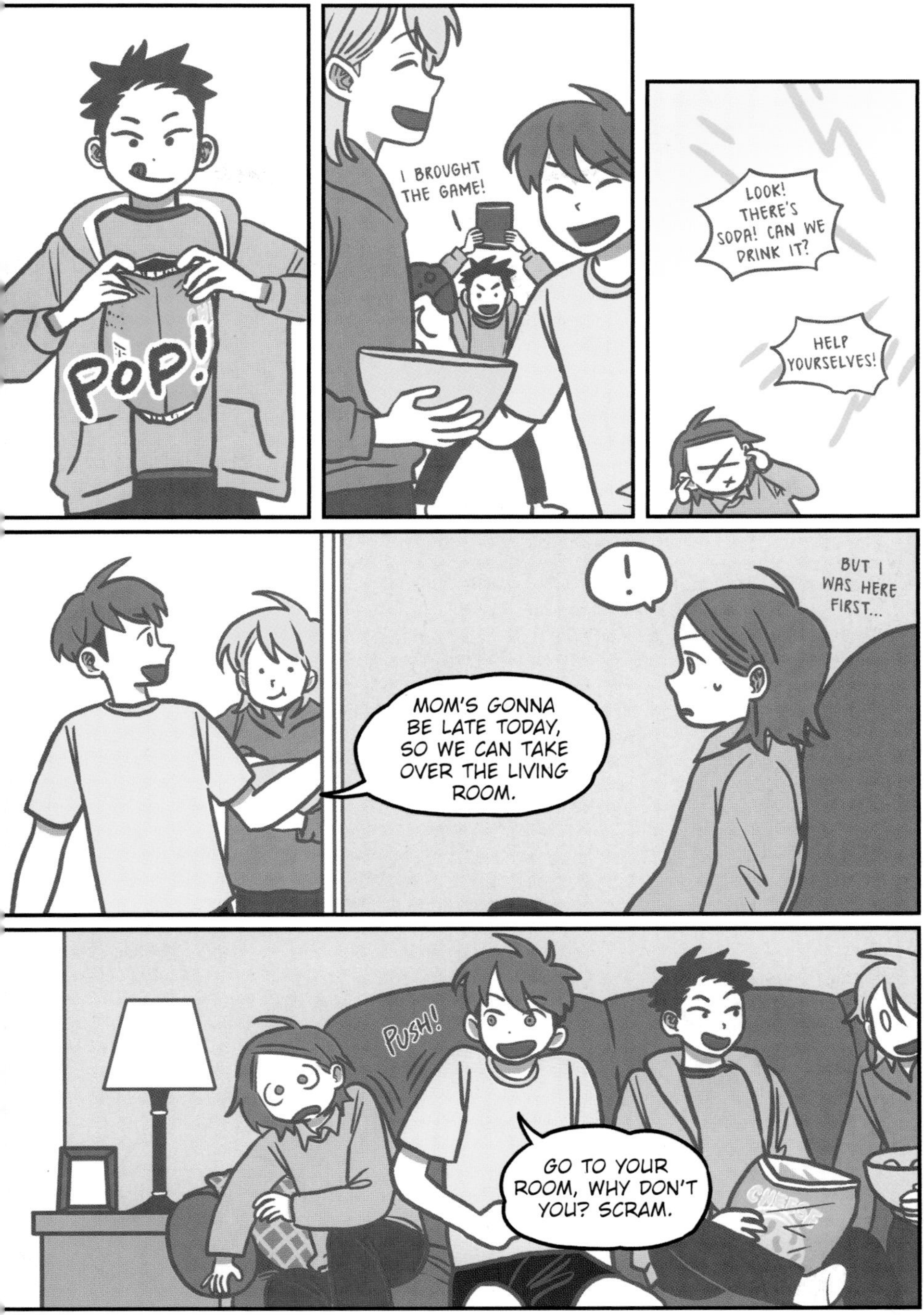
POP!
I BROUGHT THE GAME!
LOOK! THERE'S SODA! CAN WE DRINK IT?
HELP YOURSELVES!
!
BUT I WAS HERE FIRST...
MOM'S GONNA BE LATE TODAY, SO WE CAN TAKE OVER THE LIVING ROOM.
PUSH!
GO TO YOUR ROOM, WHY DON'T YOU? SCRAM.

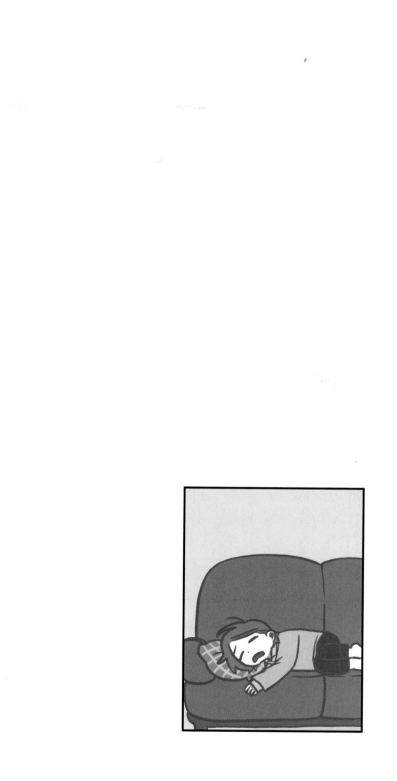

CHAPTER 8

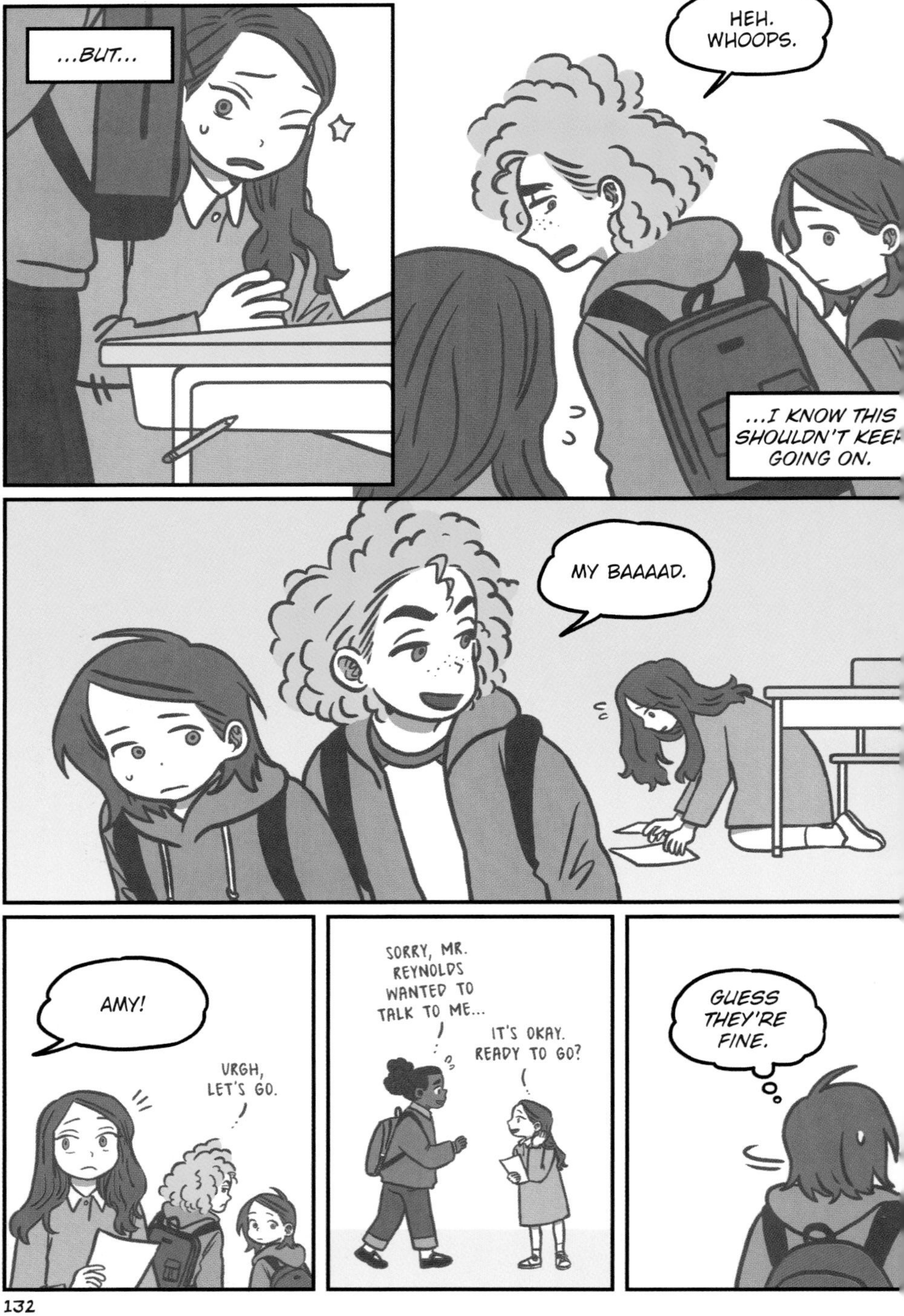
...BUT...
HEH. WHOOPS.
...I KNOW THIS SHOULDN'T KEEP GOING ON.
MY BAAAAD.
AMY!
URGH, LET'S GO.
SORRY, MR. REYNOLDS WANTED TO TALK TO ME...
IT'S OKAY. READY TO GO?
GUESS THEY'RE FINE.

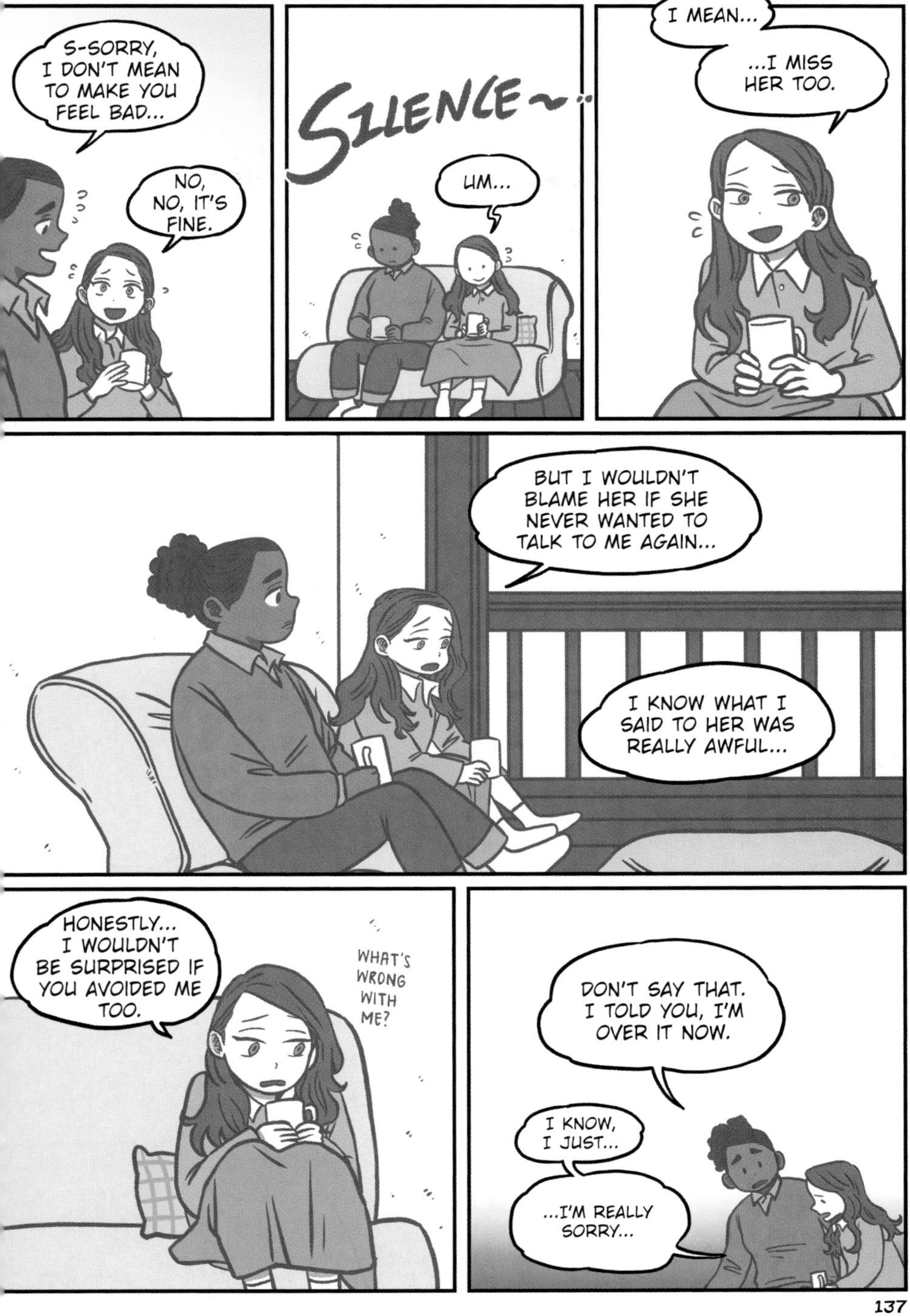
S-SORRY, I DON'T MEAN TO MAKE YOU FEEL BAD...
NO, NO, IT'S FINE.
SILENCE~
UM...
I MEAN...
...I MISS HER TOO.
BUT I WOULDN'T BLAME HER IF SHE NEVER WANTED TO TALK TO ME AGAIN...
I KNOW WHAT I SAID TO HER WAS REALLY AWFUL...
HONESTLY... I WOULDN'T BE SURPRISED IF YOU AVOIDED ME TOO.
WHAT'S WRONG WITH ME?
DON'T SAY THAT. I TOLD YOU, I'M OVER IT NOW.
I KNOW, I JUST...
...I'M REALLY SORRY...

CHAPTER 9

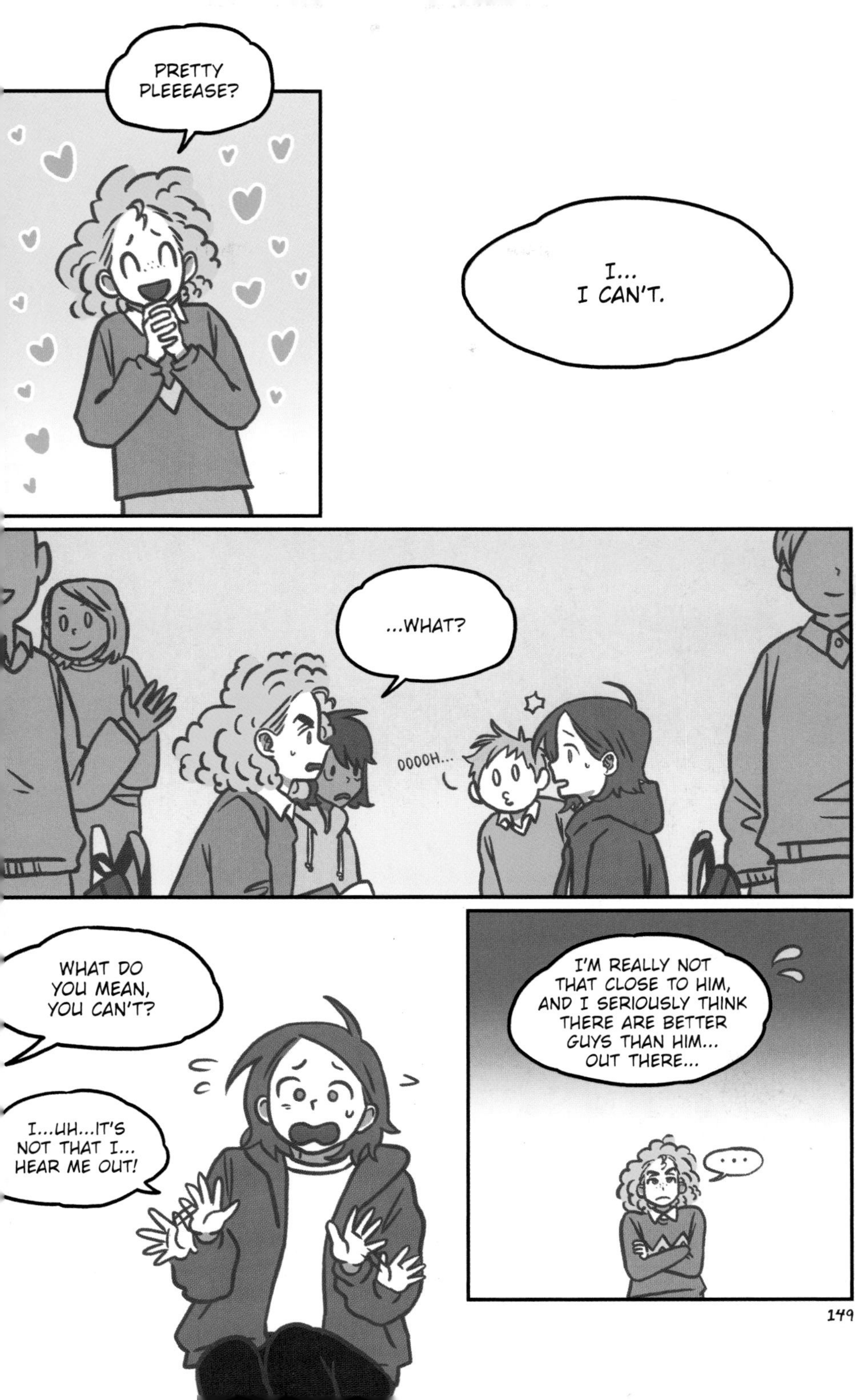
PRETTY PLEEEASE?
I... I CAN'T.
...WHAT?
OOOOH...
WHAT DO YOU MEAN, YOU CAN'T?
I...UH...IT'S NOT THAT I... HEAR ME OUT!
I'M REALLY NOT THAT CLOSE TO HIM, AND I SERIOUSLY THINK THERE ARE BETTER GUYS THAN HIM... OUT THERE...
...

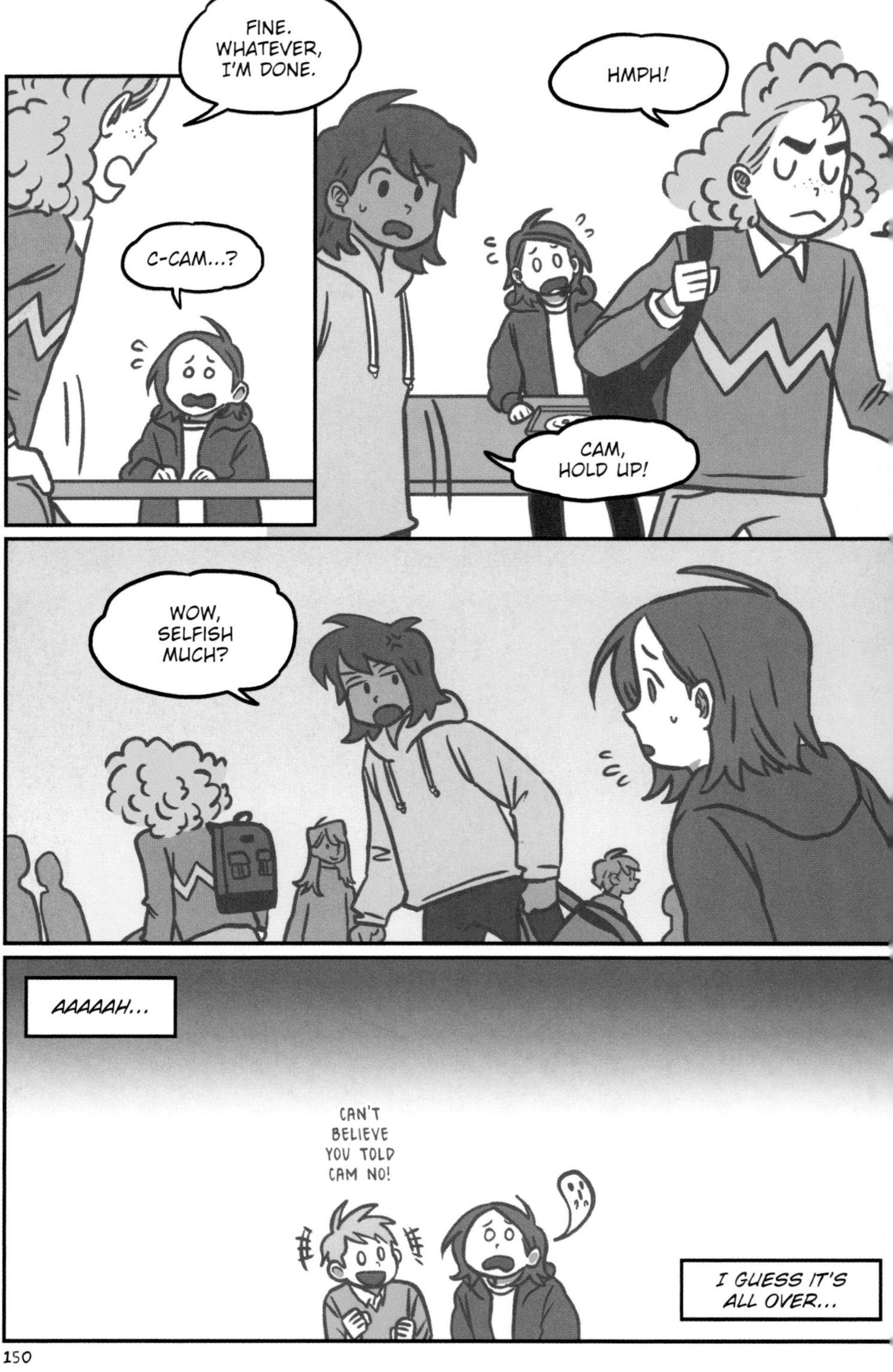

FINE. WHATEVER, I'M DONE.
C-CAM...?
HMPH!
CAM, HOLD UP!
WOW, SELFISH MUCH?
AAAAAH...
CAN'T BELIEVE YOU TOLD CAM NO!
I GUESS IT'S ALL OVER...

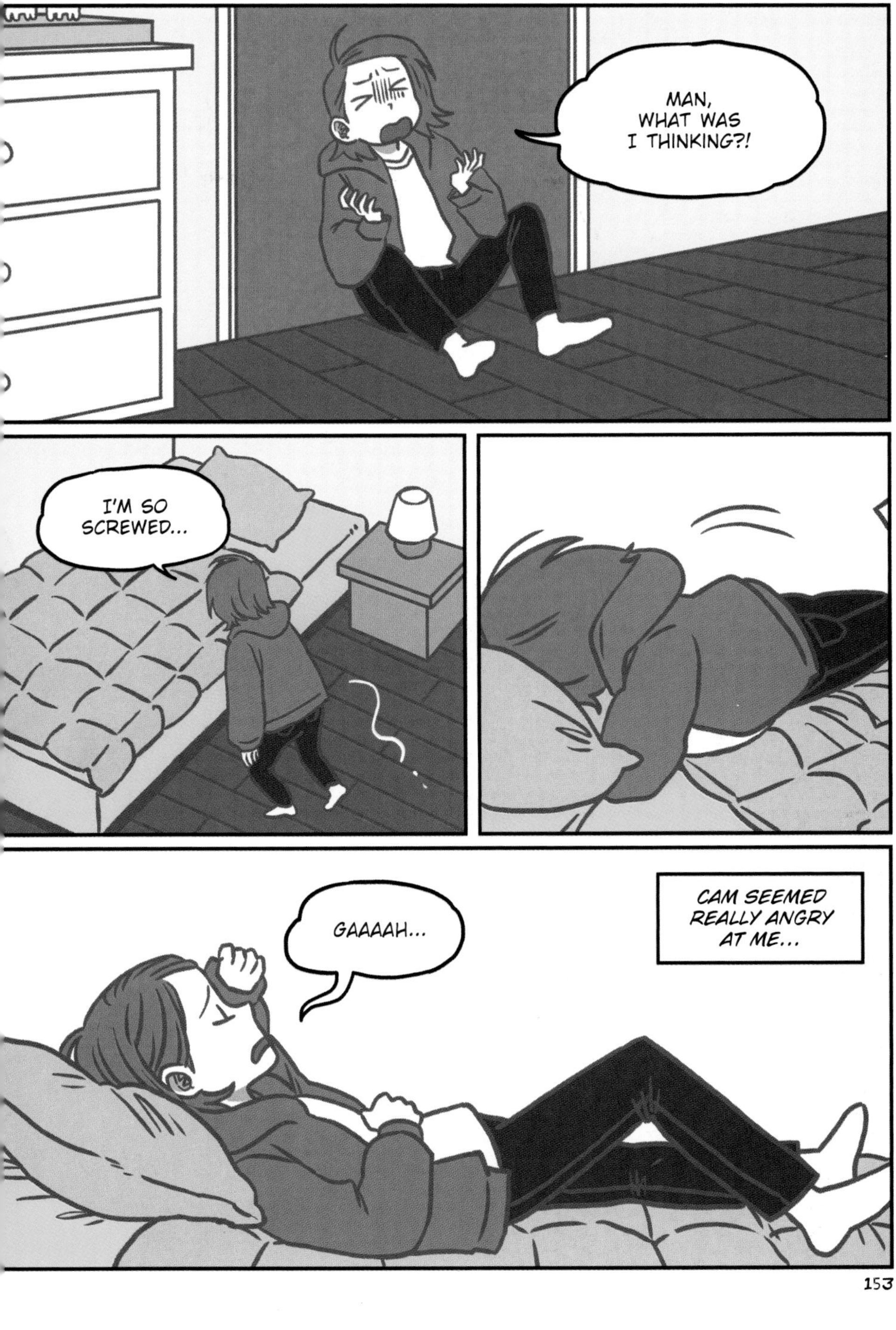
MAN, WHAT WAS I THINKING?!
I'M SO SCREWED...
GAAAAH...
CAM SEEMED REALLY ANGRY AT ME...

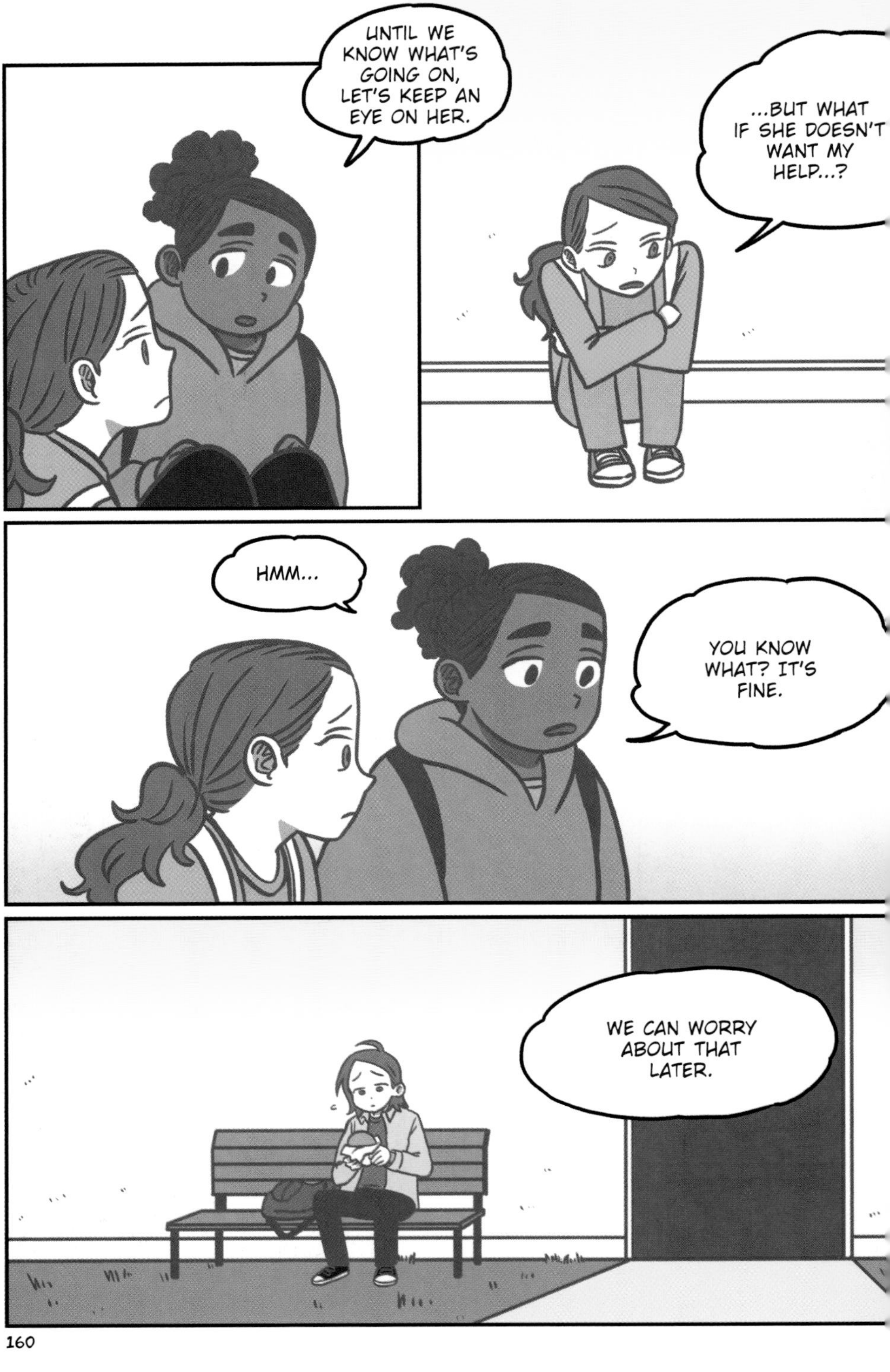
UNTIL WE KNOW WHAT'S GOING ON, LET'S KEEP AN EYE ON HER.
...BUT WHAT IF SHE DOESN'T WANT MY HELP...?
HMM...
YOU KNOW WHAT? IT'S FINE.
WE CAN WORRY ABOUT THAT LATER.

CHAPTER 10

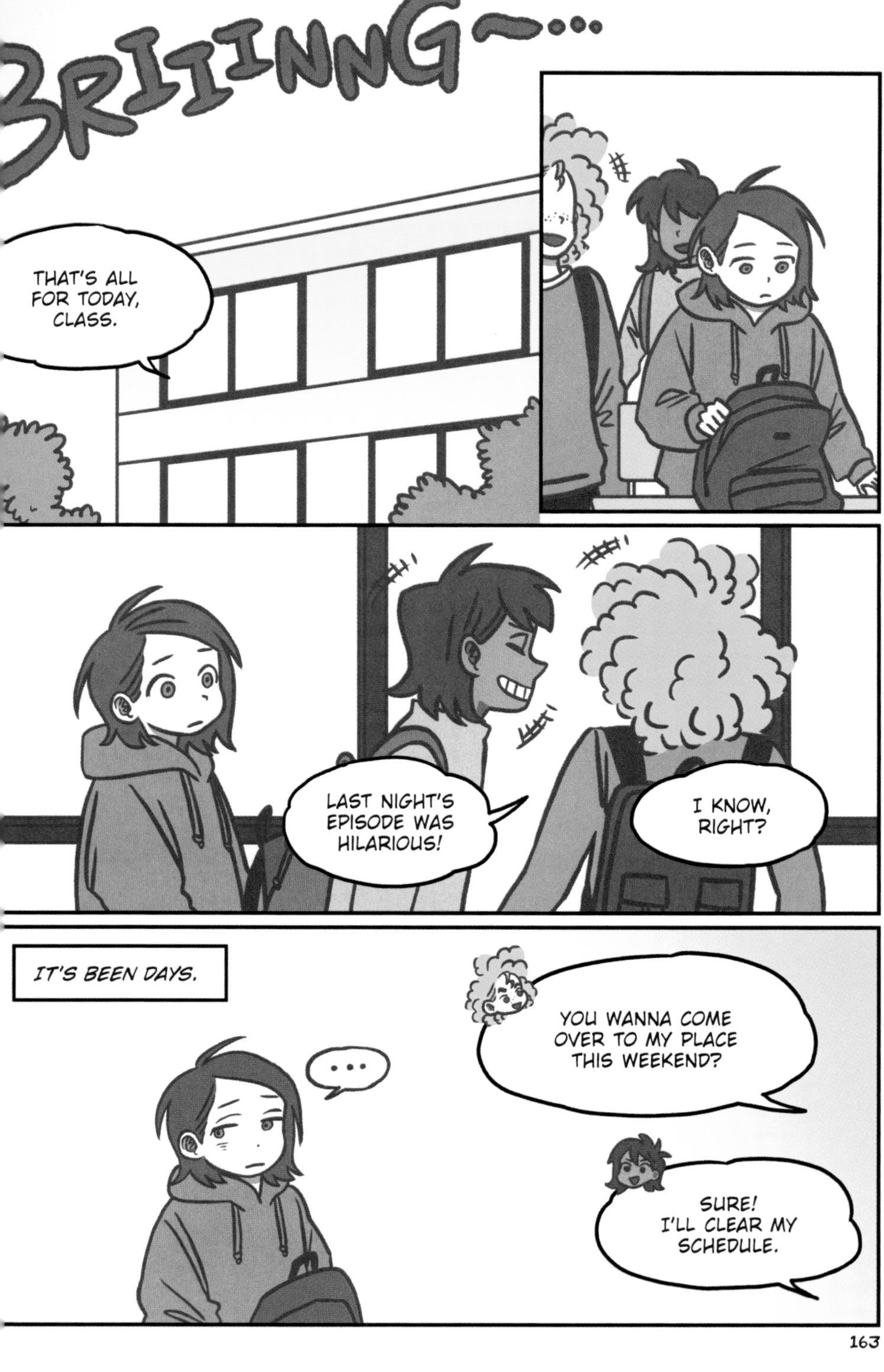
BRIIINNG~...
THAT'S ALL FOR TODAY, CLASS.
LAST NIGHT'S EPISODE WAS HILARIOUS!
I KNOW, RIGHT?
IT'S BEEN DAYS.
YOU WANNA COME OVER TO MY PLACE THIS WEEKEND?
...
SURE! I'LL CLEAR MY SCHEDULE.

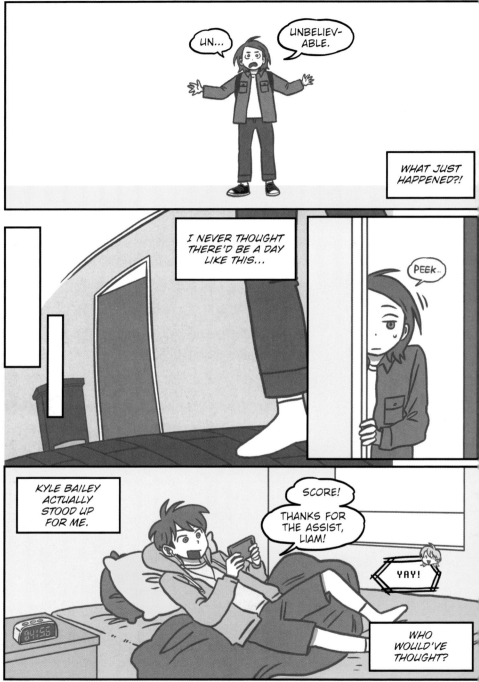

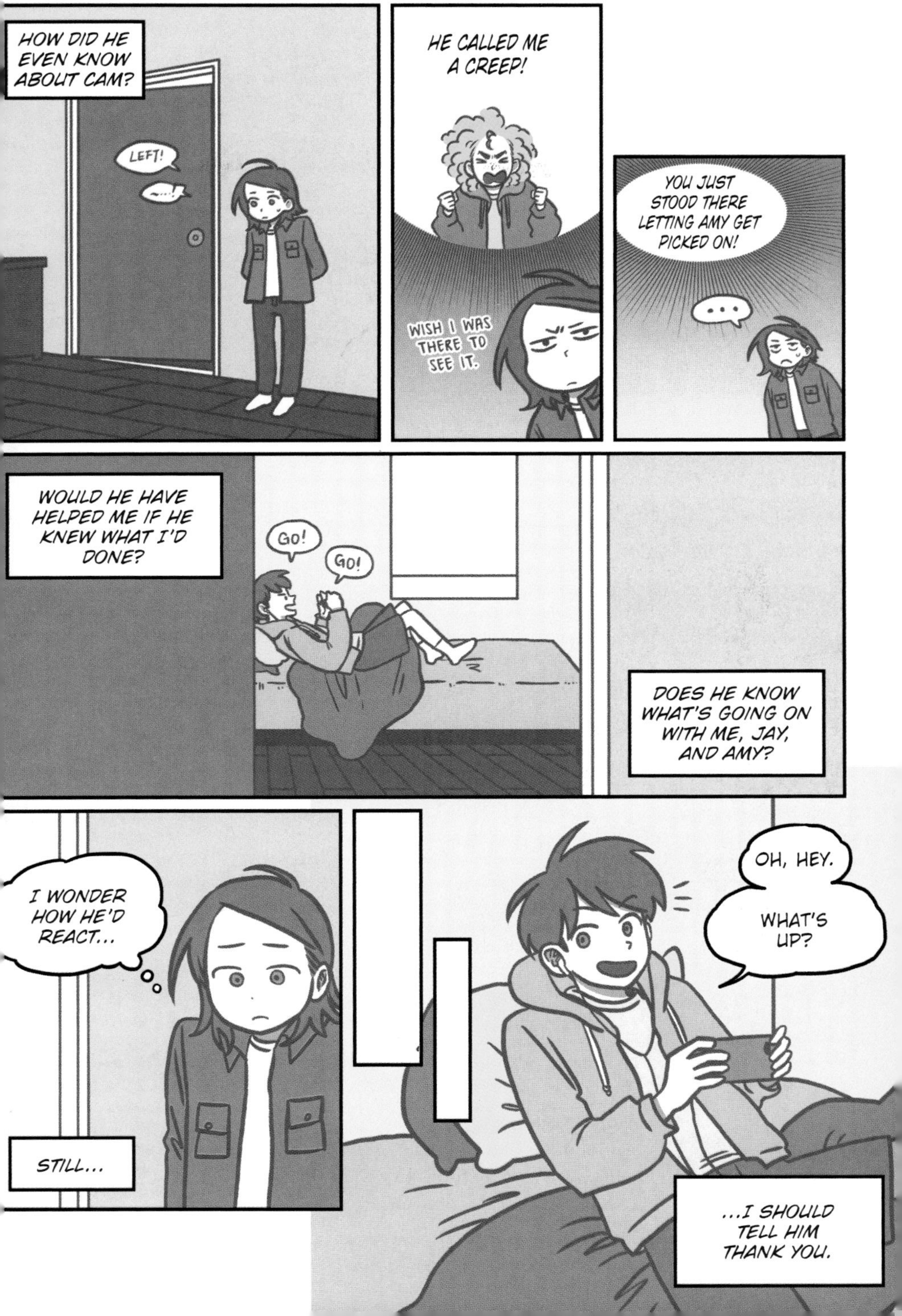
HOW DID HE EVEN KNOW ABOUT CAM?
LEFT!
HE CALLED ME A CREEP!
WISH I WAS THERE TO SEE IT.
YOU JUST STOOD THERE LETTING AMY GET PICKED ON!
...
WOULD HE HAVE HELPED ME IF HE KNEW WHAT I'D DONE?
GO!
GO!
DOES HE KNOW WHAT'S GOING ON WITH ME, JAY, AND AMY?
I WONDER HOW HE'D REACT...
STILL...
OH, HEY.
WHAT'S UP?
...I SHOULD TELL HIM THANK YOU.

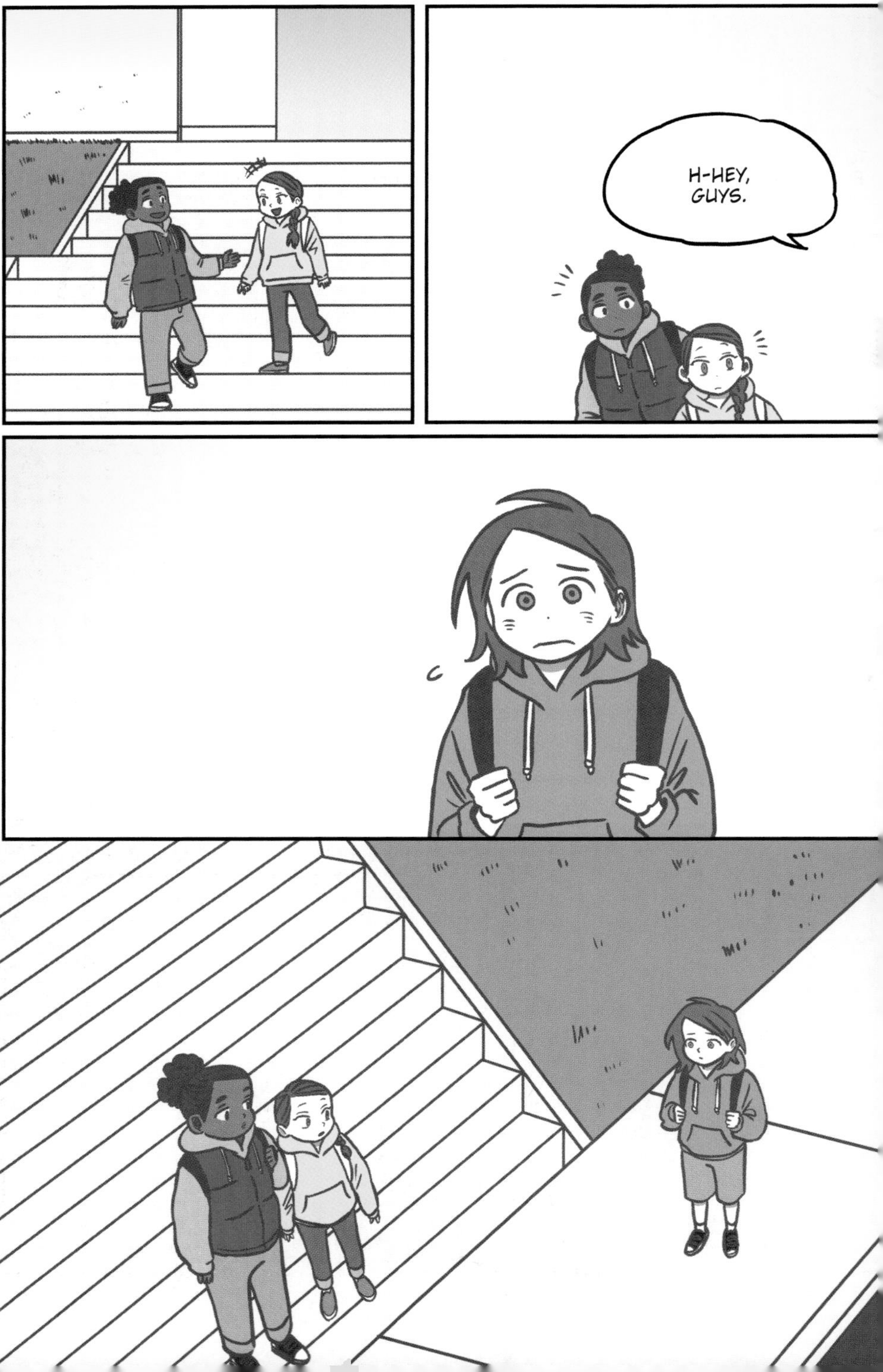
H-HEY, GUYS.

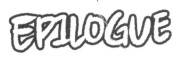

EPILOGUE

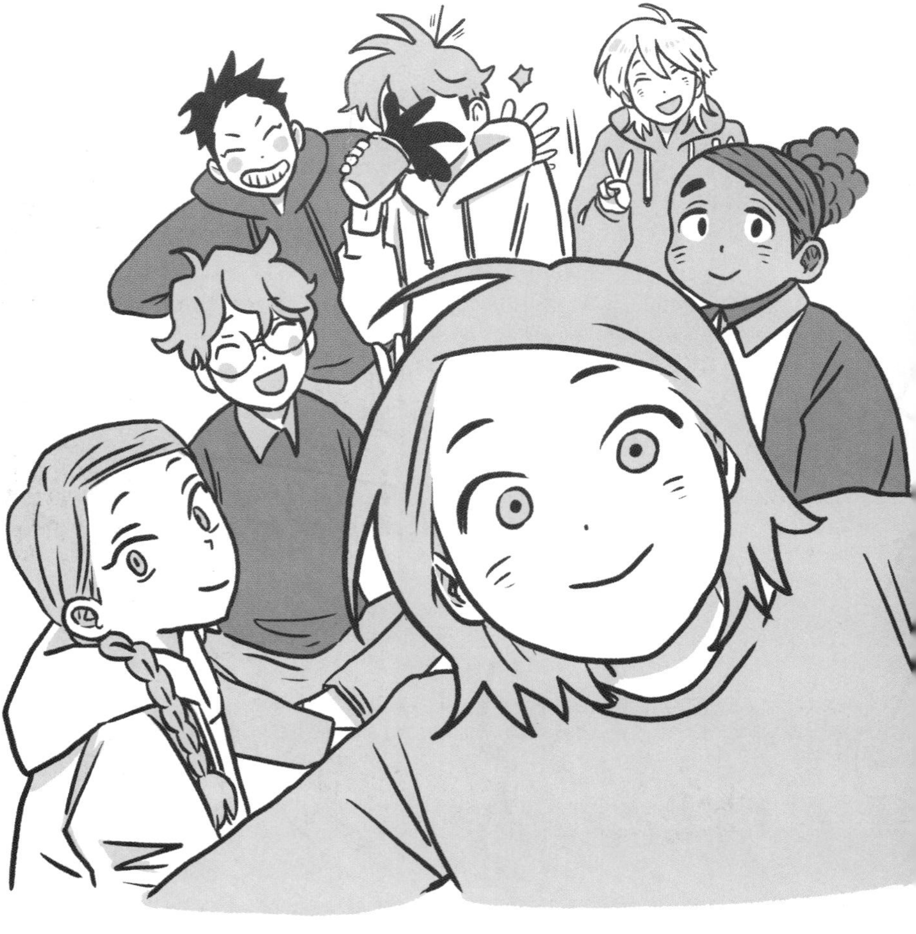

KYLE'S LITTLE SISTER

THE END

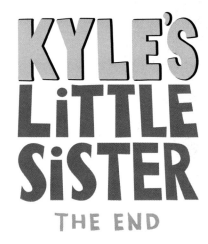

범이. (BUM)
BORN IN 2008

GRACE

CHARACTER PROFILE

MID-SHORT HAIR

THICK EYEBROWS

ROUND EYES

ROUND FACE

Hoodie Fashion

- Something Comfortable

SHARES SOME CLOTHES WITH KYLE

Likes

- Playing Games
- Fantasy Novels
- Stuffed Animals

Hoodie Colors

Favorite Pants Style

- Pants with Lots of Pockets

NOT INTERESTED IN FASHION (YET)

Grace
6th Grade

SHE LIKES TO SIT NEAR THE WINDOW

PAJAMAS:
LONG T-SHIRTS

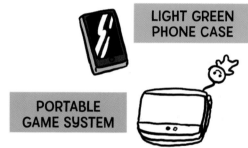

LIGHT GREEN PHONE CASE

PORTABLE GAME SYSTEM

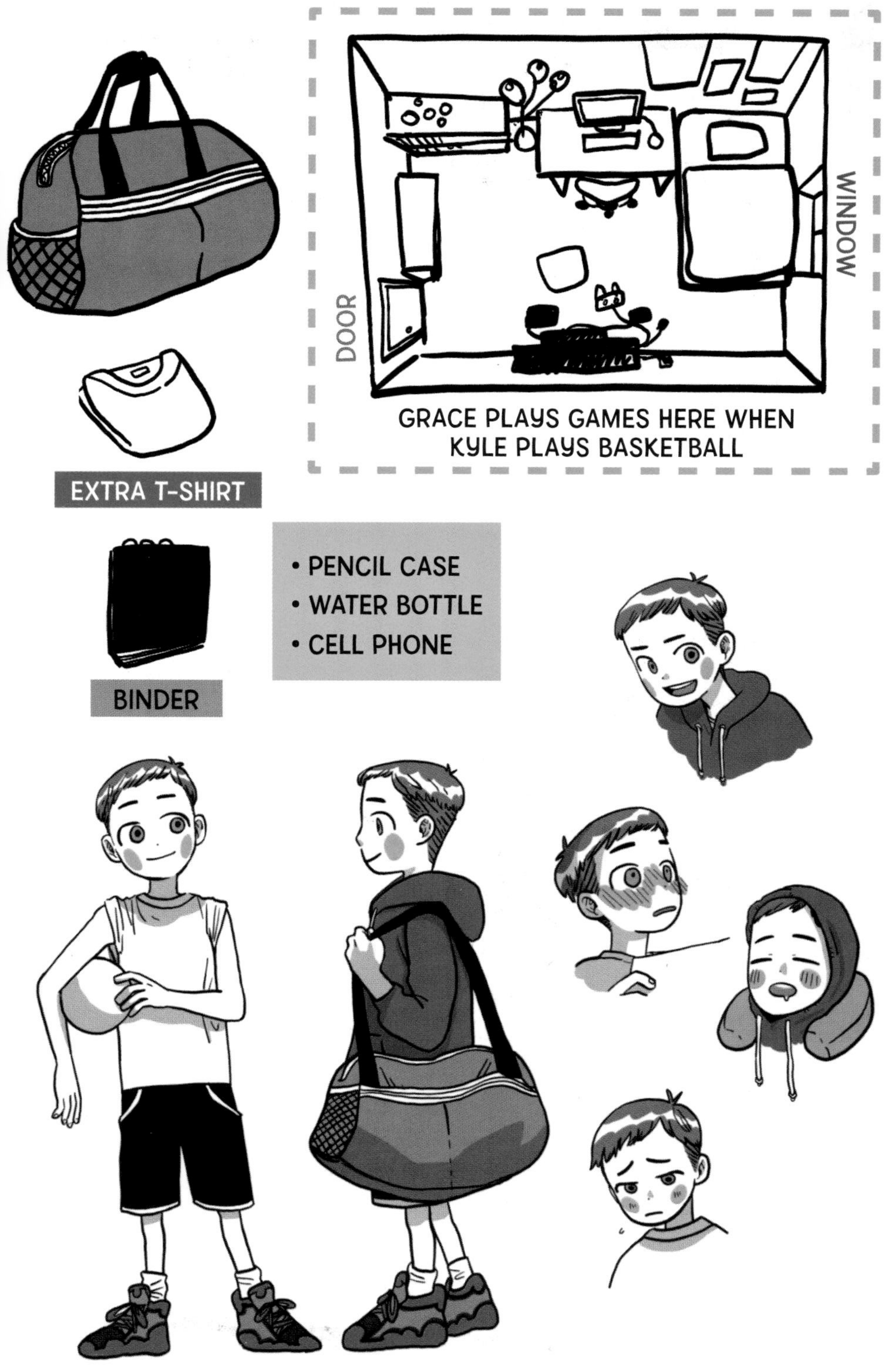
WINDOW
DOOR
GRACE PLAYS GAMES HERE WHEN
KYLE PLAYS BASKETBALL
EXTRA T-SHIRT
BINDER
• PENCIL CASE
• WATER BOTTLE
• CELL PHONE

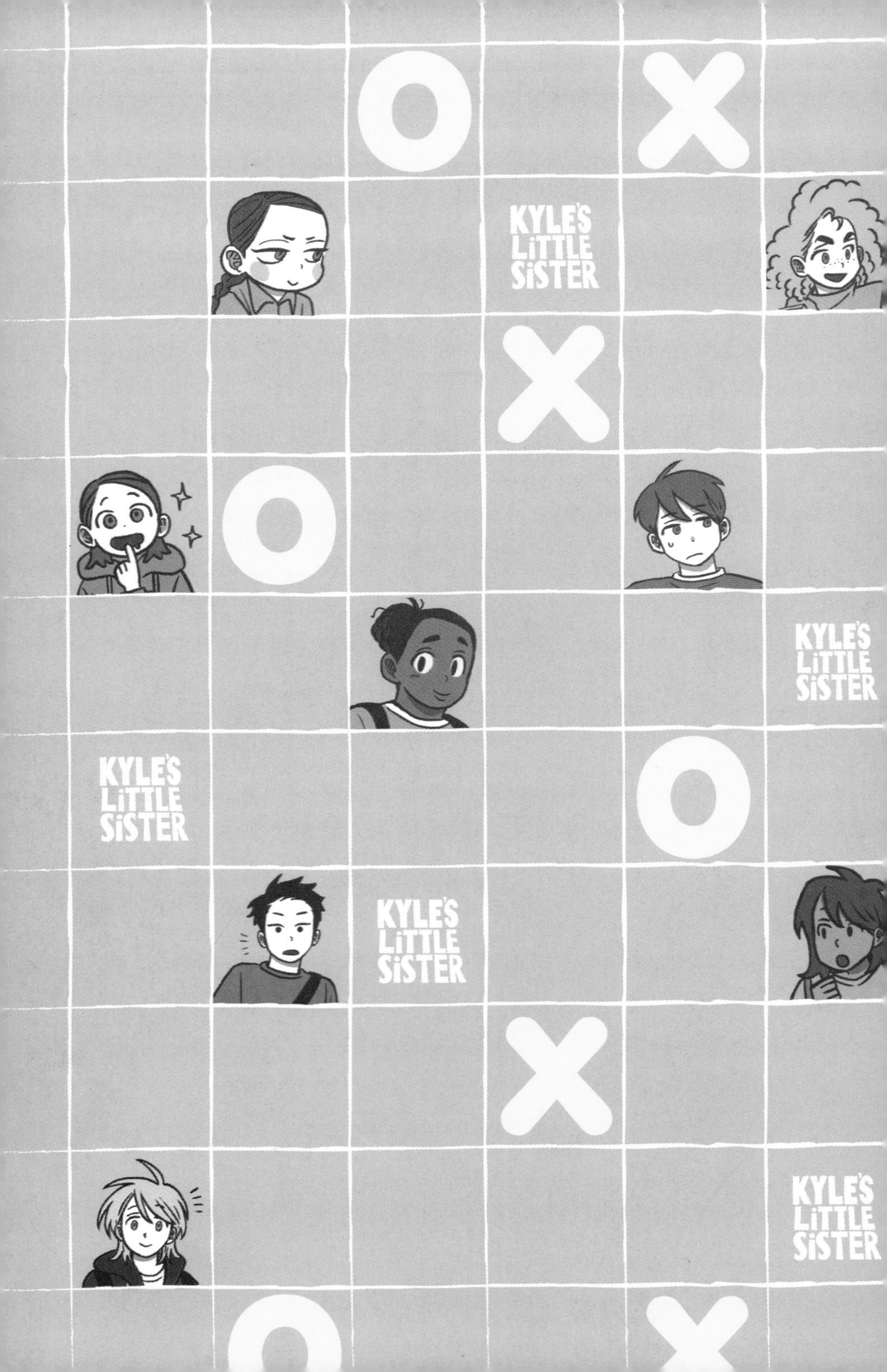
KYLE'S LITTLE SISTER
KYLE'S LITTLE SISTER
KYLE'S LITTLE SISTER
KYLE'S LITTLE SISTER
KYLE'S LITTLE SISTER